WILDFIRE OMENS

WILDWOOD BOOK 1

NICOLE GARDNER

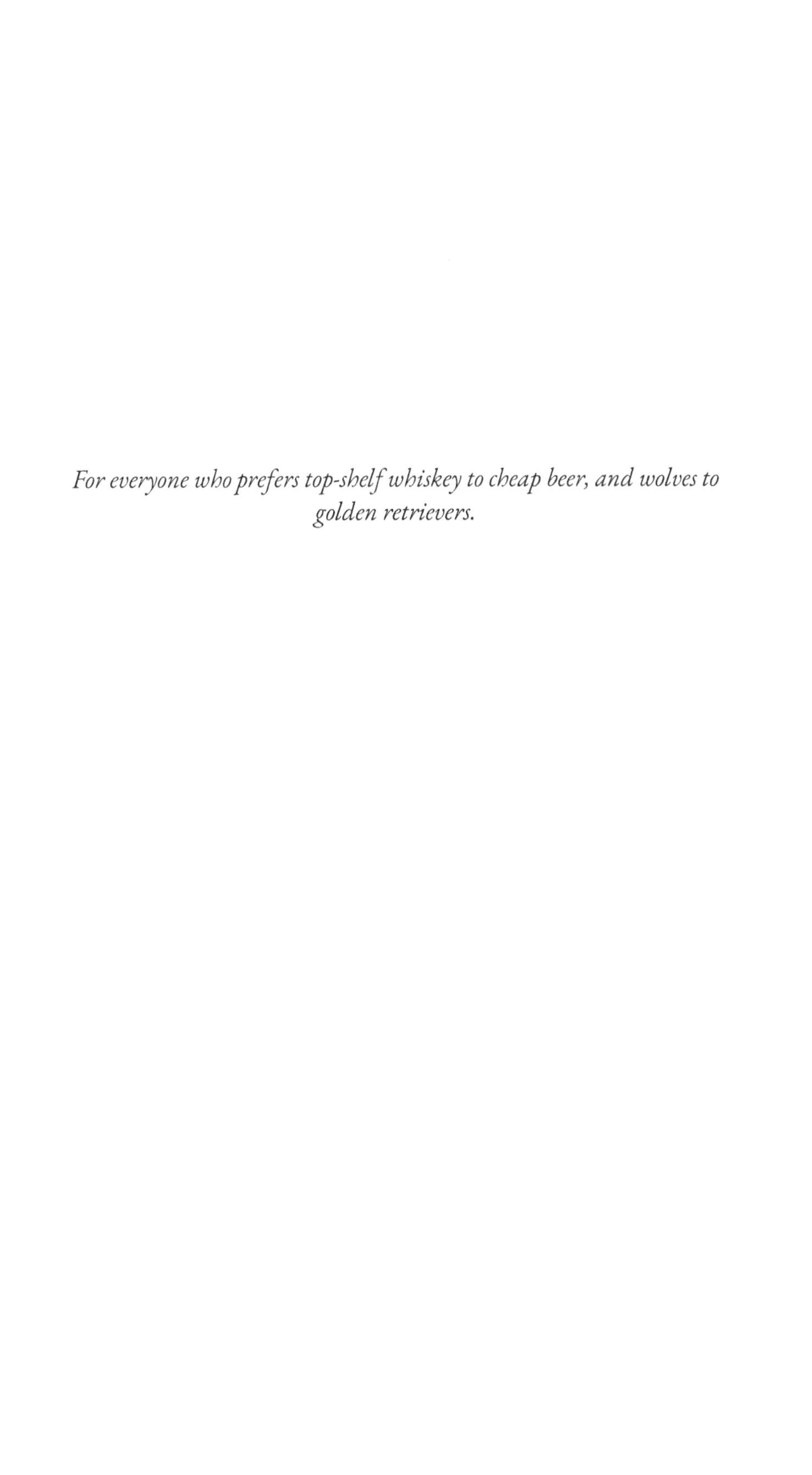

For everyone who prefers top-shelf whiskey to cheap beer, and wolves to golden retrievers.

Chapter One

Cheyenne

Smoke rose from the fire, drifting into the crisp morning air and disappearing into the still dark sky. I hugged my arms around myself and watched the flames. Something was coming. I could feel it. Could feel the tremors of it in the cold earth underneath me, could hear it in the whispers of the wind that snaked through the trees. The truth of it settled into my soul, bringing unwelcome anxiety.

Change was on the horizon. It moved as certainly as the westward winds that blew in from the foreboding sky. In my experience, change was rarely a good thing. It was loss; it was heartbreak. It was scorched earth and attempting to rebuild from the ashes. It was something I tried to avoid at all costs.

I trembled before shaking myself. Whatever was coming, it would have to wait. I had a job to do, and I needed to block out these feelings so I could focus on it. Because if I didn't, change was coming for another family, too.

And I'd do everything in my power to stop that from happening.

Sam walked over to the fire, his step dragging and his blue eyes looking bloodshot from pure exhaustion. He pulled off his wool cap and ran a hand through his tawny hair. "Hey, Cheyenne, that coffee ready yet?"

"Probably," I answered. "Help yourself."

"Thanks." He grasped the handle of the percolator with his thick gloves, filling up his thermos before walking over and grabbing mine to fill too.

"Here," he said after putting the percolator back on the fire. "Drink up. We're going to need it today." He dropped down to sit beside me, bumping his shoulder to mine.

"You think?" I took my thermos from him and sipped, closing my eyes in appreciation. Coffee was always worthy of gratitude, but there was something almost divine about steaming-hot coffee cooked over a campfire on a frigid morning.

"I've got a bad feeling about this one," Sam muttered. "Too many hours have passed."

I had a bad feeling too. But something told me mine had nothing to do with our mission.

"We never give up hope," I said, chiding him.

Sam was always the first one to get negative. But in this case, he had a point. Our average search duration was around five hours. We'd been searching for this hiker for over twenty-four—never a good sign. And we weren't even the first team to go out. The local guys had done a hasty search before calling us in, and the man's hiking buddies had searched before that.

It had now been nearly three days since Scott Fairbanks had wandered off alone without his pack, highly intoxicated from the bourbon he and his friends had shared around their evening campfire. He'd stumbled away from the group and simply vanished into the unforgiving terrain of Bighorn National Forest. We were still early in the season, with snow on the ground in the higher parts of the park and temperatures still dropping into the 30s at night even in the lower elevations. Not a great scenario for an inexperienced hiker without supplies.

I knew as well as Sam did that people sometimes died simply from getting lost while looking for a private spot to relieve themselves. It had happened to hikers who were much more experienced than Fairbanks, in areas with more foot traffic and larger search teams. Some people were never found. But we had to maintain hope, and part of my job was to hold on to that hope for all of us.

Sam gave me a pointed look that let me know he was already past the point of believing we'd find Scott alive. If he was right, it wouldn't be the first time our mission changed from rescue to recovery. And, sadly, it wouldn't be the last. But I hoped he was wrong—for the team's sake as much as for Scott and his family.

So I shook my head and gave him a friendly smile. "Just finish that coffee. You'll find your optimism again before you get to the end of that cup."

"I doubt that," he grumbled.

I stood, brushed the dirt from my jeans, and called the rest of the unit over from where they huddled in small groups, tending their horses or shoveling down food and packing up their supplies. They were all weary, and I felt a stab of empathy for them. We'd already thoroughly worked the grid and had reconvened at base camp to grab a few hours of sleep before expanding the search yet again.

"I know you're all tired," I said, raising my voice so everyone could hear me. "This has been a difficult search. But this is what we do, and we've done worse before. When it gets hard, remember why we're doing it: Scott Fairbanks. He has a family. A wife and two kids. They need him back, and he's gotta be anxious to get home to them. We're going to make that happen. We head out again in fifteen minutes. There's fresh coffee over here if anyone wants any. Do what you need to do."

I put on an optimistic face for the team, but Claire, our Sheriff's Office coordinator, shot me a knowing look. She could always see through me—probably because we'd been best friends since the day I'd moved to Wyoming as a kid. I'd been a quiet, shy, awkwardly tall eight-year-old still reeling from the dissolution of the life I'd known, thanks to my dad deciding he'd like to start a new family with someone else. My mom had packed us up and moved us to her childhood home, where we'd crammed into my grandmother's house and I'd started a new life that was absolutely nothing like the one I'd had in St. Louis.

It was the worst year of my life—and the best thing that ever happened to me. I'd met Claire Hawkins my first day in school. She was everything I wasn't—an honest-to-goodness cowgirl, born and raised on a Wyoming horse ranch, who had never met a stranger. She marched over to me that day, her mess of blonde curls only slightly contained by the sparkly green cowboy hat on her head, and announced that we'd be best friends. It was a promise she'd kept even when it would have been easier for her to break it. I loved her fiercely for it.

She meandered over now, slinging an arm around my shoulder.

"What do you really think?" she asked, keeping her voice low.

"I think it got too cold last night. It's clear he didn't do the smart thing and stay put when he realized he was lost, and I'm worried he may not have found a water source out here," I said, matching her quiet tone. "But I'm not giving up hope."

She grinned. "No, we're not."

Hank, our base command leader, came over to finalize the plan. He'd been a lifelong search-and-rescue operative, until the arthritis in his knees slowed him down enough that he recognized he was a liability on the ground and switched to running our base instead. We all loved him like a dad, and his experience was invaluable.

He put a hand on my shoulder. "How's the team holding up?"

"We've done worse," I said. It was a mantra that got us through the hard ones.

"Come take a look at the maps," he said, motioning to where he had them spread out on the tail bed of his truck. "I want your thoughts."

I followed him over and looked at the ground we'd covered, comparing it to what we'd been told about our hiker's last known location. Claire sipped coffee from her bright-red thermos as she watched me study the map.

"We've covered a lot of ground," Hank commented, shaking his head.

"We have," I agreed.

"You've got good instincts. What do you want to do next?"

A thought was beginning to form as I looked over the topography, trying to put myself in Scott Fairbanks's shoes.

"We followed some tracks this way," I said, using my finger to trace the areas we'd marked on GPS as possible clues. "If we assume he was smart enough to stop and hunker down once he realized he was lost, then, theoretically, he should be somewhere in the grids we've already searched. Somewhere in here," I said, tracing a circle over an area we'd covered twice.

"Exactly."

I bit my lip, thinking it over. This was the kind of search where we really needed a canine unit for scent work. "We could send a team or two back through some of the more dense places we've already checked or spots where it's possible he built a shelter from natural elements. Maybe it blended in and he was asleep—or unconscious—and didn't respond when they called."

"But..." Hank probed, hearing the skepticism in my voice.

"But when I interviewed his friends, that's not the picture I got of him. He was inexperienced, the only one of them who'd never done anything like this. Had never built a shelter before, and reportedly didn't have any equipment to do so. Didn't take anything except a flashlight and a roll of toilet paper when he walked off, and had been drinking enough that he wasn't thinking straight. Wasn't the kind of guy to make the safe choice even when he was."

I felt a little flicker, a nudge that I was on the right track. "I don't think he hunkered down and waited for rescue. My gut says he panicked and kept moving."

"Hmm." Hank made a non-committal noise, but it didn't bother me. He always held his opinion until he was sure.

I pointed at a spot that was a few miles from where we'd been searching. "There are caves over here, aren't there?"

Claire leaned over, looking. "Yes. That's pretty far from where he was last seen though." There was a sliver of doubt in her voice, even though I knew she trusted me.

"It is," I agreed. "Would have taken him some time to make his way over there, especially in this terrain. Add in hunger, thirst, and general weakness... I get it. But a lot of people naturally head toward water."

I traced my finger over the map, imagining his route in my head. "There's a fairly large creek that runs that way. It's a downhill path from where he was last seen, and it lines up with the clues we marked. If he wandered around in circles for a bit like this"—I showed them with my finger—"and hit *this* trail, he might have thought it was the one they were on to begin with. If he took it far enough to hit that creek, he might have kept going, assuming it would lead him to civilization if nothing else. Then if he saw the caves and was smart enough to use them as a shelter, it would explain why no one was able to spot him from the air."

There were over a million acres in this forest. It was essentially like looking for a needle in a haystack at this point, and all I had was a hunch and some wild speculation. I glanced at the group, knowing that the wrong decision would force us to expend valuable energy—and morale —looking in the wrong place. But my gut said to check the caves, and it was the first time I'd felt that on this search. I trusted it. So I tapped my finger on the map.

"I really think we need to look here."

Hank nodded, slapped my shoulder, and called everyone over. "Alright, people. It's go time. Cheyenne's gut is saying to check the area around Bear Hollow Cave, so you're heading there and setting up a new grid. Everyone okay with that plan?"

The group was exhausted, but there were only nods of assent. Tired or not, this was what we lived for.

I headed back to pack up my gear and put out my fire. Then I made my way over to my horse, Wildfire, a deep Chestnut mare. She was my favorite search companion. Not every search called for horses, but I loved the ones that did. I'd rather be out with her than on an ATV or a helicopter any day—and certainly more than trekking on foot. Besides, Wildfire offered more than companionship and steady feet on the trail. She had good instincts of her own and appeared to love the search-and-rescue team as much as the rest of us. Her gentle spirit seemed to understand why we did what we did.

"You ready, girl?" I stroked her neck as she nuzzled into me.

Claire and Sam came up beside me, both already on their horses. Even though Claire was our liaison, she participated in every search, having been a member of the unit long before she joined the Sage County Sheriff's Office as a deputy. When we divided into search teams, she, Sam, and I were nearly always together.

"You wanna take the lead?" Claire asked.

"Sure," I answered before swinging up into my saddle. I glanced at Sam and Claire. "Let's do this."

For the first time in the last twenty-four hours, I finally had a good feeling about something. My gut said we'd find Scott Fairbanks alive.

But my spirit still said something else was coming. I took one last glance at the sky, shivering as a hard wind blew through camp, rattling Hank's lanterns and sending up a cloud of dust around us all.

Yes. Something was coming.

Chapter Two

Rhett

The wind whipped furiously, making it difficult to stay on the road. I grinned and leaned into it, embracing the feel of the pavement underneath me. There was nothing like the lonely Wyoming highways for putting on speed, for feeling the throb of the engine and the way it mimicked the beat of my heart. Not another soul in sight, just me and my bike with the big sky above us and the Bighorn Mountains looming in the distance. The sun was beginning to rise, snuffing the stars out of the sky one by one.

It was a pretty damn perfect morning—if I could forget about where I was heading.

Not that home was a bad thing. In fact, I'd been missing the ranch. It had been almost two years since I'd been back, longer than my usual intervals away. Cole's wedding in Tennessee last year had given me a great excuse to skip my annual visit, since I'd seen the family there anyway. Couldn't take more time off work, all that.

Excuses were a good thing, since I tried to stay as far away from here as possible.

But as the months had passed, I'd found myself thinking about everyone more and more. My nieces had to have grown a ton since the wedding. And Cole settling down into his own life made me realize the others probably would soon, too. Things were changing.

Jonathan was eighteen now. Hard to believe my baby brother was now the age I was when I first took off. He'd be graduating soon, and who knew where he'd end up? I recognized the wildness in his soul. It mirrored the wildness in mine and in Cole's. We'd left, and he probably would, too.

I wasn't a sentimental kind of guy, but even I had some weird feelings thinking about that one.

It was good that I was making time for this. Besides, it was only a few weeks at most. I'd done a hell of a lot worse things for a few weeks at a time. I could survive living with my family for that long.

Even if doubt crept in when I tried to reassure myself about it.

I grinned again when the landscape started to change. The straight highway began to curve, and the sparse pines lining the road started to thicken as I got close to Wildwood, a damn cute town that sat in the shadows of the Bighorn Mountains. It was one of those places people flocked to from the cities to play cowboy for a week, snapping photographs of the old-fashioned storefronts and hitching posts that lined Main Street.

Suckers. Playing cowboy was a whole lot different than actually being one.

I blew through town, then opened the bike up on the last few turns, feeling an odd nostalgia when I recognized the land that belonged to my family. It was my father's now. Had been my grandfather's before that, and his father's before that. Someday, it would technically be shared by the rest of us, split evenly—on paper, anyway. We all knew that it would really belong to Travis, just like he belonged to it. Like Dad, he lived and breathed this land. It would be in good hands.

I was glad for it. Partly because I was happy for him. Partly because the land deserved someone who would take care of it. But mostly because it left me free from the responsibility of carrying on a legacy that had never been my dream.

I slowed down as I turned onto the long drive that led up to the main house, passing by the big sign that read *Falcon Ridge Ranch*, followed by the guest cabins that were tucked into the trees that lined the left side of the driveway. Dad had insisted on building the cabins there, despite Mom's belief that the guests would prefer to be out back with views of the horses. Didn't matter, Dad had said. When he was eighty, he wanted to be able to sit on his back porch, drinking a cup of coffee and watching the sun rise over his pastures without any tourists spoiling the view. Figured he had been right about that one.

The scent of sagebrush filled my nostrils as I rode straight toward the sun rising behind the mountains. I loved the ranch this time of day. The guests were usually still sleeping, since *playing* cowboy didn't require being up before dawn. But my family would be up, probably congregated in the kitchen, finishing up breakfast and pouring hot thermoses of coffee as they split up duties for the day.

I couldn't wait to see their faces when I walked in.

I hadn't told them I was coming in case I changed my mind at the last minute. But I was here now, and despite my ambivalence, it felt good to be back. Besides, they needed my help, and for once, I was doing the right thing. I could almost picture Mom getting all misty-eyed over it, proud of her boy for coming to the rescue.

Had to admit, that would feel good for a change.

The ranch house looked almost exactly the same as it had when I'd lived here—over a decade ago now. It was a modest home, considering how successful my parents had been at expanding the operation so that it could support all seven of us Hawkins kids if we wanted it to. The main house was the same one my grandfather had built for his bride. It was a two-story log cabin made of Eastern White Pine, with three stone chimneys jutting out and a sprawling front porch with old-fashioned porch swings on each end. The tourists loved it. So did I, now that I wasn't crammed into it with six other kids and not an ounce of privacy.

I parked my bike out front and strode up the curving walkway toward the porch, noting the fresh plants out front, all native to

Wyoming. That would be Beth's doing, I figured. She had a knack for that kind of thing.

I pulled out my key and let myself in through the front door instead of knocking. Didn't matter that I hadn't lived here in over ten years. I was a Hawkins, and a Hawkins didn't knock at Falcon Ridge Ranch.

I pushed my long hair back, doing a quick check in the entryway mirror to make sure I didn't look *too* rough, then strutted into the kitchen, smiling when I saw I'd been exactly right. Mom, Travis, Beth, and Jonathan were all in the kitchen, thermoses in hand, talking quietly. Two years and things hadn't changed.

Mom was the only one facing my direction, standing at the head of the kitchen island where she presided like a queen over the others. She was a tiny woman, but no one would ever doubt that she was in charge. Her long red hair fell down her back, and her green eyes glinted as she gave instructions, looking more like a Celtic warrior than the rancher she was.

Her eyes widened when she caught sight of me. "Rhett? What on earth?"

"Hey, Mom," I said, grinning. "Got any breakfast left? I'm starved."

She blinked twice, then threw a glance at Travis, who frowned. He looked at Beth, who looked at him, then at Mom. Jonathan was the only one who returned my grin.

This wasn't right at all.

Mom shook herself, then gave me a hesitant smile. "Well, goodness, Rhett, it's good to see you! Of course we have food. Ah, there are muffins over there," she said, pointing to the large white bowl sitting on the kitchen counter. "And there's still a cup of coffee in the pot. But what are you doing here?" She shook her head again, then came over and grabbed me in a warm embrace.

I hugged her tight, realizing just how much I'd missed her. "I'm here to help."

"Help?" She looked at me blankly, then threw another glance at Travis. He hadn't bothered wiping the frown off his face.

"Yeah. I figured, with Dad out of commission for a few weeks, you could use another hand around here. I was in between projects and I'm overdue for some time off, so"—I shrugged—"I thought I'd take a few weeks to pitch in."

Her face softened. "Well, that's really sweet, Rhett. We're thrilled to have you, of course."

Were they though? Because all the looks they were exchanging said something different altogether.

"Yes." Beth, my sweet younger sister, jumped in, coming to give me a hug. "You caught us by surprise, that's all."

Jonathan snorted. "Yep, that's all."

Mom sent him a sharp look.

There was definitely something going on that I didn't know about.

"Where's Claire?" I asked, realizing my other sister—and the one family member, other than Mom, that I could always count on to be happy to see me—was missing. Finn, Beth's twin, was also absent, but that was no mystery. He was a professor at the university in Montana and couldn't get away while school was in session.

Travis finally spoke up. "Claire's out on a search. I guess that makes your arrival pretty good timing. We really could use some extra help today," he admitted. "We were trying to figure out how we were going to manage things with just me, Mom, and Beth. We've got a four-hour horse tour this morning, and we like to send two people. Maybe you could be her second." He looked to Beth as if for approval, and I saw her give a small nod.

"Whoa." I threw my hands up and took a step back. "I'm here to help, but I've been awake for almost twenty-four hours. Drove all night. I've got to grab some sleep before I do something like that."

"Shocker," Travis said with a tight smile. "Here to help, but not really."

"I just need a few hours," I protested. "Then I'm all yours. But I won't be good for anything without some rest. I'm dead on my feet."

"Alright," Mom said, giving Travis a warning look. "You can crash in Jonathan's room for now."

"Hey!" Jonathan protested. "He said he's going to be here for a few weeks. Are you saying I have to share that long?"

I jerked my head back, surprised by his attitude. Jonathan and I had always gotten along well. Probably better than my parents liked, since they didn't want him turning out like me.

"Just for today," Mom soothed, checking her watch. "We'll figure something out. We'll get him set up in Jimmy's loft or an empty guest cabin. But I don't have time right now. We've got to get a move on. Jonathan, help Travis saddle up the horses before you leave for school, okay? Beth, can you help me set up the guest breakfast?"

Beth smiled and nodded, then shot me an apologetic look, like she knew this wasn't exactly the reception I'd expected. "Sorry. It's a crazy day here."

"Yeah, I see that," I said. I gave them all a tight smile. "I'll scarf this, then grab a few hours of sleep and check in with you after to see where I can pitch in."

Travis let out a strangled laugh.

Mom gave me a quick kiss on the cheek. "Get some sleep. Oh, and say hi to your father, won't you? He'll be so glad to see you."

"Sure."

But I doubted that, especially after the way everyone else had reacted. Thought I'd get a little bit of gratitude, but it felt like I was in the way.

Which, come to think of it, was half of why I'd left in the first place.

It was only a few weeks, I promised myself. Six at most. No one could expect me to take more than six weeks off of work. Maybe not even that. Maybe four would be long enough to do my duty, get them through the rough patch.

Two if they found someone to hire temporarily.

I could do anything for two weeks.

I shook my head as I headed up the stairs toward Jonathan's room. Even I didn't believe I could last two weeks here.

CHAPTER THREE

Cheyenne

MY BODY ACHED WITH EXHAUSTION AS I UNLOADED Wildfire from Claire's horse trailer. Thirty-two hours out on a search, snatching an hour or two of sleep at a time, was brutal. But it had all been worth it. We had found Scott in the entrance of Bear Hollow Cave. He was cold and scared but alive. We evacuated him and he was transported to the closest hospital for treatment, and soon, he would be reunited with his family. That knowledge made the physical toll worth it every time.

I took care of Wildfire, then headed inside, stripping off my filthy clothes to wash up quickly. I was torn between the long, hot shower I desperately wanted and the food I desperately needed. Trail food only went so far, and I hadn't been able to eat a real meal at base camp, unable to shake that feeling of dark storm clouds on the horizon even after we'd found our missing hiker. But my body was insisting on a real meal now, and one glance at my bare kitchen cabinets had me grabbing the keys to my truck.

After a long search, there was only one thing I really wanted: a greasy burger and fries from Whiskey Creek Bar. Plus, there was nothing like the drive into town to help me zone out a bit. It was a funny thing. Out on horseback, you were one with the horse, one with the world. Acutely aware of every stone on the trail and every movement in the brush. But in the truck with the windows rolled up, the world passed by in a blur. Almost like a TV show you'd seen a thousand times before, something you'd tune out but still find comforting just the same.

But this time, driving into town felt different. With every passing mile, that feeling I'd had by the fire became stronger.

Something was coming.

The closer I got to the bar, the more sure of it I became. Worse, I had a sneaking suspicion that it wasn't *something* coming.

It was *someone.*

Someone I hadn't had to face in a very long time.

I tried to reassure myself it couldn't be Rhett. Even if it was, that didn't mean I'd have to interact with him. After all, he'd come back now and then to visit his family, and we'd managed to avoid each other completely. How many years had it been, anyway? Over ten, as hard as that was to believe. So, even if my premonition was right and Rhett Hawkins was back in the Bighorns, it didn't have to involve me.

But my heart thudded with anticipation, and a familiar ache bloomed inside me. And I knew.

It had always been this way with him. Like an invisible string tied us together whether I wanted it to or not. I could feel the tension in that connection when he got close.

It had been a long time since I'd felt that ache, that burn of being close to him. At first, when I'd known he was visiting, it had felt like heartbreak. Like something was terribly wrong in the universe, because he was here but he wasn't mine anymore. Over time, it had gotten easier. A muted ache instead of fresh pain.

He had been my first love, my first kiss, my first everything. No matter what I'd done to try to cut the ties between us, I hadn't been able to.

When I pulled into the parking lot of the bar, my heart rose and sank all at the same time. The vintage panhead with leather saddlebags parked out front was one I'd recognize anywhere. It was Rhett's pride and joy, a gift passed down from his grandfather. Memories crashed through me of all the times I'd held on to him on the back of it, laughing as the wind whipped through my hair, feeling completely content simply because we were together.

I stared at the bike, wondering if I should turn around and go home. While part of me was curious, the other part of me didn't want to see him. Didn't want to feel the pain of being near him—the pain of something that had once been beautiful being so broken.

Rhett Hawkins had taught me what love was. But then he'd thrown my heart away like it meant nothing to him.

I let out a deep breath and forced myself to get out of the truck. I was hungry, and I wouldn't let him take this from me, too. This was my post-search ritual, and only a coward would turn around and run away now. This was my town. My bar.

He'd left. I'd stayed.

I wouldn't let him run me out of the place where I belonged. Rhett was the coward. Not me.

When I pushed open the door and walked in, I saw him standing at the bar with his back to me. His dark hair was still long, brushing the top of the black leather jacket he was wearing. He was stockier than he'd been, looking like a man instead of the teen I'd known, but even without seeing his face, I'd somehow still recognize him anywhere. And just the sight of him broke my heart, like the pieces he'd shattered had never quite healed.

I took a deep breath, steeling myself.

Pete waved from behind the bar. "Hey, Cheyenne! Heard about the search today. Congratulations! Want your usual?"

I forced a casual smile. "That would be great. Thanks."

Pete glanced at Rhett, whose back was still to me, then realized what was happening and threw me an apologetic look.

Rhett turned slowly, facing me.

"Hey, Cheyenne," he said. He leaned back against the bar and crossed his arms, lifting his chin so his eyes could meet mine under the rim of his black cowboy hat. There wasn't even a trace of a smile on his face.

"Rhett," I said, nodding. His name felt odd on my tongue. It was a name I'd avoided speaking for years. In the beginning, I'd ask Claire if she'd heard from him, if he was okay. I couldn't help it. I had still loved him, despite his betrayal. But eventually, I'd stopped, my pride not allowing me to ask anymore. I lived my life as if he'd never existed, as if we'd never shared what we had shared.

But here he was, standing in front of me, back in *my* territory.

I couldn't pretend he didn't exist anymore.

Chapter Four

Rhett

I could feel it the minute Cheyenne walked into the bar. Didn't know how I always knew. But I did, even all these years later. Everything in me tightened in anticipation—and dread.

I'd always known the day would come when I'd have to face her. I'd managed to avoid it all the other times I'd been home, except the times I'd *tried* to see her and realized it wasn't welcome. Since then, I'd been a total coward, doing whatever it took to stop from running into her.

But if I was going to hang around for a few weeks this time, I knew I'd run into her eventually. Wildwood was too small to avoid her forever. I just hadn't expected it to be on my first day back.

I gripped my beer and turned, facing her.

It was like a punch to the gut. Or worse, being electrocuted. Didn't know if I'd died or come back to life.

Time had treated her well. Hell, that was the understatement of the year. She was beautiful. Always had been. Always would be.

That shiny dark hair was longer than it had been, cascading in waves down her shoulders. She was as tall as a supermodel, and that body I'd once known every inch of was as lean and toned as an athlete's. She was wearing dark jeans tucked into leather boots—boots that, by the look on her face, she'd like to kick my ass with.

Her face was thinner than it had been when we were kids. It was all angles and shadows now. Not a typical beauty, but it took my breath away just the same. And those dusky pink lips, currently pursed up in a scowl, took me back to memories I'd tried damn hard to forget.

"Hey, Cheyenne," I said casual-like, though I gripped my beer even harder.

She gave me a regal nod. "Rhett." Only one word. Like she couldn't spare even another one for me. Cheyenne Snow was an ice queen. But once, to me at least, she'd been like a warm glass of brandy.

She walked toward a booth in the back, motioning to Pete to let him know where she was heading. I turned back to the bar and saw him give her a little smile before throwing me an apologetic look.

Wasn't his fault the tension between me and her was so thick you could cut it with a knife. I forced a smile and drained my beer, then threw some cash down onto the bar to cover it.

I meant to leave, give her some space. But my feet had a mind of their own, and I walked to her table instead.

She looked up, her face unreadable. She wasn't scowling anymore, but there wasn't an ounce of friendliness in her eyes. It was like she was looking at a stranger. And that stabbed deep.

I missed the way she used to look at me.

I cleared my throat. "I, uh, I'll be hanging around for a while."

"Okay." Not even a flicker of emotion.

"Dad's in rough shape. Broke his hip after a fall. So I'll be helping out for a couple weeks. Maybe more."

"I'm aware of your father's condition," she said quietly.

"Oh." Of course she'd know. She and Claire were probably still thick as thieves, even though Claire never mentioned her to me.

"Is there a point to this conversation?" she asked, raising her chin and staring me in the eye.

"Just wanted you to hear it from me."

Something crossed her face—surprise or annoyance. I wasn't even sure. But I was glad to see at least some sort of emotional reaction. Didn't know what I'd been expecting. Cheyenne wasn't the type for tears, wasn't the kind of woman to beg me to stay. Wasn't the kind of woman who'd try to get my attention.

Kind of wished she was.

She cleared her throat. "I'm not sure why you thought I'd be interested in your movements, Rhett. I've lived the past ten years without knowing where you are or what you're doing." There was another flicker of emotion. Anger this time.

"Right." I clamped my lips. This wasn't going well at all. "I just didn't want it to be awkward when we ran into each other. It's a small town."

Pete chose that moment to place her beer down on the table. She smiled at him and nodded her thanks. Jealousy twisted inside me. It had been a long time since I'd seen Cheyenne smile, but I remembered when the sight of me would make her face light up.

She turned back to me and shrugged. "Why should I feel awkward? I'm not the one who has anything to feel awkward about." She put her lips on the mouth of her cold beer bottle and tipped it up, taking a long swallow.

My mouth went dry.

I was so distracted I didn't even notice the man who'd come in and slid in across the booth from her.

"Thought you'd be here," he said, grinning.

"It's tradition." She smiled again, then looked at me. "Rhett, you remember Sam, I'm sure."

I glanced over at the man, seeing him for the first time. Of course I remembered him. Sam Barton. He'd been friends with Cole and Travis in high school. A couple years older than me—Cole's class, if I remembered right. But even if we'd been the same age, we'd have run in different circles.

He'd always seemed like some kind of goody-two-shoes to me. Clean cut, killer smile. Quarterback on the football team, homecoming king, and somehow also a straight-A student. He'd been popular and well liked, even by the teachers at our school. About as different from me as you could get.

Despite that, I'd watched Cheyenne turn to him for comfort when her grandmother died. It had been the final nail in the coffin on any hope of getting back together with her. I couldn't compete with someone like Sam Barton. Not then, and not now.

His eyes betrayed surprise. "Rhett. Didn't know you were back in town."

"Well, I am," I said, my voice coming out like gravel. "Here to help out while Dad's down."

"That's great," he said, glancing at Cheyenne. "I know they could use the help out at the ranch."

"Yep."

Cheyenne said nothing. She looked at me with an expression of mild impatience, like I was interrupting her evening.

Which, I supposed I was.

"Well. Have a good night," I said, tipping my hat to her.

Sam stuck out a hand for me to shake. "Good to see you, Rhett."

"Yeah. It's good to be back." My voice felt hollow. Because if Cheyenne looked at me like that—like I was an interruption in her life—then it didn't feel good to be back at all.

When I got back to the ranch, Claire was in the kitchen, scarfing down a small mountain of food. She squealed when I walked in, jumping up to grab me in a tight bear hug. I relaxed a little, glad at least one of my siblings was genuinely happy to see me.

Growing up, I had always gotten along best with Claire and Cole. We three were the wild souls of the family, the ones who always seemed to get ourselves into trouble. The big difference between us was that Claire stayed here, while Cole and I left Wyoming, marking us as the two family deserters. Cole had earned his forgiveness though. Hard to stay mad at a man who put his life on the line serving his country. Plus, he'd eventually settled down. Got married and had a kid. Adding a grandchild to the family was an automatic slate-wiper, it seemed.

Even though Claire had stayed, she was still a wild one at heart, which made us two peas in a pod.

"Nobody told me you were coming," she said, slapping me on the shoulder, her face all lit up in delight.

"They didn't know. Surprised them when I pulled in this morning." I leaned against the kitchen counter as she went back to her plate, popping a giant spoonful of mashed potatoes into her mouth. "Hungry much?"

She laughed. "Sorry," she said around the food in her mouth. "Just got back from a long search. I'm half starved."

"Good outcome?"

She nodded, grinning. "Yeah. Took us over thirty hours, but we found him."

"Good deal." I cleared my throat. "I, uh, saw Cheyenne at the bar. I guess she's still on the team?"

Claire's face changed. "Yeah," she said, her tone suddenly measured. "She's one of our most active volunteers and the head of our local horse team. She's actually the reason we found the guy today. If she hadn't insisted we search the caves, we'd probably still be out there looking."

"Wow." Pride bloomed in my chest. Even though we'd been broken up for ages, I was still proud of what she did.

Claire looked at me with curiosity. "How'd she react to seeing you?"

I gripped the counter behind me. "She looked pissed for half a second. Then just bored. I told her I was staying awhile and she acted like she didn't even know why I would bother telling her. Like it didn't affect her at all. I might as well have told her I'd had a muffin for breakfast."

Claire smirked. "Well, what did you expect? "

I blinked a couple of times. I wasn't even sure. "I don't know. Just thought she'd have something to say about it," I said lamely. "I'm normally only here a couple days. Didn't want things to be awkward for her if we ran into each other."

"Uh huh." Claire gave me a knowing look, then hopped off her chair and headed to the fridge. "Beer?"

"Yeah."

She tossed me one and opened hers, taking a big swig before sighing. "Man, it's good to relax after a search."

"I bet." I fiddled with the tab on the beer. "Hey, um, what's the deal with Cheyenne and Sam Barton?"

"What do you mean?"

"I mean, are they married? Dating?"

Claire gave me a sly grin. "Why does it matter?"

I shrugged, trying to look nonchalant. "It doesn't. Was just wondering."

She shook her head. "They're not together. Not married, not dating. Not anything. Just friends."

"Sure didn't look that way to me."

Not that he'd even touched her tonight. But I'd never forget coming back to Wyoming when I heard Cheyenne's grandma had died and the way it had crushed me to watch her fall apart in his arms. He'd held her while she cried by the casket, and his gaze had caught mine where I stood at the back, away from everyone else. He'd glared at me, a warning to stay away. I'd known I wasn't wanted there, so I'd turned around and left without even speaking to Cheyenne.

Claire gave me a long look, her eyes narrowing like she could read my mind. "Sam's a longtime member of the search-and-rescue team. They're close."

"Close, huh?" It was better than married or dating, but I still couldn't help the frown that slipped out.

"We're *all* close. We have to be. We train together, spend countless hours in the wilderness as a group. It's a family." She paused, then sighed. "I still don't know why you care so much. You've never even made an effort to see Cheyenne again. But Sam's got a girlfriend. Emily something or another. She came for the summer last year, they had a fling, and she never left."

Something in my chest loosened. Claire was wrong. I *had* made an effort to see Cheyenne after I left. It hadn't been welcomed, and I'd finally taken the hint. Didn't know why her being with Sam now would bother me so much, but I couldn't picture her with someone like him. Not that he was a bad guy, clearly.

He just wasn't me.

But we were entering dangerous territory and I needed to lighten the conversation, so I decided to poke fun at Claire.

"So, what about you, little sis?" I grinned. "You got a boyfriend?"

She smirked. "Like any man could tie me down."

"Don't know what I was thinking," I said, laughing. I finally popped the tab on my beer and chugged it down. "Mom said something about one of the cabins maybe being empty or being able to use the barn loft apartment. Wanna hook a guy up with a place to crash?"

"What, you don't want to share with Jonathan?"

I grinned. "He basically let me know I'm not welcome to. Thought that kid liked me."

Her face softened. "He loves you. But you remember what it's like to be eighteen."

Yeah, I did. That was the problem.

AFTER I GOT SETTLED INTO THE LOFT APARTMENT, I WALKED down to the office. I'd need a horse while I was here, and I knew I'd have to go through Travis to get one.

Sure enough, he was hunched over the desk, frowning as he looked over charts and schedules. Travis worked sunup to sundown, even when Dad wasn't out of commission. He was responsible like that. Made the rest of us look bad.

I rapped on the open door. When he didn't look up, I spoke to get his attention. "Hey, Travis."

He glanced up, nodding in acknowledgement, before flipping over the charts he was looking at like he didn't want me to see them. Cool as a cucumber, he didn't say a word. Reminded me of Cheyenne's greeting. But at least she'd said my name.

"Can I talk to you for a second?" I asked.

"Give me a minute. Let me finish up here. You can wait on the bench outside."

I frowned, annoyed at his dismissal. I might not have worked here at the ranch, but I was still family. Didn't know why he had to be so secretive. But there was no use arguing with him.

I sure as hell wasn't going to sit and wait on a bench though.

Instead, I took a stroll through the stables, checking out the horses who'd been brought into their stalls for dinner. We had a few new ones since I'd last been home, including a couple of pretty mares and two Shetland ponies. I'd almost made my way down the line when I heard Travis come out and clear his throat.

I walked back down to him and leaned on the stable gate, propping my boot up on the lowest rung. "I'll be needing a horse while I'm here. Figured I needed to talk to you about that."

He gave me a look, then walked by me, heading toward the end of the barn from where I'd just come. I followed, catching up.

"I said I'll be needing a horse."

"How long are you really staying?" He didn't even look at me.

"As long as you need me to."

He stopped and turned toward me, crossing his arms. "I needed you this morning. Hell, I needed you ten years ago."

"Hey, man—"

"Don't 'hey, man' me. We needed you. You left. Didn't even give us any warning. We counted on you, and you blew off your responsibilities and left us in a lurch. You haven't stayed more than three nights in a row ever since, and you sure haven't cared about how thin we've been stretched before. So why on earth should I believe you're going to hang around this time?"

My chest tightened. "Look, we're never going to agree about the past. But I'm here now, and I want to help."

He snorted. "Yeah, until you get a hankering to leave again. Then you'll just disappear, not caring about the fallout."

I shoved my hands into my pockets and gritted my teeth. "You going to give me a horse or what?"

He stared at me, his eyes narrowing. "You want one, you've got to earn it."

"Earn it how?"

He nodded toward the very back of the stables, where I hadn't made it yet. "Got a new one in. We named him Diablo."

"Diablo?" My eyebrows shot to the roof.

Travis snickered. "He suits you. He lets you, you can ride him. But you don't touch any of my other horses, you hear? I've already got a riding schedule made up for this week, and I better not come out here and find one of my horses missing."

With that, he sauntered off, chuckling under his breath.

I groaned. I had known Travis wouldn't make it easy on me. But this?

"Alright," I muttered under my breath. "I'm already in hell. Might as well go meet this Diablo and see what I have to deal with."

Chapter Five

Cheyenne

I ate my burger and fries as quickly as possible, barely tasting them. A few more of our teammates came into the bar for celebratory drinks. Everyone was in a great mood despite their exhaustion. We always felt good after a positive outcome.

But I couldn't force myself to share their joy. Not this time.

"You okay?" Sam asked quietly, slipping around to my side of the booth.

"I'm fine."

He snorted. "Sure you are. I know you well enough to know better than that."

I leaned my head back and closed my eyes. "Okay. I'm not fine."

He was quiet for a minute. "Is this the first time you've seen him since—"

"Since he left in the middle of the night? Yeah, it is." I brushed my hair away from my face, tucking it behind my ears, knowing I must look awful. Still hadn't showered, hadn't slept, and the emotions coursing through me over seeing Rhett made me feel like I'd aged another ten years in a matter of minutes. Not exactly the version of myself I'd wanted him to see the first time we saw each other again. But that was life. It never seemed to work out exactly the way I wanted it to.

Sam nudged me. "Wanna talk about it? We can go somewhere else."

I pushed the last of my food away, unable to stomach it any longer. "No, but thank you. I'm really tired. I'm going to head out, take a hot shower, and settle in for some sleep."

He closed his hand over mine. "Cheyenne. I remember how he broke your heart."

I shook him off. "He didn't break anything."

But we both knew that was a lie.

I stood in the shower with my face turned up to the hot spray of water, letting it run down my face to hide the tears I resented. Rhett didn't deserve them.

But they fell anyway.

When the water finally turned cold and I couldn't possibly have any tears left, I got out and grabbed a towel, drying my face. I wiped the steam from the mirror, getting a quick glance at how terrible I looked before it fogged back up again. Red eyes, puffy cheeks, and the kind of exhaustion sleep couldn't fix wasn't a pretty combination.

Just like the day I'd found out he was gone.

I hated that he could still do this to me. Ten years later, he'd somehow found a way to break my heart all over again. I took a deep breath, steeling myself. It was just the initial aftershock, that was all. I was strong. I would put myself back together, and the next time I saw him, it wouldn't be like this. I'd be ready for it.

What I certainly was *not* ready for was the knock on my door. I braced myself on the bathroom counter, groaning.

I grabbed a sweater from my closet and pulled it over my head, calling out that I'd be there in a minute. As soon as I was dressed, I went to the door, opening it to find Claire standing on my steps with a bottle of wine in her hand and an apologetic look on her face.

I sighed. "Come on in."

"I'm sorry," she said, greeting my dog with a quick belly rub as I locked up behind her. "I didn't know he was in town, much less that he'd gone to the bar tonight. You okay?"

Claire normally gave me a heads-up when her brother was around, and I'd usually find a reason to stay busy at home instead of venturing out where I might run into him. He never stayed long anyway.

"I'm fine."

"Liar. You've been crying."

I shot her a look and headed to the kitchen, pulling out two wine glasses. "Nah. Just a hot shower."

"Right." She rolled her eyes, kicked off her boots, and plopped down at my kitchen table. "I love my brother, but he makes me so mad sometimes. I don't know how he could be so stupid."

My heart warmed at her loyalty. "Let's not talk about him. Except..." I hesitated, wondering if I really wanted the answer to my question.

"Yeah?"

I poured the deep-red wine into the glass, avoiding Claire's eyes. "He said he's staying for a while to help out."

She nodded. "That's what he says."

"How long do you think it will last?"

She bit her lip. "Honestly?"

"Of course." I faced her, surprised by the worried look on her face.

"I think he's serious. I don't think he's going to rush off."

"What makes you say that?"

This time, a little grin flashed on her face. "Well, for one thing, the only horse Travis would give him is Diablo, and he's actually trying to saddle him."

I spit out my wine while laughing. "You're kidding."

She shook her head. "Travis is pretty pissed at him, obviously. Isn't going to make it easy."

"Apparently not. Diablo isn't going to cooperate with Rhett."

"Exactly." Her face darkened. "But it's more than that. I don't know, Cheyenne. I get the feeling he isn't telling us everything."

This time, I frowned. "You think he's in some kind of trouble?"

She shrugged. "Knowing Rhett? There's really no telling. But normally, the first thing he does is tell us how quick he'll be heading out again. Like he doesn't want to get anyone's hopes up about him staying for even a week. Always sets the expectation from the beginning that he'll be in and out—don't get used to it. This time, it was the exact opposite. He's even setting up in the barn loft apartment."

"Hmmm." I didn't know Rhett well—not anymore, which was a strange thing considering how we'd once known each other so well that I could read his mind from across the room. But I knew he normally blew out of town as fast as he arrived. It was interesting, that was for sure.

And complicated for me, for both personal and professional reasons.

Claire studied me. "He asked if you and Sam are dating."

I almost spit out my wine again. "Seriously? Me and Sam?"

She grinned. "Yeah. He looked relieved when I told him Sam has a girlfriend."

I rolled my eyes. "I don't know why he'd care."

Her face turned serious again. "Cheyenne, I don't know why he left. But I know he loved you. And I don't think he's ever loved anyone else since. Maybe—"

"No." I shut it down immediately.

"If he hung around, you don't think there's any chance you two would rekindle things?"

"It's too late for that. First, we have no idea how long he's really going to stay anyway. Second, I could never trust him again. Not after the way he left. Third..." I shook my head, not wanting to reveal the truth: that loving him had destroyed me and I'd never risk that kind of destruction again. "I like my life and I'm not looking for more," I said lamely.

"I figured. So I'm guessing you want me to discourage him if he acts interested?"

"Of course," I said, picking up my wine and swallowing the rest of it in one gulp.

"Okay." She rapped her knuckles on my table and stood, grinning. "I'm going to head out. We both need to get some sleep. I'm on shift tomorrow, but I'll see you Friday, okay?"

"You didn't even touch your wine," I said, laughing.

"I only brought it for you." She tugged her boots back on and headed toward the door. "Stay out of trouble—unless you invite me to go with you, that is." She gave me an exaggerated wink and tossed her blonde hair back.

"You're a terrible deputy," I said, finally giving her a real smile.

"Don't I know it," she said, laughing. "Love you."

"Love you, too."

I locked the door behind her, grateful she'd stopped by. She was the sister of my heart, and that was something Rhett hadn't taken away when he'd left.

Despite my exhaustion, I tossed and turned through a night haunted by dreams of the past. The next morning, I decided an early ride was what I needed to put me to rights before I faced what was certain to be a challenging day at work. I put coffee into a thermos, saddled up Wildfire, and hit the trail, climbing to the top of a ridge where the Wyoming plains stretched out in front of me.

Out here, I could breathe again. I slowed Wildfire to a stop, looking out over the land as a sense of peace filled my heart. This was where I belonged. It was the great love of my life now—the wind, the storms, the mountains, the sagebrush that dotted the landscape. The wild ponies, the spirit that flowed through this country. It strengthened me. Made me remember what mattered.

Once, I had wanted Rhett to be my cowboy on a white horse, taking me away from all of it.

But up here, on the mountain that was as much a part of me as I was it, I could see that it was a gift that he hadn't. That was the problem with young love. It blinded you to everything that really mattered.

And this mattered.

I had a home I loved. Work that filled my soul. A good horse. A faithful dog. Friends.

It was all I needed.

I made a vow to remember that when I had to face Rhett again today.

· · ·

TRAVIS WAS PACING OUT FRONT WHEN I PULLED INTO MY parking place at the ranch. He came straight to my window, giving me a motion to stay put.

I ignored him and stepped out of the truck anyway. "What's up?"

He put his hands on his hips and spit, disgusted. "I figure Claire told you who's here."

"She did."

"You didn't have to come today. That's the deal. Anytime he's here, you get a paid day off."

I shook my head. "Not this time. Claire says he's hanging around for more than a day or two. You're short-staffed with Walker recovering. Besides, you already had to cover for me while I was out on the search. I'm not going to leave you in a lurch today."

"We'll manage somehow. You don't have to be here."

I put a hand on his shoulder and gave him a little smile. "Thanks. But I happen to like my new job, and I don't plan on letting him ruin that."

I'd only recently started working for the ranch, but I loved it. They were completely understanding about my SAR volunteer schedule, and I got to be outside around horses all day and actually get paid for it. Beyond that, I genuinely enjoyed the work.

At first, being back here had been hard. Too many reminders of Rhett. But it had gotten easier. As long as I kept strict boundaries in place—like not coming back to family dinners, no matter how often Naomi invited me—it was fine.

When Travis first hired me, he made me a deal that Claire would give me a heads-up when Rhett was home and I would get paid days off until he was gone. It hadn't been an issue thus far though, and I had no intention of taking advantage of them now.

I wasn't a coward. I could work here and ignore Rhett. Besides, he probably wouldn't hang around for long. It would be fine.

Travis studied me, then nodded. "Okay. If you're sure."

"I'm sure. Thanks though."

"Of course." His eyes softened, giving me an affectionate look. He'd always treated me like one of his sisters, and I appreciated it. "He asked for a horse to use while he's here 'helping.' I gave him Diablo."

My face broke into a grin. "Claire told me. That should be fun to watch. As long as you trust him to not do anything that will cause a setback for Diablo, that is."

"Nah." Travis shook his head. "Rhett's got his issues, but he always knew horses. He respects them. That's about the only area where I trust him not to screw up. Diablo will be fine, but I figure it will help speed up Rhett's exit."

"Probably." I cocked my head. "But while he's here, you really should put him to work. Take advantage of him wanting to help."

Travis snorted. "I doubt he even knows how to do a day's work anymore."

I winked. "So show him. Might help speed up his exit even more."

He grinned. "You might be right about that. Maybe I'll put him on muck duty."

I fell into step beside him as he turned toward the stables. "So what do we have on the schedule today?"

"Two short tours this morning—two hours each. We're doing a big lunch here. Then we have a longer group going out for an afternoon tour."

"Four hours?" I confirmed.

"Four or five if everyone's having a good time. You good with that?"

"Yeah, I'm good."

"Great. Beth is going on the morning tours, but I think Jonathan will be your backup this afternoon. It's a half-day at school and he wants to earn some extra money before prom."

"Got it."

I tensed automatically as I saw a familiar figure storm out of the barn, cursing as he kicked a rock down the pathway.

Travis chuckled. "I'm guessing he didn't have any luck with Diablo this morning."

I couldn't join his laughter. The sight of Rhett made it difficult for me to breathe. "Does he know I work here?"

"Doubt it. We all kept quiet about it when he got here—*that* was awkward. Only one who might have said something is Claire."

But based on the way Rhett froze when he saw me walking toward him, I knew she hadn't told him, either.

Chapter Six

Rhett

Diablo lived up to his name and worse. Damn horse wanted to laze around the pasture, eating grass and strutting for the ladies, but had absolutely no intention of letting me saddle him or even lead him back into the stall. I'd tried sweet-talking him, buttering him up with treats. He was having none of it.

Didn't know why we even had a horse like that here. This was a working ranch and we needed horses that liked their jobs. No sense in paying the feed bill on a horse that didn't contribute, and this one was bound and determined not to contribute a thing.

Travis was messing with me. Trying to get me to leave.

Well, too bad for him. If he wanted me gone, I was damn sure going to stick around.

I walked out of the stables, heading toward the main house to find some food. But I stopped in my tracks when I looked up and saw Travis walking all cozy with Cheyenne.

Hell.

No wonder he wanted me to go.

I crossed my arms, gritted my teeth, and tried to force something that looked remotely like a smile as they approached.

"Morning, Rhett," Travis said, a hint of warning in his voice.

"Morning." The word came out as pure gravel, and I knew my attempt at a smile probably looked more like a snarl. "What's she doing here?"

Travis slung a protective arm around Cheyenne's shoulders. She crossed her arms and gave me a level look.

"She happens to work here," Travis said. "When Claire started working full-time, we needed someone to take over the trail rides. That going to be a problem for you?"

Both their faces made it clear it didn't matter if it was. Cheyenne wasn't going anywhere.

"Not a problem," I said between gritted teeth.

"Good."

I started to walk away, then turned. "Why the hell do we have a horse like Diablo taking up a stall space, anyway?"

This time, Cheyenne spoke. "Because I asked them to. And no matter what your feelings are toward that horse, I expect you to treat him right—or else you'll have to deal with me."

They turned away, not offering any other explanation. I stared after them, wondering when my older brother had decided to make my ex-girlfriend his own.

I was still staring when Travis turned around and smirked. "Oh yeah. Forgot to tell you. Since you've offered to help, you're on muck duty today. Once you get done with that, come find me and I'll give you your next assignment."

Shit.

Literally.

A FEW HOURS LATER, I WAS DRIPPING SWEAT AND I STANK. But damn if the stalls I'd finished didn't look fantastic. I leaned on my shovel, looking proudly at my work. Travis might not have thought much of my work ethic, but he was wrong. He had no idea how hard I'd worked the last few years.

Of course, I couldn't really blame him for that. I'd kept my life to myself, never sharing much beyond the basics with the family. Wasn't even sure why, except that they all thought I was a screwup. Made it hard to share anything real with them. It felt like they were always searching my words, looking for my mistakes. Looking for a reason to talk about me when I was gone.

No matter how much I built for myself, it never felt like enough.

But I'd worked hard. Had to, working in construction and property development. I'd busted my ass, saved, and lived simply. Now that I was tired of working for someone else, I was in the position to start something of my own. I'd given my boss my notice before heading north, using the family emergency as an excuse. Hated that Dad was hurt, but it was the kick in the pants I'd needed to finally cut ties and move forward with finding my own path. I wanted to start my own business, build my own legacy. Do the kind of projects that really mattered to me.

Wasn't going to be here though. Based on how well this visit had gone so far, I knew I should get as far away from Wyoming as possible before picking a place to lay down stakes. But with Dad down, they needed me—whether they wanted to admit it or not.

I'd gone back to my work when Cheyenne walked in, her soft leather boots barely making a sound as she strolled down the length of the stable. I deliberately ignored her at first. She came up to me and stopped, crossing her arms as she surveyed my work.

I turned and looked at her, clamping my mouth so I didn't say anything bitter or sarcastic. Seeing her here was too damn emotional. I was angry—angry watching my brother sling his arm around her like she was his, angry seeing that she fit better here than I did now. Angry that my family clearly preferred her over me.

And I hated to admit it, but behind all that anger was grief threatening to flow like a raging river if I didn't keep it walled up where it couldn't escape. Seeing her here... Well, it brought it all back. Those days when I'd felt freer and lighter than I ever had since. Days when I felt like I'd conquered the whole world because Cheyenne was mine. Nights when we'd sneak down to the barn together or take a blanket out to the back pasture to sleep underneath the stars, surrounded by the horses she loved so much.

I was glad she was here, for her sake. But it added a whole new level of hard for me. I grabbed my water and gulped it down, wishing it could satisfy my real cravings. Cravings that were eating so deep at my soul that I was tempted to run away from here again just to stop feeling them.

But I knew from experience that it wouldn't work. Didn't matter how far I ran—I'd never once stopped wanting Cheyenne.

CHAPTER SEVEN

Cheyenne

AFTER THE MORNING TOURS, I HEADED INTO THE STABLE, bracing myself before seeing Rhett. Beth had offered to let him know lunch was ready, but I wanted to do it myself. It felt important for me to face him. After today, the ice would be broken and we could simply be two coworkers who rarely had to see each other. My job primarily kept me out on the land with the tourists who wanted a taste of cowboy life in Wyoming. I knew that Travis would keep Rhett busy with grunt work in the stables.

But, today, I needed to prove to myself that I could be around him without Travis's protection.

When I stepped into the barn and saw him, my face flushed with heat as memories flooded me. This was the place where he'd first whispered those sweet words of love into my ear. The place where he'd given me my first kiss and I'd given him my heart. It all rushed back in a way I hadn't prepared for. I had to remind myself that the Rhett I was seeing in front of me wasn't the same boy I'd fallen in love with. He was a man now, a man I barely even knew.

He was caught up in his work and didn't even notice me. I stared, unable to stop from appreciating how incredible he looked in those tight jeans with his low-hanging buckle and a black button-down shirt tucked into his belt. His rippling forearms glistened with sweat, and his long dark hair kept falling over one eye.

Then he looked at me with those dark eyes that could still hold my gaze across a room. I could barely breathe, feeling like my heart might shatter all over again.

Our love had been childish, but it had been real. Seeing him again, all this time later, I wanted to weep for the years that had been stolen from us—and for the future years we'd never have. Because even though Rhett Hawkins was still the only man who could make my breath catch like that, it didn't matter. He'd ruined any chance of a future together.

Not that he wanted one anyway.

He gulped down a bottle of water, then gave me an angry stare. "Checking my work? Wasn't aware that you're now the co-captain around here."

I didn't know whether to laugh or cry. "Actually, you've done a very nice job. Didn't know you still had it in you."

"Mucking out stalls isn't exactly rocket science," he grumbled, grabbing the manure fork and moving to the next one.

"That's true. But there's a difference between someone who does a fast and dirty job just to get it done and someone who actually tries to make the space as comfortable for the horses as possible." I walked down and looked at another one of the stalls before glancing back at him. "I didn't realize you still cared about them so much."

"Of course I care. It's my family's legacy."

My eyebrows furrowed. "And yet, you left."

"And yet, I'm here."

He was. I respected it. Appreciated it. And hated him for giving me another reason to admire him.

"You need something?" His tone was clipped.

"I'm here to tell you that lunch is ready. It's out on the back lawn."

He jabbed the fork into the ground and leaned on it, giving me a wary look. "Who all is invited?"

"Everyone," I said, wanting to make clear that this wasn't a special invitation. "It's something we do for the guests. Part of the whole ranch experience."

He frowned. "That's new."

"Not really. They've been doing it for a couple of years now."

"They didn't do it when I was here. Back then, the focus was on the cattle, not on city folk who want to come out here and pretend to be cowboys."

I shrugged. "We've expanded our offerings. The tourism side of things has become a bigger player for the ranch financially than it used to be. Honestly, it's probably saved them."

"I see." He stared at me for a moment. "Guess I'll clean up and come get some food."

"Okay." I'd known he would. Even so, I felt a mild flutter of panic. Every moment I was with him felt like pouring salt into an unhealed wound.

"Hey, um." He cleared his throat awkwardly, taking off his black cowboy hat and raking his hair back behind his ears. "Are you and Travis..."

I wanted to say something sarcastic. Wanted to be angry he'd asked at all, about Travis *and* Sam, when he didn't have the right to know a thing about my love life. But something about the agony on his face made me unable to do it.

"No," I said quietly, shaking my head. "He's like a big brother to me, the way Claire is still like a sister. They've always looked out for me."

It was more than that. When Rhett had left, they'd both insisted on still being my family. I'd tried to pull away, but they refused to let me. They respected the fact that I needed distance from the family as a whole. But they kept checking on me, letting me know Rhett's absence didn't change our friendships. It was something I would always be grateful for, no matter how hard it had been at first.

"Okay. I know I don't really have the right to ask," he said, the agony on his face deepening.

"Then why did you?" I regretted the question as soon as I asked it. There wasn't an answer he could give that wouldn't hurt. But we'd never had any sense of closure. One day, we'd been together; the next, he was gone. And we'd never spoken again. Maybe if we got some of it out, it wouldn't hurt so much anymore.

Maybe someday he'd even tell me why I hadn't been enough for him.

"This is hard," he admitted. "Nobody told me you worked here. Honestly, if I'd known, I wouldn't have come back."

That stung.

"So why did you come back, Rhett? Why now, after all this time?"

"My dad's hurt. I had some free time, and I really want to help my family out," he said, those eyes piercing me. "But like I said, I didn't know they'd hired you. It's weird, being around you. If you and Travis were together, I wouldn't be able to handle it."

"I don't belong to you anymore." The words came out in a whisper.

"I know."

Part of me wanted him to say he wished I still did, that he wished things were different. That he regretted leaving. But he didn't say a word.

I LEFT RHETT IN THE BARN AND HEADED TOWARD THE outdoor buffet, grateful to put some space between us. I closed my eyes, taking in a deep breath as I reminded myself that this was the worst of it. I'd faced him and I'd survived.

This was the most painful it would be. Every future interaction would get a little easier, and it was temporary. Walker's full recovery would take time, but I knew he'd be back in the saddle the moment he got the all clear from the doctor. Six weeks tops, I imagined.

Six weeks was still a long time to have to see Rhett every working day.

Beth saw me walking and waved me over to where she was sitting perched on one of the square hay bales we kept for people to sit on. She'd already shed her cowboy hat, and her light-brown hair was pulled back in a gold clip, with loose tendrils framing her delicate face. As comfortable as she was on the back of a horse, she didn't quite fit the cowgirl persona the way Claire did. Beth seemed to belong to another time and place altogether. When she wasn't working, she had her head stuck in a book or would curl up somewhere with a notebook, scribbling down story ideas. She was a responsible, reliable member of the family who never shirked the work, but I secretly wondered how much longer we'd have her as part of the operation before she found her own path.

I motioned to her, letting her know I'd join her as soon as I grabbed a plate, then jumped in line to load up on Naomi's incredible cooking. Today's menu was chili and homemade cornbread, two things I'd never bother making myself but made my mouth water when it was Naomi cooking them. She'd grown up in the South, and her sweet Southern cornbread was practically a dessert. The guests always went nuts over it. They also went nuts over *her*. Naomi insisted on serving the guests herself, and I swore it was half the magic of the experience. She took the time to get to know every guest personally, remembered their food preferences, and always had a kind smile for everyone.

Today, she stood behind the buffet, her auburn hair looking almost golden in the bright sun. Her gorgeous skin was bare except for the tinted moisturizer she swore by and the pink lip balm she always had in her pocket. She was a woman who still looked ten years younger than her age, despite being what she called "a low-maintenance girlie." I thought it had something to do with her spirit. The good ones always seemed to age more gracefully than anyone else.

"Smells amazing," I said, smiling at her as she dished me up a large helping.

"Thank you." She smiled, but it didn't quite reach her eyes. "I didn't expect to see you here today. You know we understand if you'd rather..."

I shook my head. "I'm fine. With me working here now, it was bound to happen sooner or later, wasn't it?"

She nodded slowly. "Have you two talked yet?"

I knew what she meant. She wanted to know if we'd had any real conversation—if he'd apologized or even given an explanation. I gave her a tight smile. "We interacted briefly. It's fine, Naomi. I promise. It won't affect my work."

She gave me a sympathetic look. "It's not your work I'm worried about, honey. I love my son with all my heart, but…"

I swallowed hard. "It was a long time ago."

"You let me know if you need anything, okay?"

"I will."

She shot me a knowing look.

"I promise." I gave her a quick nod and headed over to Beth, blinking back the tears that had been threatening to spill all day.

Despite the emotions of the past twenty-four hours, I wasn't normally the type to cry. I'd shed countless tears the week Rhett had left, then none until the day my grandmother died. I'd sobbed at her funeral, but I'd never had time for tears since. There was too much work to be done. Who had time to cry for something that couldn't be changed?

But with Rhett back, my emotions felt like a swirling dark storm, threatening to let loose if I gave them leave. That was the dangerous thing about him. He'd always been able to reach a part of my heart that no one else could. It was what had made me love him before—and what made him so difficult to be around now.

I sat down on the spot Beth had saved for me and spoke first, before she had the chance to question me the way Naomi had. "Great work today," I said, giving her a smile that almost felt genuine. "I think everyone loved the tour."

She searched my eyes, then let out a little breath and returned my smile. "The kids were adorable."

"They were," I said, laughing as my eyes sought out the two little boys on the other side of the yard with their parents.

They'd both been so excited about being cowboys that they'd arrived for their ride in the most adorable cowboy boots, leather chaps, and matching red cowboy hats. The youngest one was a natural. He was comfortable in the saddle and spent the whole ride singing cowboy songs at the top of his lungs. The older one was terrified. Beth rode beside him, coaching him the whole time, but he gripped the saddle horn with both hands and never relaxed. When we finally got back to the ranch, he jumped off the horse and kissed the ground dramatically.

Beth's eyes went dreamy. "I'd love to have at least five kids someday."

"You're good with them," I commented. It was true, and it was the reason I greatly preferred having her partner with me on the trail instead of Jonathan. Beth was a natural at making the kids feel safe and keeping them in line. Jonathan was practically a kid himself and got annoyed at staying in the back with the young ones.

"Yeah." She made a face. "If only I could find a decent man."

I grinned. "Did your date with Pete not go well?"

"He's sweet," she said, sighing. "But we had absolutely nothing to talk about. All the man wants to do is talk horses and feed and farming."

"I'm guessing you get enough of that around here," I said, shooting her a sympathetic smile.

"Exactly. Besides, it's clear enough that all he's looking for is a wife. It felt more like a job interview than a date." She rolled her eyes.

"But aren't you looking for a husband?" Her attitude surprised me, since it was no secret that she had dreams of being a wife and mother.

She toyed with the button on her shirt, looking away. "Yes, but...I want more than that, too. I don't want to get married for the sake of getting married. I want love. Soulmate kind of love. I want to meet that one person who turns my whole world upside down, who makes me see everything differently... Someone I know I'll want to wake up beside every single morning for the rest of my life. And I want him to feel the same about me. Not just marry me because it's convenient and I'll make a decent ranch wife." She glanced at me, flushing. "I suppose someone as practical as you probably thinks that's silly."

"No," I said, my heart aching as I thought of how I'd once felt that way about Rhett. Like I'd found my other half, the one person who made the whole world make sense. How, after years of feeling alone in the world, he'd made me feel like I would never be alone again.

Until he left and I was worse off than I'd been before loving him.

Still, I knew what that kind of love felt like. And while it hadn't worked out for me, I hoped it would for her.

"I hope you find someone who turns your world upside down," I said quietly. "But only in the best ways."

Her face changed and she bit her lip, giving me a nervous look.

"Rhett?" I asked. Not that I needed to. I could practically feel the energy change with him near.

She nodded. "He came."

"It's fine." I had a feeling I was going to be repeating those words a million times today, and I wasn't sure how to feel about it. On one hand, I felt lucky to be cared for by this family that meant so much to me. On the other hand, their concern kept bringing my attention to the issue instead of giving me the distraction I needed. The last thing I wanted was to waste any more emotional energy on Rhett Hawkins.

"Looks like Mom is lecturing him," she whispered with a little giggle.

I smiled, despite the ache in my heart. "I have a feeling he's going to get a lot of that if he hangs around."

Beth turned to me, giving me a piercing look. "Will you leave us if he does? Honestly, Cheyenne, I don't know what we'd do without you."

I waved her off. "Let's get real. He's not going to hang around long. And if he does? It will be fine."

It had to be. Because I couldn't let him take anything else from me.

CHAPTER EIGHT

Rhett

MOM'S FOOD WAS THE BEST IN SAGE COUNTY, BUT I COULD barely taste it as I choked it down on the only free hay bale left—one that happened to be directly across from Cheyenne. I tried to look anywhere else—the sky, the trees, the guests. But my treacherous eyes kept turning, stealing glances at her as she ate lunch with my little sister.

They were totally different. Beth was like a delicate rose. Prim and proper, sweet and gentle. She was only a few years younger than me, but somehow she was still just a girl in my eyes.

Cheyenne, on the other hand, had grown into an incredible woman. I couldn't stop myself from watching as she interacted with the guests who came up to thank her for the tour she'd given them. They adored her. Two little boys even insisted on getting their picture taken with her, and she handled it all with grace.

She'd been shy when we were kids. Hell, the first couple years she and Claire were friends, I barely even knew she existed. She always seemed to shrink into herself, like she didn't want to be noticed by any of the rest of us.

She'd been different with me, once I'd gotten to know her though. Free and happy. I'd always loved how I got to see that side of her. No matter how quiet and reserved she was around everyone else, with me, she'd been completely open. Trusting.

Until I broke that trust.

As I watched her now, it was clear she'd come into her own without me. She was strong and confident. Still quiet, especially compared to Claire, but she didn't shrink anymore. Was comfortable with who she was and didn't need me by her side to draw her out. Didn't know why that surprised me. We'd all grown up. But I felt unexpected pride watching her do her thing.

Unfortunately, watching her also caused an odd ache in my heart. When I'd left all those years ago, I'd never meant it to be a permanent break between me and her. I had to get away from the ranch. Had my reasons for that. But it wasn't because I'd wanted to leave her.

I gritted my teeth and dug into my chili, trying hard not to look up at the woman sitting across from me. If I'd known I was going to have to see her every damn day on the ranch, I might not have come back at all. Maybe this was what I got for skipping confession the last, oh, fourteen years. Mom would say penance had found me anyway.

After scarfing my food, I got up and headed back to the stables to finish up the stalls. I should have had them finished before lunch, but I was out of practice and I wanted them to be perfect. Wasn't sure why I was trying so hard to prove myself, but I was. I knew no one expected much out of me.

I was bound and determined to prove them wrong.

Travis came in while I was finishing up the last one. He didn't say a word as he walked up and down, looking at my work the way Cheyenne had. I bit back the sarcastic remarks bubbling up.

"Nice work," he finally said, a look of surprise on his face.

"Thanks," I said gruffly, surprised at what his approval meant to me. "What's my next job?"

He gave me a level look. "Cheyenne's taking the next group out in about forty-five minutes. It's a longer tour, and they won't be back until dinner. We need to saddle up some fresh horses, make sure she has every-thing she needs. When she brings them over here, we'll help riders mount and get the stirrups adjusted for them. Once all the guests are settled and they head out for the tour, I need to ride over and check the cattle. I have a couple of late-season calves due any day now. I'd appre-ciate the help if you want to come."

It was the closest thing to a peace offering he could give me. Cattle were his passion. Even offering to let me near them meant something.

I nodded slowly. "I can do that."

"Okay." He gave me a nod and turned, heading out.

I followed him, bracing myself for another interaction with Cheyenne. But she wasn't there. It was just me, Travis, and the horses. He pointed out the ones she'd taken that morning. He'd apparently skipped lunch in order to take their saddles off and turn them out onto the pasture. Those horses were done for the day, so we picked out a fresh batch for the new group based on the ages and sizes of the guests registered.

"Cheyenne will want the two ponies for the littles," he said, point-ing, "and she likes to ride Stormy, the gray mare over there."

"Fitting," I mumbled under my breath.

Travis shot me a look. "Can you handle getting those saddled up?"

"Yep."

"You'll see the pony saddles in the tack room. Cheyenne's saddle is the black one. She also takes the black saddlebags with the med kit, and you'll need to add six bottles of water from the fridge in my office. Beth will carry the rest of the water for the guests, but I'll take care of prep-ping her horse."

"Got it." I turned away, hiding my scowl.

There was a time when I'd known Cheyenne better than any other person in the world. I'd known her likes, her dislikes. Her favorite movie. The way her eyes fluttered when she slept. How she always kept sugar cubes in her right jacket pocket for the horses. The way she'd throw her head back and laugh when she was on the back of my bike, reveling in the pure freedom of fast roads and sunshine. How her breathing changed when she got excited. How she tasted.

And now, my brother was the one telling *me* what Cheyenne liked, what she needed. Pissed me off.

But I gritted my teeth and got the job done, trying to block out the memories of all the times I'd saddled a horse for Cheyenne before. Despite the passing years, I found myself doing exactly what I'd always done then—checking every cinch twice more than I'd check my own, needing to know everything was secure.

When I turned and caught her staring at me, I knew she was remembering, too.

"Thanks," she said, avoiding my eyes as she came to take the reins from me.

"You're welcome."

At the sound of my voice, she turned to look at me, saying nothing. I looked into her eyes and almost got swept away in the depths of them. I had to shake myself and walk away, hoping no one noticed.

WHEN WE HAD THE GROUP ON THEIR WAY, TRAVIS HANDED me a walkie-talkie and told me to saddle up a horse for myself.

I eyed him. "Ah. I see. This whole 'help you check the cattle' thing was really just so you could laugh at me trying to saddle Diablo."

He chuckled. "As funny as that would be, no. You can take one of the others."

"Thank God. I'd rather not die today."

He scoffed. "Diablo won't kill you. But he also won't let you ride him." He pointed toward a horse near the front of the pasture. "I'd recommend Whisper, the paint horse over there. He likes working cattle."

"Got it."

I led Whisper into the stable while Travis got his own horse. Then I fell into step beside him as we headed to the tack room to grab saddles.

"So, again, I ask you. Why do we have that damn horse out here anyway? Not like you to keep a horse around that's not good for anything."

Travis was quiet for a beat. "Diablo's a rescue. Came from the Smiths' farm. Cheyenne reported Thomas Smith for animal cruelty and

Sheriff McGrath confiscated his animals, including Diablo. They all needed places to go. The local rescue didn't have a spot for him, and Chey couldn't afford to take on another feed bill. So she asked if we could take him, give her a chance to try to rehabilitate him. She offered to put in extra hours here without pay to help cover his food and board until he can earn his keep."

A whole range of emotions flooded my chest. Admiration for the woman Cheyenne was—had always been. Anger to hear about Thomas —he'd been in school with me and Cheyenne, and he'd always been a snake. Irritation that she was working for free, to cover someone else's mistakes.

"You make her do that?" I asked, unable to stop the growl in my voice.

"Of course not," Travis said, rolling his eyes. He grabbed a saddle and gestured toward one he apparently wanted me to get, then headed back out toward the horses. He rubbed his gorgeous mustang named Steel down. Then he put a blanket on its back, threw his saddle on top, and started working the cinches.

"We can cover hay for one more," he said, explaining. "Besides, I think Cheyenne's right. I don't know if he'll ever be a solid enough trail horse to use for guests, but he's got a ton of potential. And if anyone can rehabilitate him, it's her."

"I'm surprised she even let you offer him to me," I admitted. "Last thing I want to do is screw up a rehab."

He grinned. "Well, getting him used to other people is phase three of her rehabilitation plan. She's already implemented the first two phases. Besides, I know you. No matter how pissed you get, there's no way you're going to let him see it. You know horses, respect them. I knew it would be fine."

His approval meant something to me, but I ignored it and scoffed. "Seems like she skipped a step if she's on phase three and he still won't let anyone saddle him."

Travis smirked. "Oh, he lets her."

"Really?"

He nodded. "Yep. She's ridden him in the training circle several times. He's skittish but sweet as a baby with her. It's men he doesn't trust. She said it will take time for him to realize the men here aren't like Thomas."

Pride bloomed in my chest. Of course she could ride him. Cheyenne's way with animals had always been almost spooky. They trusted her. Always had.

Travis gave me a funny look. "What are you grinning about over there?"

"Nothing," I said, wiping the look from my face as I adjusted my saddle. "You ready?"

I HAD TO ADMIT, BEING OUT ON THE RANGE WITH THE horses and cattle felt good. It was something I'd always missed. There was nothing like those Wyoming skies stretching out in all directions, that feeling of trotting over the plains on the back of a good horse. I'd been all over the country, but nowhere felt like home the way this did. Ranching had never been my passion, but I'd missed this just the same.

Even though I knew it was a bad idea, part of me wished I could start my business in Wildwood and spend more days like this, out on the land that still had a hold on my heart. It would never work though. Not with Cheyenne hating me and with things always being so damn awkward with my family. The last thing I needed were the constant guilt trips I'd get if I lived here but didn't work the ranch.

When Travis was content with the condition of his cattle, he motioned back toward the ranch house.

"Race you back?" he called, grinning.

"You're on," I muttered under my breath, giving him a hard nod.

He took off like a rocket on his mustang. I tried to catch up, but in the end, it was no contest. He'd beaten me—badly.

Just like he'd known he would.

He was smirking when I finally caught up to him. "What's the problem?" he asked, ribbing me. "Out of practice?"

I leaned over on my saddle horn and smirked. "Being the first to finish isn't something for a man to brag about."

He rolled his eyes but gave me a good-natured laugh. "Come on.

Cheyenne's group will be back soon. Let's get the horses tended to, then get some dinner. I'm half starved."

"You're always hungry."

He shrugged. "Ranching is hard work. But I guess you wouldn't know much about that, would you?"

Just like that, the ease between us dissipated and tension returned like an unwanted visitor.

WE GOT THE HORSES UNSADDLED, BRUSHED DOWN, AND settled into their stalls with fresh hay. I managed to avoid Cheyenne through all of it. It wasn't that hard, considering she was doing the same thing. When she finished answering all the guests' questions and helped them snap pictures, she came over and pulled Travis aside to talk to him.

Couldn't help myself. I found an excuse to move closer to hear what they were saying. Wasn't sure what the first part had been, but as they wrapped up, I heard Travis remind her she was always welcome to stay for dinner, even if...

I knew the end of that sentence.

It made me wonder if she was still a regular at our family dinners. As kids, she'd been here every Friday night—and sometimes more often than that. She had a place at the table right next to mine, and Mom never even bothered asking if she was coming. It was just expected.

If she'd kept that up, even without me here, no wonder my family was still pissed off at me.

I didn't hear her response, but I saw her slip out, get into her truck, and leave. When she was gone, I approached Travis and asked him if she normally stayed. Hell, if I was going to mess up her routine, then *I'd* skip dinner and let her eat with the family. It was pretty clear everyone would miss her presence more than mine anyway.

But he shook his head. "She stays if we're doing a guest dinner out on the yard. Never if it's just the family. We always invite her anyway—Mom's orders."

"Which one is it tonight? Guest dinner or family?"

Mom walked over and answered the question for him. "Just the family."

I jumped, wondering how much of the conversation she'd heard. Mom had a knack for sneaking up and hearing things we didn't necessarily want her to.

She looked at me and wrinkled her nose. "Can I make a request?"

"What's that?"

"Shower," she said pointedly. "You smell like horse manure."

"That's because Travis had me shoveling shit for half the day."

She bit back a smile. "Well, we appreciate it, I'm sure. But seriously. Don't come into my kitchen until you've cleaned yourself up."

"Yes, ma'am."

She winked and turned on her heel, walking out. Mom was a petite, feminine woman with a soft voice and a gentle spirit—but all us Hawkins boys knew better than to cross her.

So I finished up my work and headed straight for my new apartment. I jogged up the stairs and saw a note pinned to my door. I walked up and ripped it off, frowning.

Leave. You don't belong here.

Two sentences that cut me to the core. I scowled and stuffed it into my pocket before heading inside to shower. I loved my family, but this was going too far.

When I was clean and in fresh clothes, I walked over to the main house, feeling like a black cloud. Everyone was congregated in the kitchen, laughing as Travis recounted how he'd told me I had to ride Diablo, then made me muck stalls all morning.

They fell silent when they saw my face. I pulled the note out of my jacket pocket and walked over, shoving it into Travis's hand.

"This your idea of a joke, too? You really want me gone that bad?"

He looked at the note, his face blank before it turned to a frown. "Where did you get this?"

"It was tacked to my door."

Mom snatched it out of his hand and read it, her smile disappearing. "Who put this there?" she asked, turning to look at each of her children in turn, a warning look on her face.

They all shook their heads. Beth came over and gently put a hand on my forearm. "I'm sorry we were laughing," she said. "But you have to know, none of us would put something like this on your door."

"Then who was it?" I growled.

Jonathan scoffed. "Maybe Cheyenne. It's gotta be super weird for her that you're back."

Mom instantly shook her head. "Cheyenne wouldn't do that. There are some teens staying in one of the cabins close to the barn, and I've had a bad feeling about them from the beginning. They're probably pulling their idea of a prank. I'll have a word with their parents tomorrow."

Travis and I exchanged looks, making a silent agreement. Whether or not that's what was going on, that's what Mom needed to believe.

So I deliberately relaxed my features and forced a grin. "You're probably right. Teenagers. I'm sure it's nothing."

"Exactly." She smiled, then walked over and pinched my cheek. "You're mine, and you *always* belong here. And by the way, without a farmhand, we *all* take turns shoveling horse shit."

My mouth dropped at her use of a curse word. I didn't think I'd ever heard her use one before. She winked at me and turned back to the stove.

"Speaking of which," I said, turning to Travis. "Why don't we have a farmhand anymore? What happened to Jimmy?"

"Had to let him go," Travis answered, shaking his head. "Caught him stealing cash from the office."

"Man. Bad timing, with Dad's injury."

"You're telling me," Travis said. "We honestly could have managed okay without him, but Dad's accident happened two days later. Two men down really left us in a pinch. It's been brutal, especially with Claire and Cheyenne getting called out on such a long search."

"That's terrible," I said, frowning.

"Jimmy's asked for his job back three times now." Travis moved to the fridge, pulled out a couple of beers, and tossed me one. "But if I can't trust him, there's no place for him here."

"Yeah," I said slowly, cracking my beer open and swallowing down almost half of it at once.

Because I knew Travis didn't fully trust me, either. And he'd never actually said he wasn't the one to put that note on my door.

CHAPTER NINE

Cheyenne

I PULLED UP TO MY REFUGE, THE LOG CABIN MY grandfather had built in the beautiful Ponderosa pine forest on the bottom slopes of the Bighorns. The two-bedroom house wasn't much, but it was mine. I loved living tucked away in the woods, far away from the tourists who came to Wildwood every summer. Today, I was even more grateful for my private oasis—and for the sight of my dog, Ash, on the front porch. She rose from where she'd been sleeping and stretched her lithe body, yawning. Then she sat down, tail wagging, and resumed her role as guardian of the house while she waited for me to get out.

This was what I loved about dogs and horses. Unconditional love.

After today, I needed that more than ever.

I walked up my front porch steps and crouched, throwing both arms around Ash's neck.

"Hey, girl," I whispered, stroking her thick, gray fur. I pulled back and she covered my face in wet, sloppy kisses. The heartache I'd been carrying all day began to ease.

I turned and sat on the porch beside her, taking in a deep breath as I sank into the peace of the quiet woods surrounding me. I only had ten acres of my own, but my land butted up against the boundaries of Bighorn National Forest, giving me a million acres of rugged wilderness for a backyard.

I loved the solitude. I would forever be grateful for the Hawkins family and how they'd made sure I was never truly alone in this world. I'd even grown to enjoy the guests who were so thrilled to experience a bit of ranch life. But at the end of the day, I was happiest here. It was home, and it brought me peace.

Unfortunately, that peace was disturbed when I heard a vehicle coming down the road. I frowned. My cabin was well out of the way, a good fifteen-minute drive to the town of Wildwood. No one came here unless it was on purpose.

I sighed when I saw the familiar beater car pull into my driveway.

Jimmy got out, his wiry frame looking even thinner than it had, desperation painted all over his face.

"Hey, Cheyenne," he said. It came out almost like a plea.

"Hey, Jimmy."

"Did you talk to Travis about getting me my job back?"

I nodded slowly. "I asked him if there was anything you could do to earn his trust again. But you know Travis. Once a bridge is burned, it's hard going back with him, and stealing from the ranch is a big deal."

His shoulders sagged. "I've got to have that job, Cheyenne."

I felt bad for him. He'd never opened up much about his home life, but I knew he'd bounced around in foster care until he turned eighteen. I also knew that the job at Falcon Ridge Ranch had been a big step up for him. They paid generously and treated their employees with respect. I wished he hadn't screwed it up, but some people seemed to sabotage everything good in their lives.

Like Rhett, but I didn't want to think of that tonight.

"Do you need money to get you by for a bit?" I asked.

He shook his head. "I'm not taking money from you. Talk to Travis again. Please?"

"I will. You know, Pete might be able to use you at the bar. Dishwashing or something?"

A disgusted look crossed his face. "It's not the same. It's not being out on the ranch with the horses."

Jimmy loved the horses almost as much as I did.

"It's something," I said firmly. "And right now, that's what matters, right? Maybe if you work somewhere, do a good job, and earn some trust back..."

He dropped his head. "You don't trust me, either, do you?"

"I don't understand, Jimmy. Why did you do it? You had free room and board, plus very decent pay for what you did. Why take from them?"

But he wouldn't answer. "Just talk to him," he repeated, avoiding my eyes. "I'll do anything."

He got in his car and drove away.

THE NEXT DAY WENT BY IN A BLUR. TRAVIS HAD SCHEDULED a full day of ninety-minute tours. They were my least favorite, as it meant retracing the same small loop over and over again. Even the horses got bored. But we often had guests who weren't horse experienced and who were afraid to commit to longer rides. So we made the best of it, even though it made the day a bit more boring. It also created more work, since we had to change over riders more frequently.

I groaned when I saw the schedule, not only because of the rides, but because it meant more opportunities for me to be in the barn with Rhett. Thankfully, it was Claire's day off, so she was helping out. With her and Beth both there, we were able to run the trail ride side of things by ourselves, while Travis and Rhett worked to repair fencing all day.

I told myself I was relieved, but even knowing he was there on the property was a distraction. I struggled to follow what Claire was saying when she tried to talk to me, and I found myself looking for him every time we turned back toward the barn. During lunch, I kept glancing around, wondering if he and Travis would show up—and felt deeply disappointed when they didn't.

When our last group finished, Claire slung an arm around my shoulder. "How bad was it yesterday?"

"It was fine."

"Why do you even try to lie to me? I'm your best friend. I can read you like a book."

I rolled my eyes but couldn't help a smile. "Okay. It was awkward. Painful. Brought back a thousand memories I'd rather forget. But I got through it, and every day will get easier, right?"

She studied me. "No part of you wants to start things up again?"

I shook my head. "That ship has sailed. Besides, there was a moment yesterday when we were alone..."

"What?" she demanded.

"Nothing," I said, shrugging. "He asked if Travis and I were together."

She almost fell over laughing at the idea.

"And he said if he'd known I worked here, he wouldn't have bothered coming back."

It stung, even now.

She stopped laughing and frowned. "He said that?"

"Yep." I turned and started unsaddling Stormy.

"Rude."

I shrugged again. "It's how he feels. He doesn't want to be anywhere near me. Obviously, something about me made him run for the hills ten years ago." I attempted a laugh, but it came out strangled. I hadn't been enough for my father, who greatly preferred the son he'd created with his second wife. I hadn't been enough for my mother, who left me behind in Wyoming when she got a job as a flight attendant, practically forgetting she even had a child here. And I hadn't been enough for Rhett, either. Clearly, the problem was me.

"Is that what you think?" Rhett's voice, dark and angry, made me freeze in place.

I turned slowly, facing him.

He stood in the doorway, his fists at his sides. Storms raged in his eyes. "You think I left because something was wrong with you? Because you weren't *enough?*" His voice was demanding.

Claire slipped backward, then turned the corner and disappeared out of the barn altogether.

Traitor.

"I didn't say something was wrong with me. I said *you* thought there was something wrong with me." I fought to keep my voice steady, and I nearly succeeded.

He went a long time without saying anything.

I waited.

"You're wrong." His face tightened, like speaking was painful. "You were everything."

He turned to leave.

I couldn't help myself. "And yet," I called after him, "you left anyway."

He stopped, clenching that fist again. Then he released it and walked away without another word.

ALL I WANTED TO DO WAS RUN AWAY. LEAVE, GO BACK TO MY little sanctuary in the woods, and forget all about Rhett Hawkins. But I'd already skipped working with Diablo yesterday. His progress had been steady, and I didn't want to miss an opportunity to move forward with him.

But first, I needed to get my head on straight. I'd always been so careful to only work with Diablo when I was my very best: calm, stable, steady. All things that described me most days. That is, until Rhett came back. Now my emotions were a rollercoaster—one I didn't particularly want to be on.

I shook myself and took a deep breath, walking through the stable toward the front entrance, planning to get myself straight. But as I walked past Diablo's stall, he reached out and nudged me with his black nose.

I stopped, smiling despite everything. "Hey, boy," I whispered, taking a moment to stroke his velvet. "Miss me?"

The horse nudged me again, in a way that almost looked like a human nod. He bent his neck down, sniffing my pocket.

"I see," I said, grinning as I slipped my hand inside the fabric and pulled out the sugar cubes he loved so much. "You're wanting something sweet, huh? Not going to lie, I could go for a dessert today, too. Maybe some huckleberry ice cream," I murmured, stroking my hand down his neck.

He nudged me again and gave a little whine.

"What do you say?" I asked, searching his eyes with my own. "Want to go for a ride?"

He nudged my pocket again.

"Alright, alright. One more." I gave him another sugar cube and made a decision. Tonight, I'd try taking him out on the trail.

He'd done well with me in the ring, but I was aware that the trail was a different story. He could be a natural, or all his anxieties could come raging back. We'd have to take it slow. Stick to the plains, where he wouldn't have to deal with any crazy terrain or trees that could hide a predator. I wanted his first trail ride with me to be as safe and controlled as I could make it.

I led him out of the stall, judging his mood today. He was wary, keeping an eye out for anyone else. As docile as he'd been with me, I knew that it would take time for his trust to extend to the rest. I wasn't sure why he'd given it to me so easily, except that I was the one who'd gotten him out of that torturous situation with Thomas. Animals had more intelligence than people often gave them credit for. When I'd witnessed the cruelty on Thomas's farm, I made Diablo a promise that I would do something about it. It was something Diablo seemed to remember.

"Here you go, boy," I said, bringing the saddle pad up to his nose, then gently brushing it along his neck.

He'd often gotten nervous about being saddled, and I'd worked hard to desensitize him. He tensed but didn't move. I kept talking to him, soothing, before finally putting it on his back. Then, I gave him another sugar cube.

"Good job," I praised, stroking his face. "You know what's next."

I brought the saddle over, going through the same steps to desensitize him before throwing it onto his back, making sure the far stirrup cleared him. He shuddered briefly but seemed okay.

"Excellent. Maybe one more treat."

I worked his cinches slowly. He'd never kicked me, but he'd attempted kicking everyone else who'd tried to saddle him, and I wasn't about to let my guard down.

He did well though. In fact, he seemed more at ease than I'd ever seen him. I swore he was going easy on me on purpose.

"You know I'm having a rough day, don't you?" I murmured, wrapping my arms around his neck.

He whinnied in response.

"Okay. Let's see how you like getting out of the ring. You ready?"

After one last quick check, I swung into the saddle. He turned toward the training ring, but I pulled his reins.

"Not today, buddy. We're going on an adventure."

He was hesitant at first but followed my lead. I took him out toward the area where we did "trail rides" for young, first-time riders. It was flat terrain with a great view and no significant obstacles for him to deal with.

After a few minutes, I could practically feel his pleasure.

"You like this, huh?" I asked, smiling.

I did, too. I felt the strain of the day begin to melt away as I relaxed into the saddle and finally breathed. It was different, riding without being responsible for everyone behind me. There was something almost sacred about being out here, just me and my horse. It was a feeling that never got old, no matter how many years I'd spent doing this, and I was grateful for every minute of it.

"What do you think?" I asked him, leaning forward to pat him on the neck. "You wanna try a trot?"

Not feeling any tension, I squeezed my legs, signalling him. He instantly picked up the pace. I grinned, thrilled with how responsive he was. He seemed as happy to be out here as I was.

After half an hour, I turned back toward the barn, pleased by how the training had gone. But when we got close, I saw Rhett sitting on the fence, watching us. His dark figure cut against the fading sunlight, washing out his features. But I'd know him anywhere.

All my tension instantly returned. Diablo felt it and backtracked nervously.

"It's okay," I said, patting his neck. "We're okay."

I took the long way around, avoiding Rhett, then took an extra-long time getting Diablo settled. But when I finally headed out toward my truck, Rhett was leaned up against the front of the barn with his arms crossed and one black snakeskin boot propped up against the siding.

"Never would have believed it," he said, his low voice startling me.

I stopped and turned toward him. "Never would have believed what?"

"That you could actually saddle and ride that damn horse. Then again, you've always had a spooky way with animals."

I jangled my keys purposefully. "I'm headed out for the night. Do you need something?"

The silence lingered a little too long before he dropped his boot to the ground and stepped toward me.

"I need you to know I didn't leave because something was wrong with you. Can't believe you'd even think that."

"Okay." I didn't trust myself to form a coherent sentence. He was standing so close to me, with that magnetic energy that had always pulled me in, looking at me with eyes that swam with emotion. It was too dangerous. Like standing on the side of a cliff in winds that threatened to make you lose your balance and fall into the depths below.

"Chey, I don't expect you to ever forgive me for leaving like I did. But we were kids, and we aren't anymore. And apparently, we're going to be working together. Think we can at least figure out a way to be friends?"

Friends. That was how we'd started once. It had quickly turned to something so much more, like a tornado dropping from an unassuming storm without warning. *Friends* was a safe word that I knew from experience wasn't safe at all when it came to me and Rhett. But what other choice did I have, really? Until he left, he was right. We had to work together. I couldn't avoid him forever.

"Friends might be too strong a word," I said carefully. "But we can at least be civil colleagues."

"I guess I'll take it," he said. "Goodnight, Cheyenne."

"Goodnight, Rhett."

I got into my truck and drove home, feeling like I'd made a deal with the devil.

Chapter Ten

Rhett

I SKIPPED DINNER WITH THE FAMILY, HEADING TO THE BAR instead. I needed to be alone. Or at least around strangers, away from the intrusive questions and exchanged glances my family seemed to think I couldn't see. Since I didn't have a thing to eat in the loft, strangers it was.

I didn't mind getting on the back of the bike for a bit, either. Helped to clear my head, process everything that had happened the last couple of days.

Like the fact that Cheyenne thought I'd left because she wasn't good enough.

Didn't know why that shocked me so much. Looking at it from her perspective, I guessed that was a logical conclusion. It just wasn't a thought that had ever crossed my mind before when the problem was me and not her.

I'd hurt her worse than I'd ever realized, that much was sure. I'd known she loved me. Hell, I loved her back. Nothing that happened after changed that. But we were kids. I'd figured it wouldn't take long for her to realize she could do a hell of a lot better than me and that my leaving was the best gift I could've ever given her.

It was why I'd asked about her less and less as time passed, eventually avoiding talk of her at all. Killed me to admit it, but I'd never wanted to know for sure. Didn't want to imagine her getting married, promising forever to some other man, and raising a family with him. It was selfish of me, sure, but a man knew what might break him.

I pulled into the bar's parking lot and parked my bike, mulling everything over. Ten years ago, I'd left Wildwood because the idea of staying made me feel suffocated—not because of Cheyenne, even though my parents were putting the pressure on there, too. But the real problem was the ranch.

Once Cole left to join the military, working for Dad became unbearable. The way he saw it, he'd already lost one son. He was bound and determined to make sure he didn't lose another. He wanted to lock me into working three hundred and sixty-five days a year at a job that was his dream, not mine. Thought if he crowded out everything else to where there was nothing left but the ranch, I'd stop talking about all the places I wanted to go and the things I wanted to do.

Showed how little he knew me. Putting that kind of pressure on me did nothing except push me away.

I had hoped to leave and get some breathing room and somehow keep Cheyenne in the process. Hadn't worked out like that. Eventually, I made peace with it. Or thought I had until now.

No other girl had ever compared to her. Not even close. And now that I'd seen Cheyenne the *woman*? I knew no one ever would.

She made me feel things no one else could. That connection she had with animals... It was like she had that same hypnotic power over me. Made me want to reform myself, settle down, and be a better man. Prove myself to her.

Downright dangerous.

I shoved those thoughts away and headed into the bar. Groaned when I walked inside and saw Sam Barton, but I decided to ignore him and head straight to the front. I claimed an empty barstool and signaled Pete.

His smile faltered when he saw it was me. "Hey there, Rhett. What can I do for ya?"

"Whiskey," I said, putting some bills on the bar. "And whatever I'm smelling to soak it up."

"That'd be the western burger. Ground bison, bacon, and barbecue sauce."

"Sounds perfect."

He gave me a weak smile. "How long are you going to be in town?"

I fought back the growl that wanted to erupt. Did the whole town want me to leave? "I'm staying for a while. At least until Dad gets back on his feet. Maybe longer."

His eyebrows shot up. "Staying?"

"Staying." If it hadn't been certain before, it was now.

His hand trembled slightly as he placed the whiskey in front of me. "Listen, Rhett. I was thinking of asking Cheyenne out. Is that going to be a problem?"

I blinked three times. Pete? Ask Cheyenne out? The idea made me want to laugh out loud. He couldn't be further from her type. He was scrawny and pale from working behind a bar instead of in the great outdoors, and his blond hair and slight build made him look like a kid instead of our age. It had to be a joke. But he wasn't laughing.

"Now, why would that be a problem?" I asked carefully.

"So, you two aren't back together?"

"Nope. Just *work colleagues*."

His face flushed with relief, apparently not recognizing the sarcasm in my voice. "Okay. I didn't want to start a problem between me and you. I know she was always off-limits back when you were here, but it's been a long time and I like her. She's sweet, you know?"

Sweet. Not the word I'd use to describe Cheyenne. But I bit my tongue and nodded. If the kid wanted to embarrass himself, that was his own problem.

I'd just taken my first swig of whiskey when Claire walked in and plopped down beside me at the bar.

"What. Was. That?" she asked, signaling Pete to bring her a drink too.

"What was what?"

She grinned. "The sexual tension between you and Cheyenne in the barn. Good grief. I thought I was going to burn alive just standing next to her when she turned around and saw you standing there, all angry and fierce."

Pete dropped the glass he was holding, turning bright red.

"I don't know what you're talking about," I muttered.

"Oh, come on," she said, elbowing me. "It's clear as day you're still hung up on her. Can't stand even thinking about her being with someone else. And the look on your face when you set her straight about how she was everything! Then you sat out there watching her ride Diablo, unable to keep your eyes off her. Never knew you were such a romantic, Rhett."

"I thought you slipped out," I said pointedly. I picked up my whiskey and downed it in a single swallow, wishing I could make this conversation disappear just as easily.

She grinned. "I was watching. From a safe distance."

"You always were a sneaky one."

"Makes me good at my job. Look," she said, turning toward me with a serious expression on her face. "I told Cheyenne I'd discourage you if you showed any interest. But you're my brother, and I love you as much as I love her. So I wanna know. What are you feeling?"

"Annoyed. At you." I signaled Pete for another drink. He refused to meet my eye when he poured it.

"I mean it, Rhett."

"I do, too."

"Come on."

I sighed. "The truth?"

"Yes."

I lowered my voice. "I hurt her. More than I ever knew. And I'm probably leaving again when Dad gets back on his feet. Best thing I could do for Cheyenne now is keep my distance."

"But..." Claire prodded.

"But I don't know if I'm that damn noble," I muttered.

Claire was silent for a moment. "You can't even think about starting something up with her unless you're staying. If you got her to let you in, then you left again..."

"Trust me, I know."

"So why are you even considering it?"

I stared at my glass. "Because she matters. Always has, even when I was gone."

Claire flattened her lips and took a deep breath. "Are you really leaving as soon as Dad gets better?"

I downed my second whiskey. "I don't know anymore."

She stared at me. "Well, until you know, you need to watch your step. I'm not trying to make you feel bad, but Cheyenne loved you. The real kind of love. It crushed her when you left."

"I know."

"No, you don't," she said, squeezing my arm.

I looked over and saw the most serious look I'd ever seen on her face.

"Rhett, I was her best friend. I was here through it all. She wasn't just sad. She *grieved,* like she'd lost her whole world. And I will root for you every single time. But I'll also kick your ass if you break her heart again."

"Understood." I was quiet for a minute, mulling it over. "I don't know, Claire. I needed to leave ten years ago. But I never stopped missing Cheyenne. Never. And part of me's always wanted to come back."

"To visit? Or..."

I didn't answer directly. "I quit my job."

"*What*?"

"Put in my notice before I headed up here. I want to start my own business. Didn't think it would be here. But I don't know, Claire." I swallowed hard, then admitted the truth—to myself as much as to her. "Maybe Dad getting hurt gave me the excuse I'd been looking for to come home."

"You never needed an excuse to come home," she said gently.

"That sounds like something Mom would say."

Her eyes went wide. "Oh my word, you're right. Don't tell her. She'd probably get all teary-eyed on me."

I grinned, feeling a bit lighter. "Nothing wrong with being like Mom."

"No." A shadow crossed her face, and I knew exactly why. Claire had the same issue with Mom that I had with Dad: the knowledge that we could never, ever live up to their expectations and also be true to our own souls. Claire had managed to walk the line a little better than I had, but the problem was the same. "Anyway," she said, shaking it off, "here's the deal. I love Cheyenne, and I have girl loyalty to her."

"I know." I was kind of even grateful for it.

"So I should discourage you," she said, biting her lip. "But..."

"But?"

This time, she was the one glancing around to make sure no one was listening. "You broke her heart. But only because she loved you so damn much. Honestly, Rhett? I think she still does."

My heart dared to hope. "You think? It's been a long time. And other than that little exchange in the barn, she hasn't shown a single trace of emotion around me."

"She's a strong woman. Puts on a brave face. She's good at that."

"Yeah, she is."

Claire looked deep into my eyes. "But I know her. She's never once gotten excited about anyone else. Has always kept her guard up. Goes on dates, keeps things casual, never lets them in. Not like she did with you."

"Because I hurt her," I said, forcing the words out over the lump in my throat.

"Because she loved you," Claire said gently. "And nothing else ever compared."

I opened my mouth to reply but stopped when Claire's face changed to disgust. I turned, looking over my shoulder, and saw Thomas Smith scowling at her.

Thomas was my age, but you'd never know it looking at him. His thinning hair and the hard lines around his mouth made him look like he was racing around the sun faster than the rest of us. He was still as lean and mean-looking as ever though, the kind of guy who'd always gotten a kick out of bullying anyone weaker than him. Didn't surprise me a bit that he mistreated his animals.

He walked up to the bar and ordered a crappy beer, shooting Claire dirty looks as he did. The big brother in me began to get pissed off, but Claire gave me a little shake of her head, letting me know she could handle herself.

Of course she could. She'd been handling herself without me around for quite some time.

"Hello, Thomas," she said, giving him a curt nod.

"Are you talking to me, horse thief?"

"Now, you know better than to make accusations like that," she chided.

"Pretty dirty scheme you've got going, huh? Taking the finest animals in the county under trumped-up animal abuse charges, then using them for free labor at your ranch. There was a time when people would hang for that." His voice was controlled, but rage glittered dark in his eyes.

Claire gave him an amused smile. "We both know there was nothing trumped up about those charges. Besides, the only horse in the county that's been taken is yours, so doesn't seem like much of a scheme, now, does it? Not to mention the fact that said horse isn't working at all."

He let out a biting laugh. "Likely story. But who could expect the truth from a Hawkins? You all think you're above everyone else, sitting high and mighty on that ranch of yours. You're the worst of them now that you have a badge to hide behind."

"Hey, knock it off," I said. Some things went too far, and no one was going to talk to my sister like that in front of me.

He stared at me for a second before recognition lit in his eyes. "Well, well, well. With you in town, I'll take back what I said. *You're* the worst of the bunch, and that girl you used to screw is the reason I lost my horse. Maybe Cheyenne needs a good lesson in what it feels like to have something taken from *her*."

My vision went red and I came off the barstool, standing in front of him with my fists clenched. "Don't even think about going near her."

He smirked, knowing his shot had landed. "Or what, Hawkins?"

"Oh, I think you know."

"You want a piece of me? You come and get it." He thumped me on my chest.

I narrowed my eyes, giving him a wicked grin. "Don't threaten me with a good time."

Claire put a hand on my arm, pulling me back. But as soon as I backed down, Thomas saw his chance and decked me across the chin.

After that, Claire didn't have a chance of stopping me. I turned and slammed my fist into his face so hard he flew backward, knocking over one of the tables.

"Stop it!" Claire said, angry now. "Both of you." She motioned to Pete. "Call the sheriff's office. Have them send somebody over here."

"On it," he said, already picking up his phone.

She pulled cuffs out from the back of her jeans and slapped them on Thomas's wrists, yanking his hand away from his broken and bloodied nose.

"What about him?" he growled.

"You punched first," she said. "His was self-defense."

"Then so is this," he said, jerking out of her grasp and lunging toward me.

She pulled him back and sat him down—hard—on a chair, then shook her head, disgusted. "Knock it off. We'll get this all sorted out in a minute. And to think, this was supposed to be my night off."

"Sorry," I said, meaning it. I rubbed my sore chin.

She waved me off. "Not your fault. He baited you and punched first, and you've got a bar full of witnesses to back that up."

I looked around, my stomach sinking as I saw the faces staring back at me. Unfortunately, this wasn't the first time they'd seen me get into a bar fight.

This might have been the first time I wasn't at least partially to blame. So at least there was that.

The next bit was a blur of making statements and feeling uncomfortable in a spotlight I didn't want to be in. My fault or not, this wasn't exactly the reputation I wanted now, especially since I was starting to toy with the idea of staying. I'd wanted to come back as someone different.

Not as the troublemaker Rhett Hawkins.

When things settled down and Thomas had been sent home with a warning and a fine, Sheriff Cade McGrath came over and shook my hand with a grin on his face. "Didn't know you were back in town," he commented. "But I see things haven't changed much."

"That's not fair," Claire interjected. "Thomas baited him."

McGrath nodded. "I know. I've heard that from everyone here. But can I give you some advice, son?"

"What?" I tried to keep my voice respectful but failed.

He leaned in. "Thomas Smith is a snake. We all know it. Nobody blames you for what happened here, but in the future, try not to take the bait. Because I'll tell you this: He's furious with your family. Now that you've embarrassed him by a sound victory in front of everyone, he's going to be furious at you, too."

"Got it."

He studied me. "Good to have you back. I know your family appreciates it right now."

Right. I wasn't sure they appreciated it at all—and I knew Mom sure wouldn't appreciate this. Didn't matter that I was almost thirty years old; I was in for a lecture just the same. But I nodded and forced a smile.

"You good?" Claire asked, moving toward me.

"I'm good."

"Thomas has to pay for the table," she said. "Pete isn't mad at you."

I glanced over at him. I wasn't too sure about that, although I knew he had different reasons to be unhappy with me since Claire had walked in making her announcement of sexual tension between me and Cheyenne.

I didn't want to burden her with that though. So I gave her a convincing smile as we walked out to the parking lot to head home.

"See you tomorrow?" she said as she turned toward her truck.

"Yeah, see you." I watched as she climbed in, pulled out, and headed toward home.

But I groaned when I walked over to my bike. Someone had let the air out of my tires.

I pulled out my cell phone and called Claire's number to ask her to turn around and give me a ride, but she didn't answer. After two more tries, I cursed, knowing I'd have to call someone else at the ranch. Travis would give me a hard time, and I wasn't ready to face Mom. That left Jonathan or Beth. Of the two, Beth was the most forgiving by far. I pulled up her number and was about to click call.

But then a familiar voice came from behind my shoulder. "Looks like you need a ride."

I turned around, relieved. "Man, am I happy to see you. But the ranch is out of your way. You sure you don't mind?"

"Not at all. Hop in."

I climbed into the front seat. "I appreciate it. Can't believe someone let the air out of my tires."

"That's a shame. Hey, do me a favor? I need a smoke. Grab my cigarettes from the glove compartment?"

"Sure thing." I leaned forward to get them, but when I did, white light exploded behind my eyes and the world went dark.

Chapter Eleven

Cheyenne

I woke suddenly, drenched in sweat with my heart pounding. Something was terribly wrong.

But as I glanced around my room and saw Ash sleeping peacefully, I told myself it was nothing. Had to have been a nightmare I didn't remember. I washed my face, then tried to go back to sleep.

Sleep didn't come easily though. I tossed and turned, sleeping in short fits before waking again, unable to shake this feeling. It killed me that I could sleep soundly in a tent in the woods but couldn't seem to rest in my own bed.

Shortly before dawn, I gave up, rising early to make coffee. I carried a cup of it to my front porch, letting Ash roam while she did her business. I tried my best to smile, to breathe in the cold morning air and let it soothe me to my bones. But no matter what I did, I couldn't shake the trouble from my soul.

It was the same feeling I'd felt the day I'd learned Rhett was here, only worse. Trouble was coming, and there wasn't a thing I could do about it. I had a feeling the trouble was named Rhett Hawkins and the storm I was trying to avoid had already begun to form in my own heart.

My hands gripped the hot mug as I lifted it to my lips, taking a slow sip as I stared past the steam that rose from it into the cold morning air. Why did that man have such a grip on me? I'd given up hope on him coming back what felt like a lifetime ago. I'd moved on.

Except, had I? Not really. I'd allowed a thick scar to grow over the wound in my heart, but I'd never let anyone else in to heal that wound. Those feelings and dreams I'd held for Rhett might have been buried, but I knew now that they had been buried only in the way of all living things: like a seed, waiting, ready to sprout new roots and erupt through the dark surface of my heart.

I shouldn't have let that seed remain. I needed a complete exorcism of all that was Rhett Hawkins.

I wasn't even sure that was possible anymore, not without giving up my life, my job, my land—all things that, unfortunately, were tied to him or memories of him. Anger flared at the thought. It wasn't fair. Wasn't fair that he could disrupt my life this way when I doubted I'd ever given him so much as a restless hour. He'd left and never looked back. Why was it so easy for him and so hard for me?

I shook my head, checking my watch. It was still early, but I needed to blow off this bad funk. Today was a rare Saturday off work—something I had Rhett to thank for, as they couldn't have managed without me had he not been there to help. The last thing I wanted was to waste the day moping over a man. Hard work was the best medicine for a bad mood, and I had plenty of chores to take care of. So I lifted my chin, put a smile on my face, and got busy.

A few hours later, I'd caught up on all the little tasks at home that needed my attention, and I had managed to do so with only an occasional stray thought of Rhett. Proud of myself, I felt a treat was in order and decided to saddle Wildfire up for a pleasure ride. Normally, I'd head deeper into the woods or maybe check out one of the canyons. But I felt a pull toward town. After all my hard work, nothing sounded better than a scoop of huckleberry ice cream.

There was a pretty little trail that cut from the back of my place to the trading post. We wound our way through the trees, down toward the open land where the town lay. As the pines became more sparse, they opened up to a wildflower meadow that was blooming with the first flowers of spring. I closed my eyes and breathed them in, lifting my face to the warm sun. I loved my little spot in the woods, but there was something special about the wide-open skies of Wyoming.

From here, you could see the town of Wildwood stretched out in the valley below. Wildfire knew the way and picked up the pace, as eager as I was to get to town.

By the time we reached the trading post, the last remnants of my bad mood dissipated, although I did roll my eyes when I spotted Rhett's bike parked across the street at the bar. Typical. He'd abandoned his family on the day they most needed him and was drinking at the bar when it wasn't even noon.

I let the irritation wash over me, knowing that it would lessen the unwelcome feelings he'd awoken. He was an irresponsible fly-by-night person and there was no sense in losing sleep over a man like that.

I tied Wildfire up and went inside the trading post, determined to put thoughts of Rhett out of my head once and for all.

"Hey, Alma," I said, smiling at the woman who ran the little store.

Alma was a widow who'd opened the store after her husband's death. She'd spent her life ranching by his side and somehow managed to keep the ranch going by herself for a few years. Eventually, it had become too much for her, and she'd leased out her land and opened the trading post.

She had to be nearly seventy, but she never seemed to slow down or show it. Today, she wore skin-tight acid-washed jeans tucked into high-heeled cowboy boots with a flouncy white shirt and an emerald-green cowboy hat. Silver and turquoise necklaces hung in layers down her chest, and she had at least six large rings on her fingers. She claimed to dress that way for the tourists. We all knew she had a flare for the dramatic and would dress to be seen whether tourists came or not.

"Well, hey there, Cheyenne." Her eyes lit up. "It's been too long since I've seen you!"

"I know. I'm sorry," I said, feeling a tug of guilt. She and my grand-mother had been best friends, and when Gran passed, Alma had been another person to step up as substitute family for me. But I hadn't been visiting her as often these days. "Work's been busy since Walker's accident. By the way, thank you for feeding Ash while I was out on the call."

She smiled, her eyes crinkling up. "Of course. You know I'm happy to do it. I'm guessing you're finally getting a day off and you're here for some ice cream."

I grinned. She knew me well. "You know it."

She bent down, scooping out an extra-large portion of the purple dessert I adored, then handed it to me. "Hank told me the rescue was all thanks to your instincts. Good work, girl."

"It was a team effort."

"Psh. Let me be proud of my girl." Alma's eyes twinkled. "Although, from what I've heard, it sounds like the man deserved more than a few days of cold and hunger. He didn't show a lick of sense out there." She shook her head in disgust.

"Everyone makes mistakes," I said before taking a big lick of the cone and sighing in satisfaction. Huckleberry ice cream had been one constant in my life, something that had seen me through every emotional crisis of being a teenage girl.

"Yeah, well, as much as I like the dollars these tourists bring into town, I wish they'd bring some common sense with them. That ice cream is on the house, by the way." She winked at me.

I smiled. "You're too good to me, Alma."

"Somebody has to be. You're always taking care of everyone else, and sometimes I think you half neglect yourself. Speaking of which…" She dropped her voice and leaned on her elbows on the counter, her face turning serious. "How are you doing?"

"I'm fine," I said, giving her a questioning look.

"I mean, since Rhett came back to town. I imagine it's been awfully uncomfortable for you at the ranch."

I shrugged, even though hearing his name struck a pang in my heart. "It was awkward at first, but it's fine. Honestly, I rarely have to see him. My job keeps me out on the trail, and Travis keeps him busy. We've agreed to be civil."

She gave me a knowing look.

"Really, Alma. I'm okay."

"What you need is to find you some nice boy to be happy with.

Never could figure out why you and Sam didn't hook up. The two of you would make awful pretty babies."

"Sam and I are friends, but there's nothing else there." I shrugged.

"Friendship is the best foundation for a happy marriage, I always say. Still, if he's not your type, maybe someone else..." She brightened. "Someone like Pete. He may not be quite as much to look at as Sam, but he's a good man. He'd be faithful and loyal. Even one of the other Hawkins boys *might* do, though I'm not sure who. Cole's already married, Travis walks around like he's got a black cloud hanging over him, Finn's life is too far from yours, and Jonathan's too young." She shrugged.

I rolled my eyes. "You make it sound like shopping for a new horse or something. This one's too old, this one's too young, this one's too spirited... As if you think choosing a life partner is on par with picking out a dependable, easygoing trail horse."

She cocked her head, thinking it over. "In some ways, I think you're exactly right there. When you're talking about a husband, you're talking about someone who—God willing—you're going to be with for decades to come. It's an investment, same as a horse, only they're not as easy to get rid of if you made the wrong choice."

"Well, I don't think it's the same at all. I believe in soulmates and that you should be with the one your soul loves, even if it's hard."

Unless your soulmate left you. Then, well, you stayed alone.

She eyed me. "And how's that been working for you? I took the practical approach and enjoyed forty-two years of marriage. You're still living in your little house all alone up there on the side of the mountain."

"I like my little house," I said, frowning. "And I'm not lonely. I don't even know where this conversation came from. I'm not looking for a husband. I'm happy on my own."

Or at least I would be, once Rhett moved on again.

I FINISHED MY CONE AND LEFT ALMA, WONDERING IF SHE had a point. If I needed to rid myself of everything that was Rhett Hawkins, maybe I did need to think about dating again.

As I was untying Wildfire from the post out front, Pete walked by. "Oh, hey, Cheyenne," he said, giving me a bashful smile.

"Hey, Pete. How's it going?"

"Good. Listen, uh, I was wondering..."

"Yeah?"

"Would you like to go out with me sometime?" The words spilled from his mouth like he'd been practicing them. He flushed with relief, then turned red, like he couldn't believe what he'd just done.

My eyes widened. Beth seemed more his type—gentle, soft spoken, effortlessly feminine and sweet. Their date hadn't gone well, but still, I'd figured he would try again with her or someone else like her.

My initial reaction was to say no—I had zero romantic interest in Pete. He wasn't my type any more than I was his. But maybe I needed to open up, try imagining myself with someone completely different. Pete was definitely Rhett's opposite. He was kind, eager to please, and the type who would never even dream of leaving Wyoming. And Beth had made it clear she wasn't interested in a second date, so I wouldn't be breaking the girl code.

I didn't want to lead him on or do anything that might hurt him. But all he'd asked for was a date. Dates could be casual.

So I overrode my impulse and gave him a smile. "Sure. I'd like that."

His face flushed again. "Really?"

"Really," I said, laughing. "What do you have in mind?"

"Dinner," he said quickly. "I'm off Tuesday night. Does that work?"

I mentally ran through my schedule. "It should, if we make it later. Maybe around seven? Of course, if I get a call..."

He held up both hands. "Oh, I know. Search-and-rescue comes first. But otherwise, I'll pick you up at your place?"

"Sure." I mustered up another smile.

"Great." He grinned. "Well, I guess I better head into work now."

I rolled my eyes. "Looks like you already have one customer."

He glanced over at the parking lot. "Oh, you mean Rhett? Nah. He left his bike there last night."

My eyebrows rose. "Did you take his keys?"

He chuckled. "No. You know I don't over-serve. Looked like his tire was flat. Claire was with him last night. He probably grabbed a ride home with her."

"Oh, gotcha." That made sense—and made me feel a little better, since it meant they weren't short two people at the ranch today.

"See ya later." He gave me another smile, then ducked across the street.

I swung up onto Wildfire, then followed him. There was a creek not far behind the bar where I could let Wildfire drink. Then we'd turn and head for home.

I glanced over at Rhett's bike as we passed it, then frowned. Pete said he had a flat tire, but *both* tires were flat. What were the odds of that?

Astronomical, unless someone had let the air out of them deliberately.

The trickle of unease that had sat with me all day came roaring back, and my heart began to pound.

I pulled out my cell phone and called Claire as Wildfire walked behind the building toward the creek.

"Hey, girl," she answered, sounding like she'd been running. "What's up?"

"Did you give Rhett a ride home from the bar last night?"

"No, why?"

"Did he show up to work today?"

She sighed. "No. Travis is pissed. I really thought things were going to be different this time, that Rhett had changed. But I guess he did what he always does and pulled out of town without saying anything to anyone."

"Claire, I think something's wrong."

"What are you talking about?"

"He didn't leave town. Someone let the air out of his tires and his bike is still at the bar."

"What?" Her tone sharpened.

"Claire... I think Rhett's missing."

CHAPTER TWELVE

Cheyenne

Two hours later, Claire, Sheriff McGrath, and I stood in a huddle in the sheriff's office, debating our options. Travis had confirmed that Rhett wasn't in the loft. Claire and the sheriff had followed up with everyone they'd seen at the bar last night. Nobody had seen Rhett leave or knew who he had gotten a ride with. They'd tracked his phone and found it tucked safely into the saddlebag on his bike, like he'd never even taken it into the bar.

"He's a grown man," Sheriff McGrath soothed. "He probably got a ride with a woman and decided to sleep over."

"No," Claire said firmly. "He wouldn't have."

McGrath gave her a look. "Seems like that's exactly the kind of thing Rhett would have done. Odds are he'll show up before the end of the day."

"I'm telling you, that's not what happened," Claire ground out.

"Look, it hasn't even been twenty-four hours," McGrath said, trying to calm her down. "We have zero evidence anything nefarious happened, other than his tires. Nobody saw or heard anything. There's no blood in the parking lot or anything that should worry you."

"Thomas was pissed," she said, giving him a pointed look.

"I know." He sighed. "Listen, I'll have a talk with Thomas. See if anything feels fishy there. Okay?"

"We need to activate search-and-rescue," Claire insisted.

McGrath gave her an exasperated look. "We don't know for sure that he's missing—it wouldn't be the first time in history someone left that bar with someone different than who they came in with. Even if he is, we have no leads to know where to start looking. I can't activate a SAR team to search all of Wyoming! Slow down. I'll talk to Thomas and we'll go from there."

She clamped her lips together and clenched her fists.

I put a hand on her elbow, squeezing to let her know she wasn't alone. "Maybe you're right," I said to the sheriff. "So if we don't hear from him in another twenty-four hours?"

He nodded, looking relieved. "Then we'll go from there. But I'm telling you, odds are he'll show up at dinner tonight with a story to tell."

I could feel Claire tensing up, so I dug my fingers into her arm and pulled her away.

"What did you do that for?" she demanded when we got outside.

"I'm trying to help you keep your job."

She looked me dead in the eye. "Cheyenne, I promise you, he wouldn't have gone home with another woman."

"Okay," I said, even though I didn't share her confidence. Frankly, I was sure there were plenty of women who'd jump at the chance to bed Rhett Hawkins.

"Tell me what you're thinking from a search-and-rescue point of view," she said, desperation in her eyes.

I sighed. "Well, the sheriff is right. We have no leads to go on, except we know he was here last night and that he didn't go home on his bike."

Her eyes filled with tears. "It's my fault."

"What do you mean?"

"He called me twice last night. I must have turned my phone to silent without realizing it or something. I didn't even see the calls until I got home, and I tried to call him back, but he didn't answer." She made a fist and brought it to her forehead, squeezing her eyes shut. "If anything happened to him..."

"I'm sure he's fine," I soothed, even though I wasn't sure at all. I was starting to think that the terrible feelings I'd had all day were less about how Rhett was wrecking my heart and more about whatever had happened to him.

That link between us... No matter how much I wanted it gone, it was there. I only hoped that somehow I could use it this time to find him.

"Is there any chance he would have walked home last night when he couldn't get you on the phone?"

Her eyes lit up with hope. "Of course. That makes sense. It's only three miles to the ranch."

"Yeah," I said, though with considerably less excitement than her. I knew that her emotions were clouding her judgment. It was odd for him to call her, then put his cell phone back in the saddlebags. If he was walking, why not carry it with him in case she called him back? She could have picked him up and shortened his ride.

Plus, if he had walked back on the highway, he should have been safely home last night. Something terrible might have happened to him —a hit-and-run accident or even an animal encounter.

The other option was that he'd tried to cut through the forest and gotten lost. This many hours later... He could be almost anywhere. If a lost person stopped where they were, that was one thing. But often, people wandered around, thinking they were only a few steps away from finding the trail again. They could get miles off track, deeper and deeper into the woods, without even realizing it—just like Scott Fairbanks. Despite the best efforts of an experienced SAR team, sometimes those people were never found alive. The Wyoming wilderness was full of danger. I'd like to think Rhett had more common sense than that, but we'd already confirmed he'd been drinking. Anything could have happened to him.

"We may not be able to officially activate a team yet, but..." Claire said.

I gave her an encouraging smile. "We're the best anyway, right?"

"Exactly."

I let her hold on to that hope instead of telling her how terrified I felt inside.

Claire and I split up. She took the highway, driving slowly up and down it to make sure Rhett wasn't lying in a ditch somewhere. I took to the woods on Wildfire. I wanted more people, more resources, more information—this was not the way to properly conduct a search. If the sheriff didn't authorize an official one soon, I'd call in favors from my team and we'd do it unofficially anyway.

In the meantime, I'd cover what ground I could and see if I could come up with something—anything—to figure out what had happened to Rhett.

I took the most direct path from the bar to the edges of the ranch's property first, keeping my eyes and ears open for any recent disturbance. When that came up empty, I turned back toward the bar, skirting the edge of the highway in case he'd walked through the woods but stuck close to the road. I'd made it about halfway back when Wildfire's ears pricked up. I slowed, listening for what had gotten her attention.

"What is it, girl?" I asked, stroking her neck. My heart rate picked up as I heard what sounded like a moan. We moved forward slowly, listening.

The noise came again.

"Rhett?" I called, my heart racing as I dared to hope.

Another groan, louder this time, though it was still faint and so far away.

I nudged Wildfire forward, scanning the area. There was a service road ahead, and it sounded like the noise had come from that direction. I headed there and listened, turning toward the left. After a few more steps down that road, I saw familiar black boots jutting out of a ditch.

My heart nearly stopped.

I jumped off Wildfire and raced to where Rhett lay before dropping down beside him. Blood was matted in his hair, and the side of his face was blue and swollen. He moaned again, attempting to open his eyes.

"Shh, it's okay. I'm here," I said, grabbing his hand in mine. "You're going to be alright. I've got you."

"Cheyenne," he said weakly, gripping my hand with a strength that surprised me.

"Yes. It's Cheyenne. I'm here." I choked up, my heart aching at the sight of him on the ground like this, broken and bloody. "Hold on, okay? I'm going to call for help."

I called Claire, gave her our location, and told her we needed medical assistance. Her relief came through the phone, though I wasn't sure how relieved she'd feel when she saw that he had been beaten badly and left for dead.

"Need... Water..." he mumbled, those eyes still fighting to open.

"I'm sorry," I said, my heart breaking again. "I can't give it to you. Not until we know what we're dealing with medically." Sticking to trauma protocol felt like a dagger in my heart.

It was one thing when the person in front of you was a stranger. Easier to say no, knowing that it was the right decision medically speaking. But when it was Rhett and his lips were dry and chapped and his voice sounded like his throat was full of gravel? It killed me not to give him the one thing he asked for.

"Thank you," he said, gripping my hand again. Those dark eyes opened for a brief moment, holding my gaze. "Thank you for finding me."

"That's my job."

"You're beautiful." His eyes fluttered closed again as his strength failed. "Never seen such a pretty sight. Never stopped loving you. Never. Had to tell you ... one last time."

"Shhh, don't talk now. You're going to be okay. Help is on the way," I said, trying to keep it professional. But there was nothing professional about the tears falling from my eyes as I leaned over him, holding on to his hand as tightly as he held mine.

Chapter Thirteen

Rhett

Clawing my way to the surface felt like the hardest thing I'd ever done. But when awareness finally dawned, she was there.

An angel, holding my hand and telling me everything was going to be okay.

I was cold. Too cold. Like I'd never get warm again. But she was a fire, a fire I clung to. The only thing that made me think I might make it through.

Everything was a blur. It took me a while to realize I was on the ground—the cold, wet ground—and that my body felt like I'd been put through a meat grinder.

"What happened?" I tried to force the question past my dry lips, but nobody answered. It was a swirl of activity. Sirens and people, and then I was moving up onto a board, being shoved into the back of an ambulance.

Everyone kept saying I was going to be okay.

But I only believed it when it was her.

I kept reaching, kept stretching my hand out, looking for that fire to cling to. And then she was back. Sitting beside me in the back of the ambulance, gripping my hand.

"Don't leave us. You hear me? You hang on. You're going to be okay."

I vaguely recognized that the words didn't come from *her*. It was my sister's voice talking, begging me to hang on.

But the hand I clung to was Cheyenne's. I'd have known it anywhere.

I forced my eyes open and she was there. Unlike Claire, who couldn't stop talking, Cheyenne was silent—white as a ghost as she stared at me. I tried to tell her I was okay, but I couldn't get the words out. And then the world went dark again.

The next time I clawed my way to the surface, the beeping noises and harsh smell of antiseptic told me I was in the hospital. I fought to open my eyes and found Mom hovering above me, her eyes red and swollen.

"Rhett," she said, sagging in relief as she grabbed the crucifix around her neck. "Thank God. He's awake, guys."

I moved my head slightly—nearly vomited from the pain—and saw my siblings standing around the end of my bed. Even Finn had come. Their faces were all pale and worried.

"You gave us quite a scare," Mom said, squeezing my hand.

"How bad is it?" I wasn't sure, but between the pain and the looks on my siblings' faces, I was concerned, to say the least.

Mom forced a bright smile. "You're going to be fine."

"Claire," I said, turning my eyes toward her. "You'll tell me the truth."

She came over, took my other hand. "Really, you're going to be okay. You took a bad blow to your head. It was ... scary. Very scary for a little while. You were unconscious for a long time, and there were ... concerns. You have a serious concussion. But the doctor says your prognosis is good."

No wonder they all looked like they were at a funeral.

"Still got all my parts?" I asked, mumbling, as my eyes got heavy.

Claire cracked up. "Yeah. You still have all your parts. But a few of them are a little worse for wear. You've got some broken ribs, cuts, and scrapes."

"What the hell happened to me?"

"We were hoping you could tell us that."

"Don't remember," I said, feeling the darkness threatening to take over again. Before it did, I gripped Claire's hand. "Where's Cheyenne?"

Cheyenne's voice, thin and strained, came from the back of the room. "I'm here."

I forced my eyes open just in time to see her step out from behind Travis.

"Need you," I managed to get out before sinking back underneath the darkness.

Chapter Fourteen

I froze. Rhett had only said the words once before drifting off, oblivious to whether I was there or not, but I didn't know what to do.

Naomi and Claire both looked at me. Claire's face showed confusion, but Naomi looked ... hopeful. Hopeful and desperate.

I couldn't refuse the look on her face. So, even though Rhett seemed to be sleeping again, I stepped forward.

"I'm here," I whispered, not sure he could hear me.

Naomi moved, making room for me to join her beside him. It was exactly where I wanted to be—and also the place I wanted to run from. Seeing Rhett lying here, broken like this... It was killing me. All I knew was that he had to get better. That I couldn't lose him again. Not like this.

Naomi looked deep into my eyes, then pulled me into a tight embrace. When she finally let me go, both our eyes were wet with tears we refused to shed.

She sniffed and shook her head. "Honey, I don't know if I even said thank you for finding him."

"You didn't have to."

"I do. If you hadn't... If he'd stayed out there much longer..."

"Don't think of it," I said as much for my sake as hers. "All that matters is that he's okay."

Someone knocked on the hospital door.

"Come in," Naomi called, some of the strength returning to her voice.

Sheriff McGrath poked his head in the door. "This a good time?"

"Of course."

He came in, shaking his head as he eyed Rhett. "Has he woken up yet?"

Naomi nodded, and I slipped back, feeling out of place standing there like I was one of the family. Claire shot me a sympathetic look, but thankfully Naomi didn't seem to notice me leaving her.

"Briefly," she confirmed.

"And? What did he tell you about what happened?"

Claire stepped in. "He asked us. Said he didn't remember. But he's still pretty out of it."

The sheriff's mouth went flat. "The doctor said with that kind of blow to the head he might not remember at all."

"Well, it doesn't really matter, does it?" Naomi snapped. Anger like I'd never seen from her flared in her eyes. "We all know who did this."

McGrath's hands went up. "Whoa, now. We *don't* know for sure."

"Oh, come on," Travis said, his words dripping with disdain. "It was Thomas. We all know it, and we're not going to let it stand."

McGrath shot him a look. "Son, we don't know anything for sure. Now, before you get your panties in a wad, listen to me. I agree with you that Thomas is a likely suspect. I've already gone to talk to him. Unfortunately, his wife gave him an alibi."

"That doesn't mean anything," Claire said flatly. "She covers for him even when he beats *her*."

"I'm aware. But without any evidence, my hands are tied. The doctor said there's multiple ways he could have gotten his injuries. He might have been attacked. But he also could have been walking on the shoulder of the highway and gotten clipped by a truck or could have stumbled and taken a bad fall. Even could have even gotten thrown off a horse. Any of your horses missing?"

"No," Travis said firmly. "He wasn't riding one of ours."

McGrath sighed. "Look, I'll keep working the Thomas angle. I know there's a good chance he was behind this. But I'm going to tell you right now"—he gave warning looks to Travis, Finn, Jonathan, and Claire in turn—"don't even think about taking the law into your own hands on this one. If it was him, we'll figure out a way to nail him. I don't need you complicating things."

The look on Travis's face said he'd prefer to take care of things himself, but he gave the sheriff a reluctant nod. It warmed my heart to see how protective Travis was of Rhett, despite the bad blood between them. When it came to the Hawkins brothers, family meant family. They might annoy or beat up on each other, but in the end, they stood together.

It meant something. I hoped they knew how lucky they were to have that.

"Call me if he wakes up and you find out anything else," McGrath added before turning on his heel and walking out.

Naomi huffed. "Well, I sure hope he's doing everything he can to find out who did this."

"Don't worry, Mom," Claire said, giving her a look that meant business. She crossed her arms and planted her feet. "If Thomas did this, I'll find a way to prove it. He's not going to get away with it."

"I don't know whether that makes me feel better or worse," Naomi admitted.

RHETT WAS IN AND OUT OF IT FOR THE NEXT TWO DAYS. THE doctor reassured us that was normal and partly due to the pain meds that kept him mildly sedated. That was what he needed, the doctor said —to stay still, with no stimulation. Lights low, very little noise, lots of rest. He was out of the woods, but he had a long recovery ahead of him.

Life at the ranch had to go on, so Naomi stayed at the hospital while the rest of us did our best to manage everything without her. Luckily, she was the kind of woman who thought ahead and had "emergency" muffins, casseroles, and breads in the freezer to feed the guests. But her absence made our short-staffed situation that much harder, and it quickly became clear we couldn't go on like this. Not with a full schedule of tourists and trail rides.

On Tuesday morning, I stopped by the hospital to check on Rhett and Naomi before heading to the ranch. It still felt strange, but thankfully, Rhett was usually sleeping, and I convinced myself I was there for Naomi's sake, not his.

Certainly not for my own sake, even though I couldn't begin to put into words the pure relief I felt every time I saw him there and knew he was going to be okay.

This time, when I walked in, Naomi's face lit up.

"Oh, Cheyenne. I'm so glad you're here. We have good news."

"Oh yeah?"

She nodded. "The doctor just did his morning rounds. Rhett is getting discharged today. It's such a relief."

"That's wonderful," I said, smiling as I gave her a quick hug. "I know you'll be glad to get back home, and I'm sure he'll recover faster being there, too."

She bit her lip. "Yes, but I have something to ask of you. I'm fully aware of what a huge favor it is. I've thought about it a lot and I feel like it's the best thing, but there are zero hard feelings if you say no."

My heart beat a little faster, as I was unsure of what she was going to say next. "You know I'd do anything for you. What is it?"

"Rhett can't stay in Jimmy's old apartment. The bed is up in a loft, and the doctor doesn't want him climbing ladders. Every guest room and cabin we have is already booked, and that wouldn't work anyway because the doctor wants him under supervision for at least twenty-four more hours. Travis is supposed to get the girls tonight for the first time all month. Walker's already set up in our room at home, and the bunk beds in Jonathan's room aren't ideal. If Rhett got confused and sat up quickly, he'd hit his head again."

"I see," I said, my heart pounding harder as I realized where she was going with this.

Naomi put her hands up. "If you say no, Claire said she'll sleep on the couch and Rhett can have her room. But that still leaves him navigating the stairs at home, and things are *never* quiet on the ranch when we're booked solid. You have an extra bedroom, and, well"—she swallowed hard—"the truth is, he asks for you every time he wakes up. My son needs you, and I have to ask. I hope you'll forgive me for it."

This time, I was the one to swallow hard. But she was right. Logistically speaking, my guest room was the best option for Rhett. That didn't even take into account the fact that I had medical training none of the rest of them had. I knew how to monitor him. And they could manage more easily without me for a day than they could without Naomi.

"It's fine," I said before I could overthink it. "I don't mind."

Relief swam on her face. "Oh, thank you. Cheyenne, I really don't know what we would do without you. I won't forget how you stepped up to help through all this, despite how strange it must be for you."

I gave her a weak smile. "You guys are family."

She squeezed my hand. "So are you."

"How soon is he getting discharged?" I asked as the reality of the situation began to sink in.

"An hour or two, the doctor said. We're waiting on some meds from the pharmacy."

"Okay." I glanced at my watch. "Why don't I head home, then? I need to pick up some supplies and put fresh sheets on the guest bed. Be sure to get a copy of his discharge instructions so I can read over them."

"Of course." She pulled out her phone. "I'll call Travis to pick us up and bring us to your place. Jonathan will have to take a day off of school to cover things at the ranch. And Cheyenne? Thank you. Again. For everything."

"It's not a problem," I said.

I wasn't sure which one of us I was trying to convince.

AN HOUR LATER, I WAS READY FOR THEM—OR AS READY AS I could be, under the circumstances. Ash eyed me as I paced my living room, waiting for them to arrive.

"I know," I said to her. "This is crazy. But I couldn't say no."

Truthfully, I hadn't wanted to. Part of me had wanted to be the one sitting in that hospital room with him every single day. I couldn't explain it. We weren't even friends—I'd insisted on nothing more than "civil colleagues." But seeing Rhett bleeding on the side of the road had shaken me.

I was used to seeing people with injuries and had even seen my fair share of dead bodies. That was par for the course as a search-and-rescue volunteer. I knew how to keep my composure, how to detach emotionally so I could do whatever needed to be done.

I should have been able to detach in this situation, too, but I couldn't. I had thought my heart was going to stop while we waited that agonizing hour for medical attention, with him drifting in and out of consciousness. I'd found myself anxious every day since, waiting for updates on his condition.

Plus, there had been guilt after Claire told me about the incident with Thomas. I'd been the one to report him. I was the reason Diablo was at Falcon Ridge Ranch.

And I was the reason Rhett had come off of that barstool, starting a war with a man who didn't like to lose.

I felt relief and panic both when Travis's truck pulled into my driveway. I opened the door and waited as Travis hopped out and walked around, opening the back passenger door. Naomi met him over there, and the next thing I knew, they were walking toward my porch with Rhett in the middle, his arms slung around their necks.

He gave me an easy grin. Other than the bruising spread over his face, he looked more like he'd had a long night at a bar than like a patient who'd just been discharged from the hospital.

"Well, hey there, Cheyenne," he drawled, his words slurring slightly. "Aren't you the prettiest sight I've ever seen."

"Sorry," Travis said, wincing. "The doc gave him a heavy dose of narcotics before the drive to minimize the pain of the bumps in the road. He's a little loopy."

"More than a little," Naomi said, fighting a smile.

"It's fine," I said, opening the door for them.

"Why are we here?" Rhett asked, looking around with his jaw hung open. "This is where Cheyenne lives. I remember. Been a long time.

She's so pretty." He turned his head toward Travis. "Do you know how pretty she is?"

"Yep," Travis answered, rolling his eyes.

"Cheyenne was the best thing that ever happened to me," Rhett said, his words turning mournful. "But she's mad at me. I love her so damn much. Always have. Travis, tell me how to make it right."

My heart actually stopped.

"I'd suggest shutting your damn mouth," Travis ground out. "Chey, where do you want him?"

"Down the hall. First room on the right," I stammered. "It's all ready for him."

"Alright. I've got this, Mom," he said, letting Naomi know she could let go.

She did, then handed me a stack of paperwork from her purse with an apologetic smile. "I'm sorry. I imagine that was awkward for you."

"It's fine. People say crazy things when they're on pain medications." I waved it off like it was meaningless.

She looked at me intently. "I think he meant them. Meds or not, Rhett's not the kind of person who says things he doesn't mean. But I'm not going to get in the middle of things. It'll be up to you what to do with that."

I was speechless, but thankfully, Naomi didn't seem to expect me to answer.

"Here's the discharge paperwork from the doctor. He said twenty-four hours of close observation. If Rhett's continuing to improve, then he won't have to be monitored quite as closely after that, but here's the hard part."

"What?"

"They want him to be completely inactive for two weeks."

"Two weeks?" My eyes widened. I knew that getting Rhett to comply with that was going to be difficult to say the least. Not to mention the fact that I hadn't expected to have him stay with me for quite that long.

She sighed. "Two weeks with low light and as little stimulation as possible. The doctor doesn't even want him watching TV. He's supposed to let his brain heal and do absolutely nothing, not even think about anything. No reading, no exercise. Nothing."

I blinked twice. "We're talking about Rhett Hawkins. Adrenaline junkie, gets bored easily, can't stand to sit still Rhett Hawkins."

"I know." She pulled a brown parchment bag out of her purse. "Meds. This should help, at least. Will keep him settled and manage the pain. His ribs are wrapped. The doctor said he'll probably deal with headaches, vision changes, and nausea for a while."

"Has he remembered anything yet?"

She shook her head. "Not yet. I hope he does though."

"Me too." I hoped for it with all my heart. I wanted the person responsible for this to pay.

"I'm going to do what I can with the guest reservations and try to get a suitable room set aside for him. When I asked you to look after him, I never meant for it to be for so long." She gave me an apologetic look. "I know none of us were expecting two weeks of forcing him to be someone he's, well, not. This isn't all on you, Cheyenne. We'll figure out how to manage this."

"It's fine," I said, knowing she already had more than enough to deal with. "I'm here for whatever you need. It's the least I can do."

Travis came down the hallway. "Got him settled. He's already asleep again. Thank goodness. Cheyenne, you going to be okay?" Doubt was written all over his face.

"We'll be fine." I put on false confidence. "I've got this. I've handled worse, and besides, he'll probably sleep for the most part. I'll check on him regularly and monitor his vitals. Don't worry about me."

Naomi gave me a long look, then wrapped me up in a final embrace before they left me alone with the man who was only a danger to my heart.

CHAPTER FIFTEEN

Rhett

I WOKE FEELING GROGGY AND WITH A RAGING HEADACHE. I forced my eyes open, then nearly jumped out of my skin at the sight of a wolf standing beside me, staring me down.

"Leave it, Ash." The words came from a familiar voice. But that couldn't be right. Because she was heaven and this had to be hell.

The wolf gave me one more intense stare, a warning of some sort that I didn't fully understand, before turning and walking away. I blinked twice. Then Cheyenne was standing in front of me, offering me a glass of water with a little straw in it.

"Must be hallucinating," I mumbled, accepting the water gratefully. She frowned. "What makes you say that?"

"Thought I saw a wolf."

Amusement fluttered on her face. "That's my dog. Her name is Ash."

I pushed myself to a sitting position, groaning from the pain. I forced myself to blink a few times before looking again at the so-called dog. She was now curled up on the floor across the room but still stared at me with that same menacing glare.

I glanced back at Cheyenne, who gazed fondly at the creature.

"That's a wolf," I said.

"No, it's a dog," she said, turning back to me with a frown. "Don't you know it's illegal to own a wolf in Wyoming?"

"Yeah, but..." I looked again, wondering if my mind was playing tricks on me. But every second I was awake, I was getting clearer, and this was no hallucination.

"Chey, that's a wolf." A wolf that looked as if she'd like to eat me for breakfast.

Cheyenne shook her head. "Nah. I think she's a blend of Alaskan Malamute, Husky, and Lab. Maybe even a little Poodle. Now, settle down. You're supposed to be resting. No more talking."

I coughed, then groaned at the pain that stabbed through my head. "That ain't no damn Poodle. Why the hell do you have a wolf inside your house?"

"Rhett Hawkins, are you accusing me of breaking the law? I've already told you it's not legal to own a wolf here—or even a wolf hybrid. Not to mention the fact that it's a terrible idea." Her voice rose, showing her irritation. "Wolves are meant to be wild and free. They don't typically bond with humans the way dogs do. Even hybrids pose significant challenges for their owners. They aren't meant to be pets, and I'd never do something so irresponsible."

"Don't *typically* bond, but you've got that spooky way with animals. If anyone could bond with a wolf, it'd be you."

Cheyenne's face twitched with a smile she tried to hold back. The wolf growled.

"Why is he growling?" I scooted back in alarm despite the stabbing pain it caused.

"Because *she* likes me." Cheyenne gave me another one of those amused smiles, then told the wolf to knock it off. The growling stopped.

"Why would that make her growl at me?"

Cheyenne looked at me with her eyebrows raised, saying nothing.

"Got it." I winced. "Your *dog* doesn't like me because *you* don't like me, so I better watch my step. Next question."

"You shouldn't talk," she reminded me. "You're supposed to be resting. Completely."

"Screw that. What am I doing in your house?"

She gave me an exasperated look but answered. "You were hurt."

"I'm aware. But that doesn't answer my question. Last thing I remember is being in the hospital, surrounded by my entire family. All three Hawkins women worrying over me and pestering the doctor to death. Now, I'm here. What the hell happened in between?"

She came over and sat down on the bed—a bed I was suddenly very aware was *hers*. Or at least had been when she was a teen. Didn't know if she still slept here or if she had taken over her grandmother's room. But this had definitely once been Cheyenne's, and being back in her bed had me wondering if I had died in that hospital and just hadn't fully figured it out yet. And if I *was* dead, I still wasn't sure what that meant about where I'd ended up. Because Cheyenne's bed might once have been heaven, but based on that wolf in the corner—and how much anger Cheyenne had to still hold for me—I was starting to think I was in for an eternity of torment.

Cheyenne frowned. "You've been on some pretty strong meds. They might have made things fuzzy."

"Catch me up, then. Please."

She sighed, relenting. "You were in rough shape. Once the doctor cleared you for release, he insisted you be monitored and he didn't want you climbing stairs or ladders. He also wanted you *resting*, not talking, and you know how loud and chaotic it can be on the ranch. Plus, I have medical training that they don't." She shrugged as if it were nothing. "Naomi asked if you could stay here, at least for a few days."

I was stunned. She hated me. Wouldn't even agree to be friends. Yet here she was, opening up her home and taking care of me anyway. I didn't even know what to say.

"That's generous of you."

Her eyes narrowed. "I owe your family a lot."

The message was clear. This was for my family, not for me.

"You're the one who found me."

"Yeah." The look in her eyes changed again, to one I'd never seen before. It was hard, with an edge of anger. "In the hospital, you said you couldn't remember what happened the night you ended up like that. Do you remember now?"

I shook my head again. "No. Last thing I remember is getting into a fight at the bar. Didn't think Thomas hit me *this* hard though."

"He didn't. At least not there." She continued staring at me with that piercing gaze. "Your tires were flat. You called Claire twice. Do you remember that?"

I tried. I thought back to that night and tried to remember anything that had happened after the fight with Thomas. But it was completely blank, as if no time at all had passed in between the fight and waking up to Cheyenne's voice in the woods. Everything after that was hazy, snippets of memories that played like a film that had been cut and spliced back together all wrong.

"My tires were flat," I repeated slowly, hoping it would jar something. But there was nothing there.

"Yes. We wondered if you decided to walk home," she explained. "I found you on a service road, just off the highway, about halfway between the bar and the ranch. Your cell phone was still back with your bike. You had your wallet on you, but there wasn't any money in it. We weren't sure if you had any in there to begin with though."

I groaned. "Had about a hundred in cash. You're telling me I spent six months in New York without a single issue only to get mugged on the side of the highway in *Wyoming*?"

She didn't answer right away, but her face made it clear she didn't believe that at all.

"What is it?" I asked. "What are you not telling me?"

"Thomas doesn't like to lose. You remember what he was like in high school." She swallowed hard. "He's the kind of guy who would hunt you down and do this to you. His wife is his alibi, but that doesn't mean anything. I'm thinking he let the air out of your tires hoping you'd walk home. Maybe he parked on that access road and waited for you to walk by."

"What a snake," I muttered. "You're probably right. Hell, he's probably the one who left the note, too."

"What note?" Her eyes narrowed.

"Second day here, there was a note tacked to my door telling me to go home, that I didn't belong here. Honestly, I thought it was from Travis. Or *you*."

She gave me a look. "As if I would ever be that unoriginal. If I had a problem with you being here, I'd tell you to your face. But it's your family, your home. You have the right to visit whenever you want."

I chuckled, then grabbed my ribs, wincing at the pain. "My apologies. And in case I haven't said it yet, thank you. Both for finding me and for taking care of me. Can't imagine either one was high up on your list of priorities for this week."

She didn't answer. Turned her gaze out the window and sighed, then asked if I was hungry.

The idea of food hadn't crossed my mind until she asked. Then it was like my stomach woke up and was ravenous. "I could eat," I answered.

"I made stew. I'll bring you a bowl, then let you get your rest. I know it's probably awkward for you to have me hanging around. You need to rest for a few more days, but you're really past the danger zone, so I don't have to hover. I'll be in and out to check on you tonight, but we don't have to talk beyond that. It's best if you sleep as much as possible."

She got up to leave, but I leaned forward—ribs be damned—and grabbed her hand. She was running away from me, but I didn't want her to.

I didn't have my whole brain back yet, but there was one thing I knew for sure. I'd let her go once, and I wasn't going to make that mistake again.

"What if I want to talk to you? Maybe I have things to say. Things we should have talked about a long time ago."

A pained look flashed across her face. "I better get that stew." Then she disappeared, the wolf following behind her.

Chapter Sixteen

Cheyenne

I closed the door to Rhett's room and leaned against it, gathering myself. This was harder than I had expected it to be. Seeing Rhett back here, in my home—in my old *bed*—brought back memories I wasn't ready to face.

Years had passed, yet it all came back like it was yesterday.

I shook off the past and went to the kitchen, dishing up a small helping of elk stew for him. It was one of the few things I cooked and was his favorite—or had been when we were young—and I'd made a quick batch in my pressure cooker while he slept, hoping he'd wake up and be ready to eat. He needed to take it slow, but if this went well, he could have a larger portion later.

It was two weeks at most, I reminded myself as I headed back toward his room with the food. Probably not even that. Naomi would figure out a situation that worked for him at the ranch and we could go back to normal. I'd be back to working the trails and probably wouldn't see him much. And by the time the two weeks were over, Walker would be that much closer to his own recovery and Rhett likely wouldn't hang around much longer.

But that thought brought sadness instead of relief.

All of this had brought up the past, but maybe that was a gift. I could face what I'd buried, let it go, and then we could put this behind us for good.

Although, I was worried Thomas wouldn't let us put it behind us at all. I had to wonder if he'd meant to kill Rhett—and if he'd try again. I hoped his anger would blow over, that the damage he'd done would be enough.

But with Thomas, you never knew.

I took a deep breath, steeling myself before knocking lightly on Rhett's door.

"Come in," he called.

I pushed the door open with my hip and carried the tray of food to his bed, propping it up over him.

"This looks great." He gestured at the food. "I love stew."

"I remember." Awkward silence hung between us for a beat before I quickly filled it. "I'll come check on you again in about an hour, but you can call me if you need anything. I'll be down the hall." I turned to leave, wanting to escape the room.

"Cheyenne, wait."

I looked back at him.

He blinked twice, like he hadn't expected me to stop. He opened his mouth to speak, then seemed to change his mind. "Thanks. Again," he muttered, dropping his eyes to his stew.

I fled the room, grateful to get some space.

An hour later, I woke from where I'd fallen asleep on the couch to the sound of Rhett stumbling down the narrow hallway. I startled before throwing off the woven blanket covering me and jumping up to go to him. His gait was unsteady, and he was leaning heavily against the wall.

"You shouldn't be up," I scolded, slipping under his shoulder to steady him and provide support. "What do you need? I'll get it for you."

"Gotta pee," he said tightly.

"Oh. Alright, well, let's get you in there."

He shot me a look. "No offense, but that's not something that requires your assistance."

"I'm trying to keep you from falling," I replied, annoyed.

"Chey." He put a hand on my cheek, caressing it with his thumb. "I was a little dizzy from standing up. That's all. I'm fine now. I don't need your help walking."

A thousand retorts were at the edge of my tongue. But standing closer than we'd been in over a decade, with his hand on my face and my arm around his waist... I couldn't seem to speak at all.

His dark eyes were clear, focused, and he gazed down at me like he was trying to read my mind. I became suddenly aware of how my breathing had grown shallow, how my heart was racing. So I dropped my arm and gave him a quick nod, moving backward, out of his reach.

"Excellent. You seem okay now. But call me if you need me."

His eyes never left mine until I turned completely and walked down the hallway, leaving him alone.

When he came back out of the bathroom, he didn't turn and head to his room like I expected. Instead, he came to the living room and sank heavily down into the first seat he came to, the old burgundy recliner I hadn't had the heart to get rid of.

"You're supposed to be resting," I reminded him, knowing that it would be the first of about a thousand times over the next two weeks.

"Got a few more questions," he said, leaning his head back and closing his eyes.

"Okay."

"These aren't the clothes I was wearing in the hospital."

"No," I said, unable to stop the little grin that formed.

He lifted his head, those eyes piercing mine again. "Please don't tell me you've had to change my clothes and ... and who knows what else."

I shook my head, resisting the urge to tease him and make him as uncomfortable as I felt. "Your mom brought clean clothes to the hospital. I'm guessing she or a nurse helped you get changed when you were discharged. You must not remember it."

He shook his head. "It's crazy how much I seem to have lost. What day is it?"

I had to think about that one for a second, as the past few days had become blurry in my mind, too. "Tuesday."

His eyes widened. "Three whole days gone. How long have I been here, with you?"

I felt a stab of sympathy for him. It must be awful to have lost whole days of your life, unable to even remember what happened during them.

"Just today. They released you this morning. Your mom and Travis drove you here from the hospital. You were pretty groggy—a combination of the injury and the pain meds they gave you. Speaking of which, you're able to have more now if you want them. It's been long enough."

"Absolutely not," he said, his mouth set in a firm line. "I don't want to drift away again. Not going to have you waiting on me hand and foot."

"I need to wait on you whether you like it or not. I don't think you're understanding the doctor's orders. You're supposed to be on complete bed rest."

"I'll rest. But no meds. I don't want to lose any more time."

I bit my lip, knowing if I were in his shoes I'd feel the same way. I should encourage him to take them, but I wouldn't force him. The meds would help keep him sedated, but they had their downsides.

"How bad is the pain?"

"Not bad," he said—clearly lying. He was still too pale, and he winced every time he spoke.

"The time will pass quicker for you if you take them. It will make it easier to get the rest you need."

"I don't want them."

"I have over-the-counter meds," I said softly. "They won't make you sleepy, but they'll help with the headache at least. You don't have to suffer. There are alternatives to narcotics."

He hesitated, then nodded.

I got up, fished out the bottle of ibuprofen from the back of my cabinets, and gave him a couple with a large glass of water.

"Thanks." His voice was gruff.

"Of course."

He opened his mouth to speak, looking like he might finally say what he'd wanted to say earlier, but was interrupted by a knock on my door.

He frowned. "You expecting someone?"

"No, but it's probably one of your family members coming to check on you. They've all been worried, and I told them to stop by any time." I went to the door and opened it, expecting to see Naomi, Beth, or Claire. Instead, Pete stood on my doorstep with a bouquet of daisies in hand.

"Oh," I said, my face flushing. I could not believe this was happening. "I'm so sorry. You probably heard about Rhett's accident. With everything that happened, I completely forgot about our date."

His gaze went past me to where Rhett was sitting in the chair. His eyes widened and he stepped back, his face turning red. "Oh."

"I'm really sorry, Pete. Rhett got released from the hospital this morning, and the doctor said he needs someone keeping an eye on him for a couple of days." I babbled on about how he had a grade-four concussion and amnesia and tried to explain why I was the most logical person to care for him, knowing that nothing I could say would fix the situation.

Pete was embarrassed and I didn't blame him. I felt terrible—and also relieved to get out of a date I didn't care about. Seeing Rhett nearly die had reminded me of how strong my feelings for him had been, and I knew that was something I would never feel for Pete. The very idea of going out with him to try to move past Rhett seemed ridiculous now.

Rhett and I were still over. But my soul was connected to him in a way I knew I'd never have with anyone else.

"I understand," Pete said awkwardly. He held out the flowers. "These were for you. You should keep them."

I took the sweet bouquet, feeling overwhelming guilt. "Thanks for understanding."

He gave Rhett a little wave. "Get well soon," he said without a trace of emotion in his voice. He turned to leave without looking back.

I closed the door, bracing myself before facing Rhett. Not that it was any of Rhett's business who I dated. Still, the situation was awkward at best.

But when I turned around, Rhett had a grin on his face. "I'm surprised you said yes."

"What?"

"The other night at the bar, Pete asked me if it was okay to ask you out. One of the few things I remember from before I got conked on the head. He's not your type though. I'm surprised you agreed."

Indignation flared. "Why would he ask your permission? You don't own me. And how would you know what my type is? You've been gone a long time, Rhett. Maybe I've changed."

At that, his face turned serious. "You're right. I've been gone a long time. And I've only been around you briefly since I've been back. But that's enough for me to know you haven't changed. Not in the ways that count. Sure, you've grown up. You're not a kid anymore. But that heart? That fire inside you? It's the same. And it would never work with Pete."

"Why not?" I demanded despite knowing he was right.

"Because Pete is like a cheap beer. Dependable. Always there when you need him, and always the same. But you? You're top-shelf whiskey. Hard, strong, but also velvety smooth and so precious you don't want to waste a damn drop. And that's a different thing altogether."

I stared at him. "That's not a kind thing to say about Pete."

He shrugged. "It's true. And there's a lot of people who like cheap beer. But not you."

"No," I murmured, though I hated to agree with him. "Not me. So what are you?"

He grinned again, then winced from the pain. "I guess we'll have to see. Now, since you're stuck with me tonight, do you have a TV in here? Or can I talk you into a game of poker?" A wicked challenge glinted in his eyes, and I felt my face turn crimson.

We'd played strip poker once as teens, just the two of us. It had ended with me buck naked underneath the stars in the horse pasture.

Not that I'd minded. Rhett had made it well worth it.

But that was a lifetime ago, and I gave him a stern look. "You're supposed to rest. No TV. And no more talking. It's time I helped you back into bed."

I expected a fight, but his eyes revealed his exhaustion.

"Fine," he said, defeated. "I'll go rest. I'm sorry. I don't want to make this any harder on you than it has to be."

"Thank you," I said, surprised by his change of attitude.

He didn't even fight me when I helped walk him to his room.

But when I got him settled in bed and turned to leave, he grabbed my wrist. "Chey, stay. Please."

I wanted to say no. Wanted to leave him the way he'd left me. But the look in his eyes tugged at my heart and I couldn't.

"Why?" I asked, my voice barely more than a whisper.

He attempted a grin, but it didn't reach his eyes. "What if I said I was feeling dizzy and needed you to keep an eye on me?"

"I'd say you're full of it."

"Fine. I miss you, Chey. I know you said we could only be civil, but I'm here. And I don't think you would have invited me to recover here if I was just a random colleague."

He sighed and rubbed my wrist with his thumb. The feeling of his calloused hand on my skin began to wake feelings I hadn't felt in a very long time, and I knew I should pull away. But I couldn't bring myself to do it.

"Then you don't know me as well as you think you do," I finally said. "I'm a search-and-rescue volunteer. I literally put my life on the line for complete strangers."

He nodded. "I know. Claire's told me some about the work you do. But how many of those strangers have you invited to your home afterward?"

I wanted to give him a number, but it would be a lie. Because he was right. My home was my sanctuary, and very few people were invited to cross that threshold.

"Alright," I admitted, pulling my hand away and crossing my arms. "You have a point."

"So does that mean we can be friends?"

Friends. The thought was still as painful as it had been before. But how could I possibly say no? I'd saved his life and brought him into my home.

"Fine," I said, forcing a smile. "Friends."

Chapter Seventeen

Rhett

Friends.

It was a bigger victory than I'd expected. I'd half expected Cheyenne to tell me to go to hell. But she hadn't. It was an opportunity and I wasn't going to waste it.

Not this time.

I knew I'd already pushed, and Cheyenne wasn't the kind of woman you could keep pushing and expect anything good to happen. So I backed off and kept things light. Told her I was ready to sleep. Thought she'd take the chance to get some space, but she didn't. She curled up with a book in the chair in my room, like she didn't really want to leave.

Crazy. When I'd come back to Wildwood, I'd never in a million years thought I'd end up back here at Cheyenne's place, actually able to call her my friend.

I probably owed Thomas a thank-you—despite the fact that he'd tried to kill me.

On the other hand, Thomas was sick in the head and he was as angry at Cheyenne as he was me. Wouldn't put it past him to go after her next.

That thought had me gripping the sheets so tight that Cheyenne jumped up and ran over to me. She felt my head like she was checking for fever and ran her eyes over my body as if looking for new injuries.

And instantly switched my thoughts away from Thomas to something else entirely.

"Are you hurting?" she asked, snapping me back to the present moment.

"Uh, a little."

She gave me a worried look. "Do you need anything? Stronger meds, something to drink—"

The corner of my mouth went up and the words tumbled out before I had the sense to stop them. "Like top-shelf whiskey?"

Her worried look changed to stern disapproval. But there was a flicker of amusement in her eyes. "Absolutely not."

"Couldn't help but try," I said, flashing her a grin to make her relax. I didn't want to tell her what I'd been thinking about Thomas. For one thing, I didn't want to worry her. For another, I was thinking it might be a good idea to stick close to her, make sure she was safe. Not that I was in any kind of shape to do that yet. But still. I remembered the look in Thomas's eyes when he'd talked about her, and I didn't like it at all.

I also knew if I told Chey I wanted to stick around to protect her, she'd be sure to boot me out the door—injuries or no injuries.

Cheyenne was a stubborn woman and I liked it. Just meant I needed to know how to work around that strength instead of against it.

I woke the next morning with another raging headache after a night of fitful sleep.

"I could kill Thomas Smith," I muttered before opening my eyes and looking for Cheyenne. She wasn't there anymore, and the disappointment hit hard.

I rolled out of bed and walked across the room, grateful to feel steadier on my feet than the night before. When I opened the bedroom door, I was hit with the life-giving smell of strong coffee.

"Thank God," I said, putting my hand over my heart and closing my eyes in reverence. I had a feeling coffee was the best medicine for me this morning. Better yet, Cheyenne would be in the kitchen, and I looked forward to that. I liked being around her, and I wanted to see what things were going to look like now that we were friends.

As I'd tossed and turned the night before, I'd thought a lot about us. How the timing had been wrong, but that didn't mean we were. Fact was, we still fit, even all these years later.

Facing death had made me think about some things. Brought some clarity to the confusion I'd been feeling over what I really wanted out of life. Made me realize what mattered and what my next steps were.

I didn't regret leaving. It had been the best thing for both of us. We'd been too young to even know who we really were, and the pressure I'd been under at the ranch was a ticking time bomb. If I'd stayed, we'd have ended up married just like Travis and his girl—and then probably imploded in an ugly mess the way they had.

Cheyenne deserved a hell of a lot more than that. And I'd deserved more than to be strapped down into building my dad's dreams and watching my own die a little more every day.

But I regretted that I'd let her go too easily. Regretted letting nearly ten years pass before trying again. Regretted letting my pride get in the way of fighting for what I really wanted.

Wasn't going to do that again.

I had no idea if she'd actually give me a second chance. But now that I knew what I wanted in life, I was going to fight like hell for one.

I walked into the kitchen, disappointed when I found it empty. I glanced out the window and saw her heading to her barn. Couldn't believe that shack was still standing all these years later. I knew she loved it, but the weathered gray building looked almost ready to give up the ghost.

I went to the cabinet where the mugs had been when we were kids and smiled when I opened it, seeing that it hadn't changed. Cheyenne's collection was smaller than her grandmother's had been—she only had three mugs lined up in a row beside an empty space I assumed was for whatever mug she was using today. I reached for one, then stopped when I saw what was tucked into the back corner of the cabinet.

I pulled it out and looked at it, flooded with memories. *Falcon Ridge Ranch.* Gold inscription on a forest-green mug. We used to sell them in our gift shop, but I knew that wasn't where she'd gotten this one. This was the mug I'd given her the first time we'd spent the night together. We'd slept out under the stars on the quilt from my bed, and I'd snuck into the house the next morning, stealing two cups of coffee to take back out for us. Travis had caught me and snickered, but he'd promised not to say anything to Mom and Dad.

Cheyenne had kept that mug all these years.

My chest swam with grief. It sucked that we'd found something so sweet together so young, when I'd been too stupid to know how precious it was.

I knew how precious it was now though. And seeing that mug gave me a glimmer of hope that maybe it still meant something to her, too. That thought cheered me up, made me whistle as I put it back into the cabinet.

I grabbed one of the other mugs and filled it with coffee, closing my eyes and inhaling the scent before taking a sip. Damn, it was good. Strong and dark, just like I liked it. Then I rustled around in her drawers until I found the ibuprofen she'd given me the night before and popped three before heading outside to find her.

She was mucking out a stall when I got there. I paused in the entryway, wondering how it was possible for someone to look so pretty while shoveling horse manure. Her tight jeans were tucked into brown cowboy boots, and her green flannel shirt was fitted enough to give a glimpse of the toned figure underneath. She had her long hair pulled back in a braid, but it had loosened with her work, and soft tendrils hung around her face. Even working, she was gorgeous and I didn't want to take my eyes off her.

When she saw me, her face brightened—a stark difference from when she'd seen me on that first night at the bar. Reminded me more of the old days, when I'd been the one to put so many smiles on her face.

Made me want to whistle again.

"You look good," she said, smiling.

"Thanks," I said, winking. "Always nice hearing that."

She rolled her eyes. "I mean you look *healthier*. Your color is better than yesterday. But you are *not* supposed to be out of bed, although I imagine the fresh air has to be good for you. How are you feeling?"

"Head's still killing me. But other than that, okay."

"I can get you some more pain meds." She put down her manure fork and moved like she was headed inside.

"Already found them," I said, putting a hand on her arm to stop her from walking by me.

She looked down at it, then at me, but didn't move away. She was silent for a moment before shaking her head and stepping out of my reach. "Great. You also found coffee, I see."

"Yeah, thanks." I studied her. She was flustered, like she wasn't sure what to do now that we were supposedly friends again. I had to admit I wasn't sure, either. There wasn't a rulebook for how to be easy and friendly with an ex.

Especially when I wanted to be more.

"Any dizziness? How'd you sleep?" It was clear she'd decided to go with her comfort zone—medical questions.

"Not dizzy anymore. Didn't get enough sleep though. When I turned in, I felt so tired I thought for sure I'd sleep like the dead. But it wasn't that easy."

She frowned. "Was it the pain? Maybe we should have gone with the heavier medicine."

I shook my head, deciding to level with her and see how she reacted. "Nah. It was being in your bed."

She flushed. "That's not my bed anymore."

"No, but it used to be. It felt weird, being back there. It's so familiar, but also so different. Doesn't look the same. Your stuff's gone. Doesn't smell the same, either—smells like laundry detergent instead of you. Like I said, weird."

Her blush turned darker. "I didn't think about that being strange for you. It's been so long..."

"There's things you never forget."

Her eyes met mine, searched them. "No," she finally said. "I guess you don't."

I stepped closer, pulled one of those loose tendrils into my fingers. "I missed a lot being gone. Missed a lot of changes in my family. Missed holidays, missed watching everyone grow up and find their own way. But you know what I missed most?"

"Don't say it," she whispered, stepping another step backward. "I'm trying, Rhett. I'm trying to be your friend. But if you..."

I stepped toward her anyway. "I missed *you*, Chey."

"You can't say things like that," she said, her voice shaky. "It's not fair. It took me too long to get over you. You can't just come back and make me confused again."

"I'm not trying to make you confused. Especially when I'm thinking more clearly than ever. There's a lot of things I want to say to you, and I guess top of the list is that I'm sorry."

"What are you sorry for?" She asked it like a challenge.

"I'm sorry that I wasn't stronger, wiser, older. I'd say I'm sorry we fell in love as kids, but I'm not. Yeah, the timing was all wrong. But even so, that time of our lives was precious. Something I'd never give up."

Grief passed over her like a shadow. "And yet, you did give it up."

"I did." I nodded. "And I can't say I'm sorry I left. It was something I needed to do. But I'm sorry I didn't handle it better. I'm sorry I hurt you. I'm sorry I gave up on us."

She stared at me for a long time before she spoke. When she did, it wasn't what I wanted to hear. "We shouldn't talk about this now," she said, her face turning stubborn. "You're supposed to be in bed. You shouldn't be thinking, much less rehashing the past like this. We can talk when you're better."

"Chey—"

"No." She raised her hands in defense. "I'm trying to be your friend and take care of you while you recover, but I can't do that and dig all this up at the same time. It's too hard. Because what I really want, Rhett, is answers."

"Answers?"

"Yes, answers. I want to know *why*. Why you left the way you did. Why you picked up in the middle of the night and took off without even letting me know you were leaving." She threw up her hands, pacing. "How you could go from spending every single day with me to never seeing me again or even calling to tell me you were okay. I was so worried. Couldn't eat for days. People break up. I get that. But what you did... It was so much worse." Her voice broke.

"Hold on now," I said, raising my voice. "That's not fair."

"Isn't it?" She stopped pacing and looked at me, eyes full of sadness.

I stared at her in disbelief, then put my hands on my hips. "No, it's not. I called you every night for two weeks straight. You wouldn't talk to me. So you can blame me for leaving, but I am not the reason we went from spending every day together to never talking again. That's all you."

Her face went white. "What do you mean you called me?"

"Don't you remember? I called you the night I left. Pulled over at a motel in Idaho and the first thing I did was call you to explain. Your grandmother answered. Came back on the line a minute later and said you refused to take my call."

Her voice was shaky when she finally spoke. "She never told me you called."

"What?" I jerked back like I'd been slapped.

"She ... she didn't tell me." Her voice was a whisper. "I never knew. I don't ... I don't understand."

"I don't, either." But I had some ideas. And I was pissed about it.

"I can't." She shook her head and walked toward the house.

"Chey, stop." Headache be damned. We were going to have this out.

She froze but didn't turn around. I went to her and grabbed her arm, yanking her around to face me. Anger flared on her face, but she didn't pull away.

"You wanted answers, you're going to get them. You asked why I didn't call, but now you know the truth. I did. So apparently you've been angry at me for ten years without even knowing the truth of what happened."

"Then tell me, Rhett. What happened?" She shook her head. "I don't know why Gran didn't tell me you called. But that doesn't change the fact that you left. You *left*. And you knew. That night, the way you made love to me... You knew." Her voice broke. "You knew you were leaving and you didn't even say goodbye."

"Yeah, I knew." I spit out the words. "I knew, and it was killing me. I couldn't tell you because I knew you'd ask me to stay and I wouldn't be able to say no. Not to you. But I *had* to leave. You may not understand that, but it's true."

"Why? Why'd you have to leave?" she demanded, crossing her arms.

I gritted my teeth. "I was eighteen. Still a kid. I watched Travis get married right out of high school. Then a year later, they're expecting a kid of their own. Dad started asking me about when you and I were going to get married and put me working full-time at the ranch without giving me a choice in the matter. Talking about freaking retirement savings and all that. Pressuring me to pick a plot of land, like Travis had, and start building a house for me and you."

"Would that have really been so bad?" She choked out the words. "I thought we were happy. What about life with me would have been so awful that you had to run away from it?"

My voice softened. "It wasn't you. I loved you."

"Then what was it?"

"It was the rest of it. You know what Dad was like after Cole joined the forces. And I didn't even know for sure what I wanted out of life except that I didn't want the ranch. The idea of staying there, of doing the same job day in and day out for the rest of my life, was suffocating me. You know it was never my passion the way it is theirs."

She swallowed hard. "Yeah. Yeah, I know."

I felt desperate for her to understand. "I saw my life going down the same exact path as Dad, as Travis... But I'm not them. I wasn't ready for all that. I wanted something different. Here, I was always going to be in Travis's shadow, and I'd never live up. I wanted to be someone on my own. I needed that. And I wanted to see more of the world."

"You've always had the soul of a wanderer," she said softly.

"Exactly." I let out a breath. "I had to leave, Cheyenne. I knew you wanted to get married. I knew how much you loved the ranch. But the idea of spending my entire life in Wyoming, working seven days a week, three hundred and sixty-five days a year made me crazy. I'd have felt trapped. Eventually, I'd have resented you, and that wouldn't be fair. Our marriage would have blown up like Travis's. His was already on the rocks two years in. The handwriting was on the wall. I didn't want that to be our story."

She gritted her teeth. "Did you ever once *ask* me what I wanted?"

I blinked again. "What do you mean? It was obvious what you wanted. You loved the ranch. Loved my family. You fit there. I knew you wanted those things, and I couldn't give them to you."

She shook her head. "Rhett, I wanted *you*. I didn't want the ranch and the picket fence and the seven kids and everything your parents have. I just wanted *you*. Forever."

The truth of it was in her eyes. My chest swam with sorrow and grief for what we'd lost, what we'd never have. "I wanted you, too."

"Then why didn't you ask me to come with you?"

"I couldn't."

She jabbed my chest with her finger, hard enough to make me wince. "Why not? If you're telling me the truth, if it wasn't about me and you really did try to reach out after, then why did you never ask me to go? How was it so easy for you to walk away?"

"Easy?" My eyes widened. "It wasn't easy. It was the hardest thing I've ever done. But I had to. I didn't ask you to go with me for two reasons. One, you loved it here, and if you left, you'd have resented me as much as I'd have resented you if I'd stayed. Second, Gran was dying. She knew, and she asked me not to take you away from her in her final days."

Shock rippled over Cheyenne's face. "What?"

I nodded. "I guess she saw the warning signs in me, knew I was getting ready to bolt. She'd already been diagnosed and knew she only had about a year to live. So she begged me to leave you with her so she wouldn't be alone."

Cheyenne was shaking. Her face was white and pinched, and she looked like she was going to burst into tears any moment. "She never told me. Never told me any of it. How could you have kept that from me?"

My shoulders sagged. "I thought I was doing the right thing. I don't know what else to tell you."

"How could keeping me in the dark ever have been the right thing? How could leaving me in the middle of the night ever be the right thing?" The words came out in a cry, and tears flooded her eyes.

I grabbed her, pulled her into a tight hug even though my ribs screamed in pain. "I'm sorry," I said, whispering the words into her hair. "I thought I was doing what was best for everyone. Gran needed you.

And you loved it here. You *are* Wyoming. It flows through your veins, Cheyenne. You're more connected to this land than anyone I know, including my dad, who spent his whole damn life on that ranch. I couldn't ask you to leave for me. And when I thought you were never going to speak to me again, well, I couldn't come back here, to a land where every sunrise, every storm reminded me of you."

She didn't say a word. I held her anyway.

But after seconds stretched into minutes, she pulled away, refusing to meet my gaze.

Then she walked away without looking back.

Chapter Eighteen

Cheyenne

I walked away from Rhett, away from the house, away from all of it. I climbed the trail behind my house, tears dropping as I pushed my body at a grueling pace, needing distance almost as much as I needed him.

I wanted to scream and cry and rage at the wind. How could Gran have done that to me? She had seen my tears, my shattered heart, and never said a word. Never told me the truth, that he hadn't tried to slice the bond between us in one swift move after all. How could she have let me believe that when it was killing me?

I could barely breathe. If Rhett was telling the truth, then I'd believed a lie all these years. It was unfathomable.

Wasn't it?

The truth hit hard as I remembered how she'd encouraged me to stay outside with the horses. How she told me to leave my phone behind, that it would only cause more pain to not hear it ring. How she called Claire to take me camping, had called other friends to sit with me at night. Had encouraged me to start training with the search-and-rescue team. Had counseled me that the best medicine was found in sunshine, in earth, in sitting underneath the stars.

And I'd listened, never once thinking that she might be hiding Rhett's calls from me.

I stopped, sinking to the ground as I wept. I would never understand. She'd loved me—I knew that. It had to have been some misguided attempt at protecting me.

But if she'd really known me, she would have understood that the worst pain of all was from believing that the love of my life could walk away without a word.

Just like my father had.

I pulled my knees into my chest, rocking back and forth as I tried to make peace with it all. After all, I couldn't change it now. The years had passed. But I knew that those years would have passed differently if I'd known the truth—if Rhett and I had been given the gift of those conversations. It would have hurt, but I would have understood. I'd seen the tension between him and his dad on the ranch; I'd known that it wasn't really what he wanted. We could have made it work long-distance while Gran lived out her remaining days. Then I could have joined him wherever he was.

Everything would have been different if I had known the truth.

But as I thought over the things Rhett had said, I realized he'd never actually intended for me to join him after Gran passed. He, too, seemed to think I belonged here. That this was what I wanted more than anything.

The two people I'd loved most in the whole world had broken me, both apparently thinking they were doing the right thing. Neither of them had bothered asking me what *I* wanted.

Rhett talked about my connection to the land. How could he not understand that I was connected to *him,* too? The entire time he'd been gone, it was like my heart lived in two places. Here, on the land that was part of my soul, and with him. Forever divided, forever broken. Forever unable to move on.

It was infuriating and heartbreaking all at once. But Rhett had been right about one thing. This land and I were one. Ten years ago, I would have left in a heartbeat to be with him, and I'd have lost something else that meant everything to me. Losing him had been the greatest loss of my life, but at least I hadn't lost this.

I dried my tears, knowing I should get back to the house. The last thing I needed was Rhett attempting to come after me and potentially falling and hurting himself. I didn't want to face him though. My thoughts and emotions were swirling all over the place. It made me feel weak and irrational, two things I hated feeling and refused to let him see.

So I put on a stony face and headed back down the trail to the house.

We were supposed to be friends. That was all. I'd agreed to it, and I wasn't the kind of person who went back on my word. I wasn't ready to forgive him for keeping me in the dark about his plans and Gran's illness. But if he was telling the truth now, everything had just gotten more complicated. Because knowing he'd tried to call me changed the story I'd been telling myself for ten years. It mattered.

And with Rhett living in my house, I couldn't deny the fact that I was still ridiculously attracted to him, drawn to him like a moth to the flame. The more time I spent with him, the stronger my connection to him became. I'd spent a decade trying to kill it only to find it flaming back like a raging wildfire.

My only defense was to avoid him as much as possible. Thankfully, that wasn't too difficult. He'd improved dramatically overnight, but he was still tired—too tired to force a conversation I wasn't ready for, thankfully. He gave me a worried look when I got back but seemed to read my mood and let the conversation drop. He mostly stayed in the guest room, and I kept myself busy with chores around the house.

WHEN I WAS STARTING TO THINK ABOUT DINNER, I WAS surprised by a knock at the door. I opened it to find Beth standing on my porch with a smile on her face and a basket in hand.

"I brought dinner, courtesy of Mom," she said. "Spaghetti and meatballs, salad, and breadsticks."

My mouth started watering immediately. "That sounds amazing. Come on in. Will you stay and eat with me?"

"I was hoping you'd ask," she said, stepping inside and bending down to give Ash an affectionate scratch. Ash loved Beth and Claire as much as I did, and her tail thumped the floor even as she sat politely.

"Here, I'll take that," I said, taking the basket from her and heading into the kitchen with it.

She followed me, slipping out of her jacket, then tossed it over the back of one of my kitchen chairs. "How is he today?"

"Better. His color looks good and he's been less dizzy. He's only taking ibuprofen for the pain, and he's spent most the day resting."

Beth raised an eyebrow. "Did you have to knock him out again to get him to rest?"

I grinned. "No. Not yet, anyway."

"How has it been ... otherwise?" She gave me a pointed look.

I sighed, wondering how long it would take for his family to stop asking me if I was okay. On one hand, their concern was touching. On the other hand, it made it harder to pretend I was fine.

"It's been okay," I said, even though it was a lie. But I couldn't tell her my heart felt battered and broken. "It's awkward, obviously. But he apologized for the past and asked if we could be friends, and I'm trying."

She couldn't hide the surprise on her face. "Rhett apologized? Seriously?"

"Yeah." I pulled out plates and began putting one together for Rhett.

"That's not like him."

"Maybe he's finally growing up. Ten more years and he might catch up to Jonathan," I said, winking.

She laughed and shook her head. "I don't know. I think he deserves more credit than that already. Is that for him?"

"Yeah, why?"

"I'll deliver it. Then you and I can eat together and I'll catch you up on the plan."

"The plan?" I asked, curious.

"You didn't think we'd completely abandon you to deal with him alone, did you?" She grinned again as she took his plate out of my hands. "We like you more than that. Make me a plate, too, would you? I'll be right back."

I put together plates for both of us and pulled out the rest of the wine Claire had brought over the week before, the night Rhett had shown up. Had that really been less than a week ago? It felt like a lifetime had passed in the blink of an eye.

Beth came back minutes later with a smile on her face. "You're right. He does look a lot better. He was sleeping, but he woke up when I went in. You must have the magic touch. I never expected him to comply with the doctor's orders to rest."

"Me either," I admitted. "But I think he's still hurting more than he lets on."

"Probably," she agreed. "Anyway, the plan. First of all, I didn't just bring dinner. I'm here to give you a break. After we eat, I'll stay with him and you can do whatever you need or want to do. Go to town, take a long bath, get some space—whatever you need."

"Thanks," I said, feeling unexpected relief. It wasn't exactly that I was in a hurry to get away from him. In fact, I'd barely seen him since that morning. But distance felt like a good thing.

"Of course. And Mom's coming to sit with him tomorrow so you can work. She prepped the food for the guests in advance, and Claire's off, so the plan is for you and Claire to handle the trail rides and I'll take over for Mom."

"That works," I said, cheering internally even more. A day out on the trail was exactly what my soul needed. The hours on horseback were certain to help me find peace and clarity.

"That way, you and Claire can go to training tomorrow night."

I blinked. "You're right. Tomorrow's Thursday. I didn't even think about it." Our SAR group trained most Thursday nights.

"It's easy to lose track of the days when your schedule's all messed up," she said easily.

"It is. Well, I sure appreciate the rotation. Not that I mind sitting with him. He's been easy," I said, feeling sudden guilt for the way they were rearranging their lives. It wasn't only for my sake though, I knew. They loved him and wanted to be with him, too.

"Well, I'm glad you don't mind, because Mom wanted me to ask you for another favor." Beth suddenly looked nervous.

"What?" My stomach dropped.

"The neurologist called today. Rhett has a follow-up appointment on Friday morning. We have a bridal party coming in that morning for brunch, so Mom really can't get away. It's been on the schedule for months at this point. But we don't have any trail riders scheduled, so we were able to block that off easily. Would you be able to take him to the appointment?"

"Oh, of course," I said, relieved that's all it was. "That's not a problem."

"Good. Thank you." She breathed a sigh of relief. "Mom said to tell you that we're paying you for your time like we would if you were working every day at the ranch. She knows what an imposition this whole thing has to be."

"It's really not," I said gently—and realized, with a bit of surprise, that I meant it. "You guys are family. No matter what happened between me and Rhett in the past, I still care about ... all of you."

I swallowed hard, knowing I still cared entirely too much.

Chapter Nineteen

Cheyenne

I stopped at the bar first, feeling like I needed to apologize again to Pete. He gave me a guarded smile when I walked in.

"Hey, Cheyenne. Didn't expect to see you anytime soon." He polished the shiny wood bar with a rag, rubbing a bit harder than was necessary.

I slid onto one of the black leather barstools. "I have backup tonight. Listen, Pete, I'm really sorry about yesterday."

"No worries," he said, though his smile didn't seem sincere. "Things happen. Maybe we can reschedule?"

I groaned inwardly, wishing he hadn't asked. The last thing I wanted to do was hurt his feelings. But it would be worse to lead him on and hurt him even more later.

"I don't think that's a good idea," I said slowly.

He turned crimson. "I see. I guess ... I guess you and Rhett are back together, then?"

"Whoa," came a voice from behind me. "What's this about you and Rhett?"

I turned around to see Sam and his girlfriend standing there, and it was my turn to blush awkwardly.

"We're not," I said, looking first to him, then to Pete. "I'm helping until he gets better. That's not why, Pete. But let's not talk about it now, okay?"

"Or ever," he suggested, red-faced as he turned and disappeared into the kitchen.

I sighed and propped my elbows on the bar, resting my head in my hands. I regretted ever having agreed to go out with him at all.

"What's all this about?" Sam asked, confused. His girlfriend, Emily, snuggled into him, giving me a strange look.

"Rhett was injured," I said, spinning around to face them as I attempted to explain. "Long story short, he's recovering at my house. Pete and I had a date scheduled for last night, and I forgot about it. When Pete arrived and saw Rhett, he jumped to conclusions."

"Ah. I see," Sam said, though his face said something different. I wasn't sure if his clear disapproval was about Rhett staying at my place or about my date with Pete.

"Rhett..." Emily said, letting the word linger on her lips. "I don't think I've met him."

"He's Claire's brother. He doesn't live here," I explained.

"Ahh," she said, her eyes twinkling. "Another sexy Hawkins brother. I think I remember hearing about him actually. Is he the ex who left you?"

"That would be the one," I said, forcing a smile—though I was irrationally annoyed at hearing her call Rhett sexy.

"So, you two are shacking up, huh?"

Make that very annoyed. "I have some medical training. I'm just helping him recover."

"Recovery from what?" she asked, cocking her head.

I sighed, not really wanting to get into all of it with her but knowing that Sam likely wanted an explanation too. "He has a head injury. A grade-four concussion. Right now, he's on bedrest and we're monitoring him. His sister is sitting with him right now to give me a break."

Her eyes bugged out of her head. "Oh my gosh. That sounds terrible. I hope he'll be okay."

"He will be. Thanks."

Sam was giving me a look like he could see right through me—which, honestly, he probably could. You didn't work with someone so closely for so many years without them learning to read your cues.

"That's a lot, Cheyenne. Are you doing okay with all of it?" he asked gently.

"I am." I knew that my face probably betrayed the truth—that it was complicated and I was a mess. But I also knew he'd respect the fact that I didn't want to get into it here.

"If you need anything, call," he said, putting a hand on my shoulder. "I'm not far away. I can take a turn sitting with him, give you a break. Whatever you need. Even if it's just to talk."

"Thanks," I said, giving him a grateful look.

"We better let you get back to your man," Emily said, winking. "The whole thing sounds awfully romantic to me. Nursing him at his bedside? It's the stuff of romance novels. Maybe fate is bringing you two back together."

I stared at her, biting back the words I wanted to say. Romantic? For someone you cared about to nearly die?

Hardly.

Now I remembered why I always avoided Sam when she was around.

Sam squeezed her arm and pulled her away, giving me an apologetic look. And I decided ice cream in a different building was better than the whiskey I'd planned on having here.

"Cheyenne! It's been so slow today I was about to close up and head home early. But since you're here, you'll help me get through the last twenty minutes of the day." Alma's eyes twinkled. We both knew she never took a day off or closed early, even though she threatened it at least twice a week.

"Glad I can help you pass the time. A scoop of huckleberry, please,"

I said, tossing some bills down onto the counter as I pulled a stool up to the counter.

She scooped it out of the chest and handed it to me, ignoring the money. "Should I ask why you're back for ice cream so soon? That's usually a bad sign."

I chuckled. "You know me well. It's been a long few days."

"I heard about what happened to Rhett. Guess that's probably made things rough at the ranch."

"I'm sure it has," I agreed.

She cocked her head. "I meant for you, silly. You guys were already stretched thin. Now, with Naomi having another injured person to tend, I'm guessing you're pulling triple duty. Surprised you're off shift already."

"Oh, I guess you didn't hear. I've actually been off the last couple of days. Rhett needed a place to recover, and my house made the most sense, so he's been staying with me."

Her face showed her disapproval. "Cheyenne..."

I held up my hands in protest. "It's not a big deal, Alma. It was easier for them to cover my job than for Naomi to watch him while the rest of us fumbled around in the kitchen, trying to prepare food for the guests. Trust me, we tried that while he was in the hospital. It wasn't pretty."

"Naomi isn't his only family member," she pointed out. "I know Claire's tied up being a deputy, and Walker's down, and Travis can barely catch his breath. But that still leaves Beth and Jonathan. One of them could have kept an eye on him. I can't believe they forced you to do that." She shook her head, frowning.

"They didn't," I said, feeling the need to defend them. "You're forgetting that Jonathan is a senior in school and can't sit around watching Rhett during the day. Besides, it's not just about who's the easiest to replace. Rhett's on physical restrictions right now and I don't have stairs. Plus, my house is a lot quieter than a ranch fully booked with tourists. I was the best choice."

She pointed a sharp finger at me. "You're playing with fire, girl. That boy about killed you when he left, and I can tell by the way you keep blushing that your heart is already getting caught up again while he's got you playing nurse. I don't like it at all. Next thing you know, he'll be trying to worm his way into your pants again, and then where will you be?"

"It's not like that," I insisted. "I'm not doing it for him. I owe his whole family for the way they've helped me over the years. Plus, he got hurt because he was defending me."

She frowned. "What do you mean?"

"We're pretty sure Thomas is the one who did this. He's got an alibi, but it's his wife, and—"

"And she won't even turn him in for beating her." Alma's face wrinkled in distaste.

"Exactly. Rhett and Thomas got into a fight at the bar. You know how much Thomas hates me. I guess he made some threat about teaching me a lesson, and that's what started everything. Then, when Rhett was alone, Thomas tried to finish it."

"That's not your fault."

"No, but I owe him," I said quietly. "But you don't have to worry. He's past the danger zone and it won't be long before he's able to move back to the ranch. He and I agreed to be friends, and that's all there is to it."

"Friends is a dangerous thing with a man like that, honey."

She had no idea.

"Trust me, I know. I'm not interested in a fling, and Rhett's not the kind of guy to hang around. I learned that lesson a long time ago, and I won't forget it."

Her eyes softened. "You know I love you like you're my own. I just don't want to see you get hurt again. Couldn't bear to see your heart broken like it was ten years ago."

"I promise, my heart's fine," I said.

It wasn't. But I hoped I was convincing enough to reassure her.

Chapter Twenty

Rhett

I'D SCREWED UP.

My apology to Cheyenne seemed to have made her mad, something I couldn't begin to comprehend. Women. They didn't make sense to me at all.

I tried to earn some brownie points by being a model patient. Spent the whole damn day in bed resting, even though I was about to go out of my mind with boredom.

And what did I get for it?

Cheyenne avoided me all day and turned me over to Beth that night. Worse, she'd apparently called in my *mom* for the next day.

Nothing said "I want to be as far away from you as possible" as calling in Mom to take over.

If I'd thought boredom was bad during my mind-numbingly slow day with Cheyenne, the day with Mom was infinitely worse. She vacillated between refusing to talk to me at all and questioning me about how Cheyenne was doing with the whole thing. Twice, she even started lecturing me on how I should thank Cheyenne for opening up her home to me. How grateful I should be.

Dammit, I was grateful. But there was nothing like a lecture to stop those feelings short.

When Mom brought me a dinner tray that night, I asked if Cheyenne would be back soon. Framed it as wanting to thank her again, just to get Mom off my back, when what I really wanted to know was when I was going to get a break from the lectures.

Mom shook her head, fussing over the tray and straightening the blankets on the bed. "Not for a few hours. She trains on Thursday nights."

"Trains?"

"Yeah. The search-and-rescue group trains every week."

"What kind of training do they do?" I asked, suddenly interested.

She pointed a finger at me. "You're supposed to be resting." She turned to leave.

"Please, Mom. I'm dying of boredom. All I'm asking for is a few minutes of conversation that isn't about my poor life choices and how grateful I need to be." I gave her a pointed look.

She paused at the door and her face softened. "Was I that bad today?"

"Whatever you're thinking, you were worse."

"I'm sorry," she said, coming over to sit on the edge of the bed. She sighed heavily as she began smoothing the patchwork quilt. "You don't know what Cheyenne means to us. She saved us when we were drowning at the ranch. The guests love her. She keeps Claire grounded and helps Beth break out of her shell. I honestly don't know what we would do without her."

It stung a bit. On one hand, I was damn proud of Cheyenne. She had built an amazing life for herself, and she was adored by my family. On the other hand, it reminded me of what I'd given up—and how, when it came down to it, my family would always prefer her over me.

"I get it," I said, my voice rough.

Mom gave me a long look, like she was trying to see deep into my soul.

Damn uncomfortable.

"So tell me about the training," I said, trying to change the subject.

"First, I need to tell you something else," she said softly. "We're grateful to Cheyenne for what she does at the ranch. But do you know what I'm most thankful for?"

"What?"

She touched my cheek. "That she found *you* and saved your life."

I swallowed hard. "I'm pretty thankful for that myself."

"You weren't around to see how broken she was when you left. She could have done the same to you and left you in that ditch."

I shook my head. "No, she couldn't have. Cheyenne doesn't have that in her."

"You're right," she said, smiling. "She doesn't. Rhett, whether you see it or not, she still cares for you. Maybe I've gone too far, said too much. But I think you still care for her, too."

I stared at her. "I do," I said, the words coming out all strangled over the lump in my throat.

"Whatever happened... Is it something you can get past?"

I waited a long time to answer. "I can. I'm not sure if she can though. " I hesitated, then told her the truth. "She's pretty angry at me right now. There were some misunderstandings about what happened back then. We talked about it some yesterday. I think it made things worse somehow."

Mom sighed. "I'm sorry to hear that. She hasn't said anything to me about it, but she wouldn't. I've always tried to let her know that I'm there for her, but she keeps everyone at arm's length."

"Yeah, I know."

"Everyone except Claire, that is," Mom said with a small laugh. "And you, back in the day." She was quiet for a moment. "You two were always good together. Even if I didn't approve of the choices you made." She raised an eyebrow and gave me the mom look.

Even now, at almost thirty years old, it made my heart stammer. "Uh, I don't know what you're talking about."

"Oh, I think you do," she said, winking. "You weren't as smooth and discreet as you think you were."

"I wasn't smooth at all," I admitted. "Mom, I've got to tell you... I don't know if there's a second chance for us. But if there is, I'm going to fight for it."

She squeezed my hand. "I'm glad to hear that."

"I'm sorry I hurt her, but I'm not sorry I left. It was the right choice for me. I needed to get out of here, figure out who I was outside the family. Needed to grow the hell up, become the kind of man who had something decent to offer a woman like Cheyenne. But I've had a lot of time to think things over in this bed, and I'm going to try to be that man now."

She gave me a smile, her eyes watery. "I hope, for both your sakes, that she sees what I see—that you're a wonderful man with everything in the world to offer. I don't tell you often enough, but I'm proud of you, Rhett. You may not have taken the path your father planned for you, but in some ways, that makes me even prouder."

"Really?" I gave her a skeptical look, waiting for the punchline.

But she was serious. "Yes. You were strong enough to forge your own path, to chase after your own dreams. I think I always knew the ranch wasn't for you. Not long term, anyway. Your father loves it so much he can't imagine any other way of life, but that didn't mean it was right for you."

I stared at her. Wasn't sure I'd ever heard anything like that from her before.

"You're a *good* man," she continued. "And while I may not like the *way* you left, I do understand why you did it."

"You do?"

"I do." She nodded.

"That ... that means a lot."

She squeezed my hand. "We love you, and we're proud of you. And we'll keep loving you and being proud of you whether you and Cheyenne get back together or not. I don't want you to ever think any differently."

"I love you, too, Mom," I finally said over the lump in my throat.

"So, the training," she said, sniffing as she changed the subject. Even she wasn't comfortable with long, drawn-out, emotional conversations. So she filled the time by telling me all about the things the SAR group did—and left me even more in awe of Cheyenne and the incredible life she'd built with me gone.

Cheyenne was in the kitchen when I made my way down the hallway the next morning in search of coffee. I lit up when I saw her, glad it was her instead of another one of my family members there to babysit. I loved my family and was grateful for their concern. But after years of living alone, it was all feeling like a bit much.

Oddly enough, Cheyenne never made me feel that way. Having her around all the time was different.

"You look happy this morning," she commented, giving me a little smile.

"First time I've woken up without a headache." It was true. Just not the whole truth.

"That's great," she said, beaming. "Perfect timing, too."

"Why's that?" I reached past her to get a coffee mug, letting my fingers brush her arm as I did.

She stared at me quizzically but didn't move away. "You have a doctor's appointment. Didn't your mom tell you?"

"Must have slipped her mind."

I found an excuse to touch her again, putting a hand on her hip as I stepped around her to the coffee pot. This was fun. Almost like a dance. Reminded me of the way my parents used to be when they thought us kids weren't looking. Always finding a reason to touch each other even while they were doing the simple, everyday things, like pouring a cup of coffee before starting the day.

"What are you doing?" she asked.

"Getting coffee." I gave her a quick wink before pouring my cup. "What are you doing?"

"I mean, what are you doing touching me?"

I turned toward her, leaning a hip on the counter as I looked her dead in the eye. "I like touching you. But if you want me to stop, say the word and I'll never touch you without your permission again."

She held my gaze. But she didn't tell me to stop.

"We need to leave in an hour," she finally said, cutting her eyes away from mine. "I have a couple of chores to do outside. Your mom left you a clean change of clothes. I put them in the guest bath. Figured you might want to shower before we leave. I can help you rewrap your ribs after if you want. There are some muffins in the fridge, courtesy of your mom. Do you need anything else?"

"Well, I don't know," I said, speaking slowly. "I haven't tried taking a shower yet. That's a long time to stand up without any assistance. I might get dizzy, you know, with all the hot water. Maybe I need some help in there." I stared into her eyes, letting her see the heat in them before giving her another wink.

Her lips twisted into an amused smile. "Then make it a cold one and make it fast, because my nursing duties don't extend that far. Unless you need me to call Travis? I'll ask him to give you a sponge bath."

I fisted my hand and held it to my heart. "You wouldn't."

"Don't try me." She winked and flounced out, leaving me grinning as I watched her go.

A shower and clean clothes made me feel like a new man, and the hour-long drive to the appointment felt great. I wasn't used to being so cooped up, and the fresh air and change of scenery lifted my spirits.

Just like the woman in the driver's seat.

She didn't talk much on the drive, reminding me that I was supposed to rest. But it gave me plenty of time to study her. I found myself wanting to memorize her features, comparing the woman in front of me to the girl from my memories. They were both gorgeous, but present-day Cheyenne was something else. That long hair, that lean body, the strength she'd built doing what she did every day. She was incredible, and I could have stared at her all day long.

"What are you doing?" she asked, eyeing me as she repeated the question from earlier.

"Looking at you. I like it almost as much as touching you."

She rolled her eyes. "You're such a flirt."

"Only with you."

She snorted. "I doubt that."

"Dead serious, Cheyenne. You're the only woman I have any interest in flirting with."

For a moment, she was silent. Then she changed the subject. "Where do you live now?"

I took a minute before replying, wondering if I was really ready to commit to staying. But one more glance at the incredible woman beside me and I knew I was.

"Wildwood, Wyoming."

She rolled her eyes again. "I meant when you're healed up and you go home. Where do you really live these days?"

"I'm not leaving."

She glanced at me with a question on her face. "You're not?"

I shook my head. "Nope. Decided I'm staying."

"Why?"

I shrugged. "Lots of reasons."

"Hmmm." She let out a deep breath. "I'm not sure what to say about that."

"No need to say anything at all." I leaned my seat back and put my hands behind my head.

"Where did you live before this?"

"Austin, Texas."

She glanced my way again. "That's where you went when you left Wyoming?"

"Nope. Headed to Idaho first. Then Montana, Flathead Valley area. Then I went to Seattle, tried the city life there. Made my way down to California, but that didn't last long. Ended up in Texas, minus a brief stint in New York."

"Wow. You've really seen a lot."

"I have." Though none of it seemed quite as pretty as the view in front of me right now.

She was quiet again before asking her next question. "Do you have a girlfriend ... or wife ... or—"

"No," I said, interrupting her.

"Ever married?" This time, she stared straight ahead, like she couldn't bear to look at me while she asked.

"Never. Not even close. You?"

She shook her head. "Not even close."

"Just another one of the ways we're alike," I murmured. "You're the only girl who ever made me even contemplate the idea of settling down, setting up house."

"Rhett..."

"I know. We can talk when you're ready."

She fell silent. But it didn't last long. "So, are you going to work for your parents? You know, if you really stay?"

"Nope. You know ranching's never been my dream."

She glanced over at me. "When we were kids, you always dreamed of renovating houses. Did you ever do anything like that?"

This time, my grin was proud. "Yeah, I did. I've been working for a developer down in Austin. He buys the properties; I go in and remodel them. He sells, then we split the profits."

"That sounds great," she said, smiling.

"It has been. I've learned a ton and made good money doing it. But I've been saving up and I'm ready to start my own business. My partner has always been focused on the commercial space or flipping properties that turn into vacation rentals. I want to restore historical properties and create homes that people actually live in. I don't need a partner anymore, and that gives me freedom to move where I want."

"You've always loved your freedom." A bit of wariness crept into her voice.

"Damn right. Going into business for myself has been a long time coming, and I've decided to do it here." And it was only partly about the woman sitting next to me. It was her, it was my family, and it was more. I couldn't explain it, but it was like the mountain was calling me home. I was tired of wandering. I wanted to be here in the wild, untamed land that spoke to my soul.

"But this is a small town." Her voice was full of doubt. "You really think you can make enough here?"

I snorted out a laugh. "Haven't you heard? Wyoming is about to be the new Texas."

"What do you mean?"

"It's projected to have serious growth over the next few years. More people moving here means more buyers in the market. Besides, I have ways to diversify the business." What I didn't tell her was that I'd also made bank over the past ten years and had never seen a reason to spend any of it. I could almost retire, except that I'd be bored out of my mind in about ten seconds.

"Hmm."

"What?"

"I don't know." She glanced over again. "It's just hard to imagine you really settling down here. I guess I'll believe it when I see it."

"Cheyenne. I'm not leaving."

But the look she gave me said she didn't believe me.

Chapter Twenty-One

Cheyenne

RHETT REACHED FOR MY HAND WHILE WE WALKED ACROSS the long parking lot toward the hospital's neurology clinic.

"Are you dizzy?" I asked, thinking he was having a hard time with the walk.

"No. Why?" He glanced at my face, then down at our hands. "Oh, that? I told you. I like touching you. But if you tell me to stop, I'll stop."

My traitorous mouth refused to form the words.

Falling for Rhett was a huge mistake. No matter what he said, I knew he wouldn't hang around Wyoming. He had the heart of a wanderer, always wanting to see new places. Always had. Ten years wouldn't be enough to get it out of his system.

He'd get bored and move on. Just like before.

But I *was* falling for him again, and I couldn't even fully explain why. He was exasperating. Cocky. Stubborn. Impulsive.

But there had never been another soul on this earth that made me feel more at home.

So I let him keep my hand in his, and I didn't say a word when that hand slipped around my waist as he guided me through the hospital doors.

Didn't say a word when we got into the elevator and I pushed the button for the third floor, with his fingers trailing up and down my spine.

I knew I should tell him to stop. That all he was doing was confusing me, making me long for things I could never have. That he was setting me up for heartbreak again, and I should be angry about that.

But I couldn't be angry, because part of me felt like everything was exactly as it should be. For the first time in over a decade, the pieces of the puzzle that made up my life had finally shifted back into place. It felt like the most natural thing in the world to start my days with him, to go with him to his medical appointments, to have him holding my hand as we walked.

I had to remind myself that this wasn't normal at all.

As we waited to see the neurologist, I could tell that Rhett was nervous, even though he was trying to hide it. His foot tapped impatiently and he squeezed my hand a little tighter than he had earlier.

"Everything's going to be fine," I whispered, trying to reassure him. "It's just a checkup."

"I know."

But his tone was clipped. I felt a pang of empathy for him, knowing that it must be hard for someone so independent and physical to be at the mercy of an injury. What if they told him he needed even more than the two weeks to rest? He'd go out of his mind.

Thankfully, that wasn't how the appointment went at all. The neurologist explained that, while the admitting doctor had followed old-school protocols, concussion treatment had changed. He actually wanted Rhett to start getting back to normal activities, slowly at first, adding on a little each day until he was back to his normal pace. Now that he was out of the danger zone, there was no need to restrict his activity for two entire weeks.

I'd never seen Rhett so relieved.

When we stepped back outside the hospital, he looked like a man who'd been released from jail. He grinned and grabbed me, pulling me into a tight embrace. It was friendly, quick, and no different than if Claire had hugged me.

Except for the way it made my heart soar.

He grabbed my hand like it hadn't just happened and whistled as we walked back toward my truck. "Can I drive home?"

"No."

"Why not?"

"Because you're supposed to ease into mental activities, not dive right back into something where a mistake would endanger both our lives. Besides, I happen to like my truck." I gave him a teasing grin as he opened my door for me, a habit that seemed as natural to him as it had been a decade ago.

"You're right," he said, his tone easy. "Man, I'm glad I don't have to go back to lying in a dark room all day."

"Me too." I started the engine, wondering if I should broach the subject of his returning home. Based on this appointment, it didn't seem necessary for Rhett to stay with me. It was the news I'd been waiting for, yet it didn't make me happy. But that was the exact reason I *needed* to bring it up. Better to rip off the Band-Aid sooner rather than later. The longer I got used to having him around, the more it would hurt when he left again.

"So," I said when he hopped into the passenger's seat. "I guess you're probably pretty anxious to move back to the ranch."

He looked back at me, a question in his eyes. "If you want me to go, I'll go. But I'm not in a hurry to leave."

"Because?" I left it hanging there, my heart picking up speed as I wondered what he might say.

I could feel him looking at me while he decided how to answer.

"I could make up a bunch of excuses. Tell you I didn't want Mom and Beth worrying over me—true, by the way. Say I wasn't ready to manage all the stairs. That one's a lie. Say I sure as hell don't want to share a room with my eighteen-year-old brother. That's totally true. But none of those things are the real reason."

"What is the real reason?" I kept my eyes on the road, my heart pounding out of my chest.

"Because the last few days are the most I've been around you in over ten years, and I had to spend almost all of it in bed. Which wouldn't have been so bad had you been with me."

"Rhett—"

"Because I want a chance for us to get to know each other again. Because I'm not ready for you to disappear back out on the trail, only seeing you as we pass like ships in the night."

My heart caught in my throat. He was saying all the things I wanted to hear. And even though I knew it was a terrible idea, I wanted those things, too.

"You can stay a little longer," I said, still avoiding his eyes. "It would probably be good for your recovery to avoid the chaos of living at the ranch. After all, the neurologist wanted you to ease into things slowly. Considering you've been on total bedrest, it wouldn't hurt for you to take a week to get used to being up a couple of hours at a time before you head back."

"Right," he said, disappointment clear in his voice.

I knew that it wasn't the answer he was looking for. He'd put his heart out there and hoped I would give him something in return. But he couldn't realize what a giant step it was for me to agree to let him stay. I was risking my heart, too. I just wasn't ready to admit it yet.

Saying it out loud would make it entirely too real.

When we got back to my place, Sheriff McGrath was standing on my front porch, knocking on the door. He turned and waved when he saw my truck pull into the driveway.

"That can't be good," Rhett muttered.

"The sheriff's on your side this time," I said, laughing.

Rhett had been on the wrong side of things too many times as a teenager, even though I knew what nobody else seemed to realize: that every time he got into trouble, it was because he was trying to right a wrong for someone else. Rhett's heart had always been in the right place, but his way of handling things got him into trouble.

I swung out of the truck before Rhett could make it to my door and headed straight up to the porch.

"Cheyenne," Sheriff McGrath said, rocking back on his heels as he stuck his thumbs into his belt loops. "I'm here to speak to Rhett."

Rhett put his hand on my shoulder. "Anything you need to say to me, you can say in front of her."

McGrath's eyebrows shot up. "I see. Can we go inside to talk?"

"Sure," I said, sticking my key into the lock and opening the door. Ash slipped past me, sniffing McGrath before running out front to do her business.

I gestured to my couch. "Have a seat."

"Thanks." McGrath stepped inside and sat down, looking relaxed and casual even though this was clearly an official visit.

Rhett was still tense. I gave him a reassuring look and sat down on the loveseat, hoping he'd follow suit. Instead, he stood with his arms crossed, looking like a tiger ready to pounce.

"What's going on, Sheriff?" I asked, hoping to break the tension.

"Well, I have some good news."

"What kind of news?" Rhett's voice was flat.

"Found a witness who saw Thomas come back and let the air out of your tires while you were still in the bar that night. That was enough to get a search warrant for his vehicle. Tire iron in the back had blood and black hair on it. Sent it to the state crime lab. Could be a while before we get results, but it's obvious it's going to be a match for yours and that's enough for me. We took him into custody this morning."

I let out a breath, feeling unexpected relief. But it was quickly followed with worry. "Any chance he'll get out on bail?"

McGrath sighed. "I'm hopeful the judge is going to deny it or set it pretty damn high, considering his history and the violent nature of the crime. But yeah, there's a chance, and the judge often goes lighter than what I'd prefer. Arraignment is set for Monday morning. We'll know after that."

"Thanks for letting us know," I said. It gave me some reassurance, but it didn't feel like enough. Knowing Thomas, it might make him more angry. If he thought he'd gotten away with it, he might let it go. But getting caught would infuriate him. If he made bail... I didn't even want to think of it.

McGrath eyed Rhett, then stood. "How are you feeling, Rhett?"

"Improving." His arms remained crossed and his face flat.

"Glad to hear it. You sure look a hell of a lot better than you did in that hospital bed. Cheyenne, we'll be seeing you. Take care now."

"Thanks, Sheriff." I saw him out, letting Ash back inside in the process, then locked the door and turned to Rhett, who'd sunk down into the recliner, looking exhausted.

"What was that about?" I asked, bewildered. "The man arrested your attacker, but you acted like he was here to arrest you."

"I don't know," Rhett said, shaking his head. "Seeing him again made me feel weird ... anxious. Can't explain it."

My eyebrow furrowed as I studied him. "You might have a touch of PTSD. That's pretty normal, considering what you went through. He was there that night after the fight and also in the hospital. Maybe you associate him with what happened."

"Maybe. Look, I don't want to talk about it," he snapped.

"Okay," I said, holding my hands up.

His face softened. "I'm not mad at you."

"I know."

He ran his hands over his face. "Chey, I just want to get back to normal. But when I saw the sheriff, my heart started racing like it was going to blow up. All that good news from the neurologist disappeared and it felt like nothing was ever going to be the same again."

My heart broke for him. Rhett had always been such a strong, hard one. I wasn't sure I'd ever seen him as vulnerable as this. Without even thinking, I walked over and dropped to my knees in front of his chair, taking his hands into mine.

"It's all going to be okay," I said, soothing him. "One step at a time, okay? I'm here."

He looked at me with tired eyes. "This isn't the way I want things to be."

"I know."

"No," he said, shaking his head. "You don't. I don't want you to take me back because you feel sorry for me."

I blinked twice, taken aback. "I don't—"

"Yes, you do," he interrupted. "I can see it on your face right now. In your eyes. And I get it. But that's not how I want things to be between us. Look, I'm going to get some rest, okay? The trip tired me out more than I expected."

"That makes sense," I said, swallowing hard. "You haven't had this much activity since ... before."

He gave me a long look, then got up and walked down the hallway without a word, leaving me wondering if our short second chance was already over.

CHAPTER TWENTY-TWO

Rhett

I TOSSED AND TURNED FOR HOURS. MY BODY WAS exhausted, but my mind wouldn't stop racing. When I had seen the sheriff, I'd flashed back to that night in the bar. Nothing I didn't already know—just the parts where I got into it with Thomas. But it played like a film strip, nagging at me like I was forgetting something important. Something had happened that night that I needed to know.

And if that hadn't been bad enough, Cheyenne's pity made me feel ten times worse.

I wanted to stay with her and make a go of things. But I didn't want her letting me stay because she felt sorry for me. Sure as hell didn't want her to take me back into her heart and her bed because I was a broken shell of a man she needed to take care of.

I'd leave again before doing that to her.

I wanted her to love me again. But not out of pity. Because of who I was.

The way I loved her.

Because I did. I knew that now. The flashback earlier wasn't the only thing haunting me. All day long, I'd had this weird feeling that this was almost exactly what life would be like if I'd stayed. That I had been dead wrong about things blowing up the way they had with Travis and Missy —that Chey and I were different.

It was the damndest thing. I'd always thought leaving was the right thing for both of us. But I was starting to wonder if I had been wrong about that. I couldn't regret the lives we'd built apart. Life alone had helped me grow up. And she'd blossomed into the strongest woman I'd ever known. But part of me wondered if maybe we could have done that growing together and still ended up in a good place. I'd left because I wanted to live a life with no regrets. But all of a sudden, I had some.

Worse, I was getting addicted to living here with her. Oh, I wanted to make some tweaks. Wanted to move into her bed instead of this one. Wanted my old strength back. Wanted her to look at me the way she used to instead of with that damn pity in her eyes.

More than anything, I wanted to be able to call her mine.

When the sun was getting low in the sky, I finally pulled myself out of bed, realizing I'd dozed right through lunch. My rumbling stomach let me know that at least one part of me was working fully and I needed to get something to eat. I stopped off at the bathroom, muttering in the mirror about how I looked like hell. Still had cuts and scrapes on my face, and the bruises were turning a nasty yellow color. It wasn't an ideal look for winning a woman's heart, that was for sure.

"Not much you can do about that," I told my reflection before heading to the kitchen.

Cheyenne was sitting at the table, eating something that smelled delicious.

"I didn't cook," she said, her voice flat without a trace of pity in it. "Your mom brought over enough food to feed an army. There's three kinds of leftovers in there: spaghetti and meatballs, chili with cornbread, and some sort of casserole thing with chicken and rice. I'd offer to heat you up something, but I figure you'd rather do it yourself."

I opened the fridge and peered inside, choosing the casserole dish. "Was I an ass earlier?"

She was quiet for a moment. "No. I actually get it. I don't like pity, either, and I'm sorry for making you feel that way."

"You've got no reason to apologize," I said, my voice coming out in a growl.

"You're right. I really don't," she said, laughing.

I turned to look at her and saw a smirk on her face. It was exactly what I needed to lighten the heavy feeling in my chest.

"Sorry for how I acted," I said.

"You've got no reason to apologize, either." She gave me a friendly smile. "I understand how you feel. I'd feel the same way. And ... since the neurologist said it was okay, I can offer you a whiskey to go with that casserole. Consider it a peace offering."

"You're an angel."

"Hardly." She laughed again and stood, getting out two whiskey glasses and pulling a bottle from a lower cabinet. "It's not top-shelf by any means. But it's not bad."

I eyed the label. "Not bad at all. I'm a big fan of rye whiskey."

"Me too." She poured a glass and handed it to me. "Remember when we stole a bottle from your dad?"

"Yep." I groaned. "I paid for that in so many ways. First, the vomiting. So much vomiting. Had a headache the next day that was almost as bad as the one ol' Thomas gave me. Then Dad found out what I'd done and I paid for it all over again."

She grinned. "Did he know I was involved?"

"Never. You know I'd never rat you out."

"Probably good. He might not have hired me if you had." She poured a small glass for herself and touched it to mine. "Cheers. To your recovering health."

"I'll toast to that." I took a sip and groaned again, this time in pleasure. "That's good."

"It is. I like to keep a bottle around for—" She cut off as Ash let out a low growl. "What in the world?"

Ash stood at the back door, her nose pointed toward it and her body on alert as she growled, low and fierce.

Cheyenne moved to the window and looked out. "I wonder if there's a bear out there. Or a wolf."

I took another sip. "Probably a bear. Seems like if it was a wolf she'd be a little friendlier, seeing as it's one of her own kind."

Cheyenne rolled her eyes. "She's not a wolf."

"So you keep saying."

Ash's growl grew louder.

Chey stared at her with a worried expression. "That's not like her," she said.

"You worried about it?"

"A little." Cheyenne moved to a closet and pulled out a rifle.

"Whoa, Annie Oakley," I said, holding up my hands.

"I'm going to take a look."

"Don't you think you should just wait, let whatever it is move on?"

She gave me an impatient look. "I have a horse out there. If there's a predator on my property, I need to protect it."

"Then let me." I reached to take the rifle out of her hands, but she stepped back.

"No way. This is my gun. I don't even know if you still know how to shoot."

I rolled my eyes. "Some things are like riding a bike."

"Even so, the answer is no. My gun. My property. My rules."

I gritted my teeth. "You're as stubborn as you were at nineteen."

"Oh, I'm way more stubborn than I was then." She chambered a round and headed for the door.

"Well, I am too, and I'm going with you."

Cheyenne walked out onto the back porch, watching carefully, with a finger up to tell me to be quiet. Ash let out a low growl as she stared toward the back of the property.

"Go find it," Cheyenne said quietly to the dog.

Ash bounded off the porch and headed straight for the tree line, sniffing the ground in a path that only made sense to her.

"It's not near the barn," Cheyenne said softly.

"And Wildfire is okay," I said, matching her low tone as I pointed toward the dark silhouette of the horse in the pasture.

Her shoulders sagged in relief. "Probably an animal."

But I was starting to wonder. "Does Ash alert to animals often?"

"Not unless they're threatening us."

"Hmm."

Thomas was in jail, I reminded myself. Couldn't get to me or Cheyenne.

But the cold sweat pouring down my back said a different story.

"You okay?" Cheyenne asked, looking at me with an odd look.

"I'm good." The words were forced, but saying them reminded me it was true. Thomas was in jail, I was here with Cheyenne, and everything was fine.

But the air felt heavy with an unseen presence.

We waited until Ash relaxed and came back, wagging her tail.

"Whatever it is seems to be gone," Cheyenne murmured.

"Yep. Still think it was an animal?"

"What else would it be?" She shot me a questioning look.

I didn't answer. But I couldn't shake the feeling that we were being watched—and that the predator waiting for us was of the human variety.

CHAPTER TWENTY-THREE

Cheyenne

RHETT WAS SPOOKED ABOUT WHATEVER WAS IN THE backyard. He'd been off ever since Sheriff McGrath came by, and Ash's alert had only made it worse. But he'd gotten so irritated when he thought I pitied him that I knew asking him about it would only make things worse.

I understood that. Dealing with trauma was a necessary part of SAR. We joined because we loved pushing ourselves and because we wanted to help save lives.

We stayed because we saw what happened when we failed.

Everyone on the team dealt with trauma differently. Some people used humor as a coping mechanism, making stupid jokes to distance themselves from the reality of seeing death up close. Others turned to each other, taking time to debrief and talk about the feelings that came up on a recovery or a search gone wrong.

But I was more like Rhett. I usually kept it to myself, dealt with it on my own. Claire and Sam would always try to draw me out and get me to talk, and I knew that was probably the healthiest thing to do. But I didn't like letting the difficult things we did touch the rest of my life. I tried hard to leave it all on the field, to put up emotional guardrails so it didn't creep out into my friendships and my job.

I imagined that was similar to how Rhett was feeling now. Something awful had happened to him, but he didn't want to feel like a victim. It might not be the healthiest way of dealing with it, but I respected it anyway.

So we went back to our whiskey and leftovers and reminisced more about the past. I made sure to keep the memories to the time before we had been a couple, preferring not to dive into those emotions again. Thankfully, there were plenty of memories to choose from. From the time Claire had chosen me as her new best friend, I'd spent about half my time at Falcon Ridge Ranch. Claire and Rhett were only a year apart, and the three of us had run around like an unbreakable trio. I'd shared an innocent childhood friendship with Rhett—until I turned fifteen and our feelings for each other changed. Then Rhett had given me my very first kiss and the entire world had shifted on its axis.

After dinner, we headed out to the front with the bottle of whiskey. We sat in the dark, legs dangling off the porch—just like we used to when he would come to visit and we wanted to talk out of Gran's earshot. It brought back a thousand memories, and I realized they didn't hurt quite as much as they used to.

Rhett put his hand over mine. "Tonight was fun."

"Yeah." My heart fluttered. "It really was."

"Do you have to work tomorrow?"

I stared at our hands, still connected, and realized I didn't want to pull away. "I really should. I haven't touched base with Travis yet, but Saturdays are big tourism days at the ranch. Since the neurologist gave you such a good report, I should probably get back to my normal schedule."

It was the best thing, but it brought a pang of regret. Spending the day with Rhett had been so nice that I no longer wanted to put distance between us.

All I wanted was to be with him.

"Maybe I could go with you," he suggested.

I shook my head. "You know you aren't supposed to ride yet, and the doctor wants you to ease back into things, not jump in full force."

He waved me off. "I'm not talking about working cattle or even going out on the trail with you. As bored as I was these past few days, I bet Dad's going nuts having to be cooped up for weeks. Maybe I'll go play cards with him or something."

The idea caught me off guard. "Would you really do that?"

"Sure. Why not?"

"You and your dad have never really gotten along that well." I couldn't keep the skepticism out of my voice.

Walker was a good man, one I genuinely liked. But he and Rhett were like oil and water. Walker had never understood why Rhett, Cole, and Finn couldn't love the ranch the way he did, and he'd never known how to connect with them the way he connected with Travis. I had always felt frustrated by how little he tried to reach out to his other sons. He was their dad, yet he put the pressure of the relationship on them.

As someone who'd been abandoned by my own father, his attitude toward them made it hard for me to fully respect him.

"I know." Rhett took a swig of his drink and looked away. "But it turns out that when you think you're going to die, you see things differently. Maybe I want to try again."

My heart melted. "I think that's great. You know, Walker's changed over the years, too. He's not as hard as he used to be. Maybe it's a good opportunity for you guys to build a new relationship."

"If he's softer, it's probably because Travis has taken on so much of the burden of the ranch." Rhett frowned. "I honestly hadn't realized how much of that weight he carried."

"It's his dream."

"It is. But he reminds me of how Dad used to be. Stressed, miserable, always juggling too many things. Only Travis doesn't have a woman like Mom easing that burden."

I was surprised by the worry on his face—and touched by how concerned he was for his brother. "Why, Rhett Hawkins, I think you're turning into a softie," I said, teasing him.

"Ain't nothing soft about me, honey." He grinned, wiggling his eyebrows suggestively.

My face flushed crimson.

"Well, on *that* note, I think I'll head to bed," I said, pushing off the porch and standing.

"Want company?" He grinned again.

"I think not." I shot him a look. "We're friends, Rhett. That's it."

His grin fell. "And what if I want to try again there, too?"

I felt caught, torn between my head and my heart. My head said it was a terrible idea and would only end with me broken again.

But my heart had already fallen back in love. It had happened so easily that I wasn't sure I'd ever really stopped loving him at all.

"I don't know," I whispered.

He stood, facing me. "What's it going to take? I know you don't trust me. I know you think I'm going to pack up and leave again without even saying a word. But I'm not. I'm here, and I'm not going anywhere."

"I want to believe you." I wanted it so badly that it broke my heart in two. "And it means something to me that you tried to call all those years ago. It really does. But you still gave up. You gave up, and when you came back to visit, you never even tried to see me. I just—"

"That's not true, either," he said, anger flaring in his eyes as he shook his head.

I crossed my arms. "Rhett, I wasn't hard to find. If you wanted to see me, you could have."

"The first time I came back to Wyoming, I drove straight here," he said, taking a step toward me. "Hadn't even slept yet. But you were gone. Gran told me you were out camping with Sam."

I jerked my head. "She said *what*?"

"You heard me. Seemed like you'd moved on pretty damn quick."

"No." I shook my head. "Gran encouraged me to join the search-and-rescue team. Claire and I did it together, and Sam tried out at the same time. We trained together and became good friends. Any camping trip she mentioned would have been SAR training. But that was *all*. It's never been more."

He gazed at me with a look that was unreadable. "Never more? What about when Gran died? When Claire told me, I got on my bike and rode all night so I could be here for the funeral."

My heart raced. "You weren't there." I couldn't believe it, yet... Hadn't I felt him with me that day? Hadn't that ache bloomed even deeper because I'd sensed him near?

"Yeah, I was." He stepped forward again, dangerously close. "You wore a black turtleneck dress that went all the way to the ground, but you still had on your cowboy boots. Your mom was there, but she'd brought a new boyfriend and didn't even attempt to comfort you. You held on to a single rose from the casket, gripping it like you were holding on for dear life."

My breath caught. He *had* been there. But it didn't make sense. I shook my head. "But... Why didn't you talk to me?"

"Because you were there in the front row, with Claire on one side and Sam on the other, both guarding you like they were your personal protection. After the service, I started to walk up to you. But they were lowering Gran into the ground, and you started crying. Sam pulled you into a hug. He saw me. Gave me a glare that told me to back off. I knew I wasn't wanted, so I left."

Tears came before I could stop them. "I can't believe you came."

"Cheyenne, I may not have wanted to get married and settle down into life on the ranch, but that doesn't mean I didn't love you. I knew Gran's funeral was going to be the hardest day of your life. She was the only real mom you had. Nothing would have stopped me from showing up and being there for you. But when I got there, it seemed like you didn't need—or want—me after all. Sam had taken my place."

I turned away from him, not wanting him to see the tears that fell down my cheeks. I was so angry. Angry at Gran for what looked like deliberate sabotage. Angry at Sam, which wasn't fair at all.

And angry at myself for believing the worst when I had known Rhett better than that.

"So tell me what I did wrong," he said. His voice let me know he was angry too. "Because it seems like you've been mad at me for all these years over something I didn't even do. Tell me, Cheyenne: What should I have done different?"

"You should have asked me to go with you," I whispered before turning to walk away again.

He grabbed me, yanking me to him. Thunder clapped, like the pure electricity between us had sparked, spurring one of Wyoming's famous storms. We both glanced at the sky before looking back at each other as rain drops began falling onto our faces.

"I'm asking you now," he said. He closed his eyes and brought his forehead to mine, gripping the back of my neck with his hand. "Cheyenne," he breathed before putting his lips over mine.

It was everything—and somehow more. As familiar as it had once been and yet new at the same time. The way his lips fit mine, the way he held me, the way it felt to be pressed up against him... So familiar. But this Rhett was different. Older. More sure of himself. He kissed me like he knew exactly what he wanted, exactly where this was going. It was passion and a promise.

And so help me God, I couldn't stop myself from melting into it. From almost sighing at how utterly wonderful it felt to be held by him again, to be *loved* by him again.

I ran my hands up his back as he wrapped an arm around my waist and pulled me closer. His fingers slipped underneath my shirt, tracing the skin on my lower back and sending shivers up my spine.

"Rhett." I breathed the word like a prayer.

"Please say yes," he said before covering my mouth with his again so that I couldn't say anything at all.

So I simply nodded.

He grabbed my hand and pulled me toward the porch, then into the house. Ash followed, shaking herself when she got inside and sending a spray of water over us. We both grinned. Nothing could dampen the pure joy that surged between us.

He interlaced his fingers in mine and tugged me toward my bedroom. When we got to the doorway, he gave me a hesitant look. "Tell me if I'm crossing any lines here. I don't want to screw things up again."

"You couldn't," I said in a whisper.

He gave me a look so full of meaning I thought my heart was going to explode.

"I've missed you," he said tenderly, tucking my hair behind my ear.

"I've missed you, too." More than I could possibly say.

He led me inside, then pulled me to him, kissing me again. "I used to imagine this," he whispered against my neck before trailing kisses along my collarbone. "Used to think about what it would be like if we ever got together again."

"I did, too. Until it became too painful to even imagine."

"I'm sorry." Regret filled his eyes.

"Me too. Rhett, even at Gran's funeral... I wanted you. I wanted you so much that when I felt you there, I convinced myself I was just aching for it. Sam was only ever a friend. Never more. If I'd have known you were there..." My voice broke at the words.

"Shhh," he said. "It doesn't matter now, does it? Even if you had been together, it doesn't matter. We can't change what happened. We can only start from here. It's the future that matters now. You and me."

"You and me," I whispered in agreement.

He tugged off my wet shirt, then kissed me again as I began to unbutton his. We moved together toward the bed, too eager to make up for lost time to slow things down. One by one, every piece of clothing came off, until it was just us, skin to skin. He lifted me onto the bed and trailed kisses down my body, each one a prayer of sorrow for the years we'd lost and of gratitude for the truth we'd just found.

Tears leaked from my eyes as I ran my hands over him, remembering the boy I'd loved, and trying to memorize the man he had become. Rhett kissed the tears away, gripping my hand in his, holding on to me like he would never let go again.

Joy and sadness turned to heat as we began to move together, finding a rhythm that was new and familiar at the same time. With my hand still in his, we rode the waves, finding release—and something deeper.

He gazed into my eyes and stroked my cheek. "You're so beautiful," he said.

I wrapped my hand around his wrist. "Stay with me," I whispered.

"I'm not going anywhere," he promised.

Chapter Twenty-Four

Rhett

I woke up the next morning with Chey in my arms, her hair splayed across my chest. Ash stared at me from eye-level, like she was mad I was in her place. I reached over to scratch her behind the ears, trying not to move and disturb the beautiful woman in my arms. But Cheyenne's eyelashes fluttered against my chest and she gave a lazy yawn, then sat up, pulling the sheet with her.

"Oh," she said with a guilty look at the clock. "I slept late."

I looked over at the clock and snorted. "It's five thirty-seven. That hardly counts as sleeping late."

"It does for me." She leaned down and gave me a shy kiss. "I need to shower before we head to the ranch."

"Why?" I asked as I played my fingers over her ribs. "You're going to get sweaty and dirty at work and have to come home and take another one."

She threw a pillow at me. "Because I'm already a mess, thanks to you."

"You're welcome."

Her face softened. "It was fun, wasn't it?"

"That's an understatement if I've ever heard one." With one quick tug, I pulled her back down on top of me and gripped her face, pulling it in for a kiss. "Good morning."

"Good morning." She grinned.

"Skip the shower. We've got better things to do." I began to move against her, showing her exactly what I had in mind.

"Okay," she murmured in between kisses. "You convinced me."

When we pulled into the ranch, I could tell Cheyenne was nervous.

"Relax," I said, giving her hand a squeeze.

"I don't know if I'm ready to tell them," she said, glancing over at me.

I shrugged. "Then we wait until you're ready. I'm not going anywhere either way."

"You're really staying?"

"I really am."

Her face flashed with a bit of doubt.

I squeezed her hand again. "This is where I want to be. Minus a few trips to keep myself from going stir-crazy. I'll work for myself, remember? So I can set up shop here but take off and travel a few weeks each year. And before you ask, I'll always ask you to come with me."

She didn't say anything in reply, but the smile on her face told me all I needed to know.

"Let's go," I said, eyeing Claire and Travis, who had emerged from the barn and were staring at Cheyenne's truck. "We've got an audience, or I'd kiss you."

Actually, if we hadn't had an audience, I'd have done a lot more than that.

"Good luck with Walker," she said, raising her eyebrows and giving me a quick wink.

"It's gotta be better than shoveling horse shit," I joked.

Though I wasn't really sure about that.

Cheyenne deliberately ignored me when we got out of her truck and walked straight to Claire. They headed into the barn together, with Claire shooting me funny looks the whole time.

Travis glanced at them as they walked away, then back at me. "Shouldn't you be in bed or something? You look like hell."

"Gee, thanks."

"You know what I mean." He winced, looking at my face. "I know it's healing, but it looks even worse now."

I rolled my eyes. "Great."

"What are you doing here?"

"Neurologist cleared me to start easing back into things. Thought I'd start by coming over, hanging out with Dad for a while."

His brows furrowed. "Hanging out with Dad?"

"Yeah. Play cards or something. Catch up. I haven't really seen him since I got here." And what had been a purposeful choice to avoid him now made me feel as guilty as hell.

"That's good. He'll like that."

"Yeah, well, maybe not. But where's he going to go?" I snickered.

"True." He grinned. "Good luck."

"That's what Cheyenne said."

He clapped me on the back. "That's because you'll need it."

Before I made it upstairs, I was intercepted by Mom. Cheyenne had updated her on the neurology appointment, but she was still surprised to see me—and even more surprised I'd come over to hang out with Dad. Her eyes got misty when I told her.

"I have to warn you," she said, her mouth going flat. "He's been in a bit of a mood lately. You know your father. Keeping him off his feet is about to kill him."

"I get it."

She squeezed my shoulder, then gave me a quick peck on the cheek. "I know you do. That's why you're probably the best one to be with him right now. If you're feeling up to it, come down for lunch at noon. We're grilling bison burgers today, and I'll have hot potatoes roasting in the fire outside."

"That sounds delicious." My mouth started watering at the thought of it.

"If you haven't eaten yet, there's leftover breakfast casserole. I just took some up to Walker and put the rest in the fridge. Want me to heat you up some?"

"Nah, I'll do it. You're already cooking for half the country today."

She smiled. "Not quite, but it feels like it sometimes. I'm assuming Cheyenne drove you here and that you didn't steal her truck and leave her stranded at home?"

I laughed. "That was one time, Mom."

"Still have to check." She gave me a wink. "So since you two rode together, do you think if I invite her to family dinner she'll say yes?"

She gave me a questioning look that I knew was about more than dinner.

"I don't know for sure," I admitted. With Cheyenne wanting to keep things quiet, she might not be ready for a family dinner.

Mom's face fell.

"But she might," I added. "You should ask her."

She brightened. "I will. I'll do it before they head out." She pulled off her apron and gave me another peck on the cheek. "I'm glad you're here, son."

"Me too."

My stomach cramped as I climbed the stairs to Dad's room. The man still made me nervous all these years later. As much as I liked to pretend his disapproval didn't matter to me, it did.

A lot.

I knocked on the door of the bedroom he shared with Mom.

"What?" His voice was gruff, like I'd disturbed his peace.

I poked my head in. "This a good time? If not, I'll come back later."

He blinked a couple times. "Rhett? Hell, son, it's good to see you upright. Didn't know you were here."

I walked in and plopped down on the chair sitting in the corner. "Thought I'd surprise everyone."

He looked me over and shook his head. "You look rough."

"So do you," I said, smirking.

"Trust me, I know," he said, groaning. "I'm sporting some new hardware too. Screws in my pelvis and a metal plate running down my femur. At least my face is in one piece though." His face hardened. "Still can't believe Thomas did that to you. He's lucky I'm stuck where I am, or else he'd have to deal with me."

I chuckled. "He wouldn't know what hit him."

"Damn right." He picked up his coffee, took a swig. "I guess you've been going as stir-crazy as I have been."

"It wasn't too bad. The doc says I can start getting back to normal activity. I'm hoping to be back to one hundred percent here in a few days. I bet you're ready to get back on a horse again, huh?"

"You can't even imagine."

I reached into my pocket and pulled out a deck of cards. "Seeing as how we're both on restrictions, how about some poker?"

He grinned. "I'll wipe the floor with you, son. You never had much of a poker face."

"Yeah, well, maybe I've improved."

"You're on."

I dragged my chair over to the bed and put his tray in between us, then started shuffling the deck. "So how much longer until you're back to normal?"

He grimaced. "They say it could be a couple months before I've got my full strength back. I can get around a bit with the walker now, but I have to be careful how much weight I put on that leg. Physical therapy comes by every day, makes me do their stupid exercises."

"Not stupid if it makes you stronger."

"Yeah, yeah. That's what your mom says." He rolled his eyes.

I dealt our hands. "What happened, anyway? It's not like you to fall."

"Bad luck, I guess. I was up on the extension ladder, repairing a spot on the barn roof. The lock failed, the extension fell—fast—and I lost my balance. Hit the ground hard enough to shatter my hip."

I frowned. Bad luck, bad timing—or something else? "Dad, any chance you were sabotaged?"

His face blanked. "Sabotage? What do you mean?"

"I mean, do you think someone sabotaged the locks on the ladder deliberately?"

He picked up his cards and gave me a look like I was crazy. "Who'd want to do that to me?"

"Oh, I don't know, maybe the same person who left me for dead on the side of the road."

He scowled. "Thomas."

"This happened after you'd already taken Diablo, right?"

"That's right." He nodded.

I shook my head, disgusted. "That man blames everyone but himself for losing that horse. If he was willing to attack me over it, I wouldn't put it past him to arrange for an accident for you, too."

Dad glanced at the clock. "I'll have Travis look at the ladder, see what he thinks. If he thinks something looks off, I'll call Sheriff McGrath to check it out, see if he needs to add anything to the charges. Thomas is in jail, right?"

"Yeah. He's in jail."

"Good." Dad's face flashed with relief.

But I didn't share it. Jail or no jail, I wasn't convinced this was over.

Chapter Twenty-Five

Cheyenne

As soon as we stepped into the barn, Claire punched me lightly on the shoulder.

"You guys slept together," she announced.

My face turned crimson. "Shhh," I said, looking around to make sure no one was around.

"Sorry." She grinned, letting me know she wasn't sorry at all. "Considering it's my brother, I should feel totally creeped out. But it's Rhett, and it's you, so we all knew it was just a matter of time."

"Oh really?" I asked, giving her a look.

"Yep. And I'm so happy for you. I'd ask for details, but you know. It's my *brother.*" She made a disgusted face.

"I wouldn't give details anyway. Except that... We're okay."

"Really?" The look on her face changed to curiosity. "So it wasn't just a one-time thing?"

I couldn't hold back my smile. "No, I don't think it is. It turns out we both had some misunderstandings about what happened all those years ago, and now that we've talked about it, we can move forward." I shrugged.

Her smile became wistful. "That's great. I'm so happy for both of you. Mostly him, because he's definitely getting the better end of this stick. But I'm happy for you, too."

I glanced around. "Can we keep this to ourselves though? I don't know if I'm ready for everyone to know. That feels like a lot of pressure, especially when things are so new."

"Got it," she said, using her fingers to zip her mouth closed. "Your secret is safe with me."

"Oh, Cheyenne!" Naomi flagged us down, jogging toward us.

Claire leaned over and whispered in my ear. "But no promises she won't figure it out on her own."

Naomi was grinning from ear to ear when she reached us. "Rhett's playing cards with Walker."

Claire's jaw dropped. "Really?"

"Really." Naomi beamed. "I can't tell you how good it feels to have him here, safe, and on the mend. Thank you, Cheyenne, for everything you did for him."

"It was my pleasure," I said—then blushed furiously, realizing I'd chosen my words poorly.

Claire nearly choked.

A sly smile crossed Naomi's face. "Stay for dinner tonight, won't you? It will do my heart good to have Rhett here for longer, so I can lay my worries to rest and see that he's really getting better. Plus, we'd love to thank you for being there for him."

"Um, sure," I stammered. "Thanks."

"Wonderful." She gave me a meaningful look, then pulled me into a firm embrace.

When she walked out of the barn, I looked at Claire. "Think she knows?"

"She definitely suspects," Claire confirmed.

"I don't know if I'm ready for that."

. . .

I LOVED MY JOB, BUT FOR ONCE, THE MORNING RIDE FELT unbearably long. I found myself counting down the minutes until I saw Rhett again. I missed him, but more than that, I worried about him. Walker could be intense. Depending on what kind of mood he was in, their morning of cards could be exactly what Rhett needed or it could push him to run again.

When we finally trekked back to the ranch, I caught a glimpse of Rhett standing by his mom, grinning as he helped pull foil-wrapped potatoes from the campfire. He looked up, catching my gaze, and winked at me.

My heart felt like it might flutter right out of my chest, and I couldn't begin to hide my smile.

Claire rode up beside me. "No way you guys are going to be able to keep things secret for long."

I laughed, feeling lighter than I had in years. "You might be right."

"Except from Travis and Jonathan," she mused. "Sometimes I think they're blind to most of what happens right underneath their noses. But Beth will know before the day's over. You can count on that. She won't say anything though."

"No," I agreed, "she won't. She's too respectful of boundaries to mention it. Unlike *you*." I gave her a good-natured grin. I loved Claire with my whole heart, even if we had completely different personalities—maybe even because of it.

Claire threw her head back and laughed, the sunlight catching on her blonde curls. "It's a good thing I've found a job where I'm supposed to ask questions and not feel awkward about it."

"Yes, that is a good thing."

Claire urged her horse to a trot, heading to the dismount block ahead of us so she could help guests as they arrived. I stayed back with the group, letting them fully enjoy the last few minutes of their ride. Rhett never took his eyes off me and walked over to meet me as I came off Stormy.

"Wish we didn't have to keep this secret," he said under his breath, deliberately brushing my body as he took the reins from me. "I'm dying to have my hands on you again."

Delicious shivers went down my spine. "I'm dying for that, too," I whispered.

His dark eyes met mine, sending heat right through me. "Soon."

"Soon." I bit my lip. "By the way, I told your Mom we'd stay for dinner. Is that okay?"

"It's great, except that it adds an hour or two to how long I have to keep my hands off you, and I don't know if I can make it." His low voice made me tremble. "The truth might slip out."

"Claire already knows," I said. "And your mom suspects."

"Does that mean you're done keeping secrets?"

"I don't know." The idea of everyone knowing sent a surge of panic through me.

"Well, tell me when you are. I'm ready to let the whole world know you're mine." His grin turned wicked, leaving me speechless as he walked away with my horse.

"Ready to eat?" Claire asked, coming up behind me and putting an arm around my waist. "Or should I play guard and keep everyone out of the barn for half an hour?"

I laughed and turned, heading toward the courtyard and dragging Claire with me. "Food. Definitely food."

I was digging into my potato when Rhett strode over and motioned with his head for Claire to move so he could have the spot beside me.

She rolled her eyes and shook her head. "Why are you guys even pretending to hide this?"

He plopped down beside me, plate in hand. "Yeah, Chey, why are you pretending to hide this? Wouldn't it be nicer if I could sit down beside you and plant a big kiss right on that pretty mouth, here in front of everyone?"

I shoved him with my shoulder. "So much for giving me time to get used to this."

"We've already lost too much time," he said, his voice turning seriously.

My heart fluttered. "I know. But this is my job. It matters to me. If things between us go wrong..."

He shook his head. "They won't. Not this time."

"But if they do..."

He sighed, deflated. "Alright. We take as much time as you need."

"Thank you."

His grinned returned. "But I can't hide the fact that you're my favorite."

I smiled. "You're my favorite, too."

WE HAD AN AFTERNOON OF SHORT TOURS. I NORMALLY hated those, but today, I was grateful for them. The mindless loop allowed me to let my mind drift to all the places it would rather be.

One night with Rhett had washed away all the pain of the past ten years. I couldn't even grieve the time apart anymore. It had turned us into the people we were—people who could actually make this work. But we were together again, and my soul felt at peace. He had told me he was in this for the long haul, and I wanted to believe it.

But I still didn't want to tell Naomi and Walker. I didn't mind if Claire, Beth, and Travis knew. They would be supportive but also understanding about the whole thing.

Naomi and Walker knowing added a whole new pressure—pressure that I worried would make Rhett pull away again. If Walker's insistence on him settling down had made Rhett take off before, would history repeat itself?

Walker might never understand Rhett's desire to live here but run a business completely separate from the ranch. The ranch was Walker's whole life. It had to be in order for him to make it work.

But it would never be Rhett's passion.

I worried that, if Naomi and Walker knew, they'd start pushing for Rhett to make a commitment. Pushing for him to stay on at the ranch and build a life there. Maybe even offer land for us to build a house again.

I didn't even want that. I loved my cabin in the woods.

Naomi would understand, I reassured myself. But Walker...

Walker could make things very complicated.

When the day's work was done, I stopped by Diablo's stall to give him some sugar cubes.

"Hey, boy," I said, stroking his velvet nose. "Missed you."

He nudged my pocket and whined.

"I know. I'm ready for another ride, too."

"Me too." Rhett's voice surprised me, coming out of nowhere. He came up behind me and wrapped his arms around my waist before dipping a hand into my pocket and pulling out a sugar cube for Diablo.

Diablo gave him a wary look, then gobbled up the treat from Rhett's hand.

"He let you give him a treat," I murmured. "He doesn't even take them from Travis."

"He's yours," Rhett said simply. "And he knows I am, too."

I rested my head back against his chest.

"What's wrong?" he asked, pressing a kiss to the top of my head.

"I'm happy."

He chuckled, that low voice sending vibrations through my body. "You sure seem down for someone who says she's happy."

"I *am* happy. And that's scary. Because that's usually about when I lose everything."

"Not this time."

I didn't answer. Because even though he'd told me he was staying, I didn't want to ask for a promise he couldn't keep.

"Let's head in for dinner," I suggested. "Everyone will be wondering where we are."

"I bet they know exactly where we are," he said, chuckling. "Why else are they all steering clear of the barn right now? No one will care if we're late for dinner, but we'll go if you want."

"I'm nervous," I admitted.

"Why?" He let go of me so I could turn around and face him.

"I haven't stayed for dinner since ... before."

"It's just dinner," he said gently. "It doesn't have to be a big deal."

"It's never just dinner with the Hawkins family."

"Do you want to go home instead?"

"No." I shook my head. "I already said we would stay."

He interlaced his fingers with mine and gently pulled me toward the main house. "Then we go. I've got you."

"I know." But I was a ball of nerves as we approached the house. I pulled my hand out of Rhett's as we walked in the front door, and I couldn't help looking at everyone when we made it to the dining room, wondering if the truth was as obvious to everyone else as it had been to Claire. Thankfully, if anyone else noticed anything, they didn't mention it. Naomi beamed when she saw me but didn't make a big deal out of it.

And nobody said anything when I took my old seat right in between Rhett and Claire.

But the feeling was so surreal I couldn't shake it. The last time I'd sat here for dinner, Rhett and I had been together. Two silly teens, hopelessly in love. I'd been so happy—and so blissfully unaware of the heartbreak ahead of me.

Somehow, we'd found ourselves picking up right where we'd left off. But that added to my unease. Was I walking straight into heartbreak again?

Like he could read my mind, Rhett squeezed my knee underneath the table. I looked over at him and he gave me a wink, as if to say I worried too much.

I took a deep breath and tried to put the doubts out of my mind as we dug into dinner, chatting about Jonathan's upcoming graduation and Claire's latest adventures as a deputy. After a while, I finally relaxed and began to enjoy myself.

The rest of us were almost finished eating when Travis walked in, looking exhausted. He tossed his hat onto the kitchen bar, then plopped down at his dining room chair with a heavy sigh.

"Everything okay, son?" Naomi asked, giving him a thoughtful look.

He reached for the green beans and heaped a mountain of them onto his plate. "Had a calving go wrong today."

"Oh no. Did you lose them?"

He shook his head. "No. Made it to them on time, but it wasn't pretty. That, on top of burning the candle at both ends lately, and I'm just worn out." He grabbed the corn and looked at Rhett. "You're looking better."

Rhett grinned. "I'm feeling better."

"I guess you'll be moving back into the loft soon and easing back to work? I tell ya, I'll be grateful for the help."

Naomi cleared her throat. "Rhett can start easing into work an hour or two at a time whenever he feels ready, but I'm afraid the loft is no longer available."

Every head at the table jerked to attention.

"No longer available?" Travis asked blankly. "What do you mean?"

"You're drowning," Naomi said firmly. "I decided it was time we gave Jimmy another chance. Hired him back on. He starts tomorrow, and he'll be moving back into the loft."

She turned to me and Rhett. "I'm sorry," she said, her voice apologetic. "Rhett, unless Cheyenne's willing to extend her hospitality for a little while, I'm afraid you'll need to bunk with Jonathan temporarily. I have a cabin we can block off as yours in about two weeks, but until then..." Her voice trailed off and she shrugged helplessly.

Rhett looked at me. His face was solemn, but laughter danced in his eyes. "Well, Cheyenne? You mind rescuing me from bunking with Jonathan? It seems I have no place else to go."

Based on the way Naomi had her mouth set, like she was fighting a smile, I had a feeling she knew I wouldn't mind at all. In fact, I was pretty sure she'd orchestrated this whole thing on purpose.

I knew I'd have to thank her for it someday.

"That's fine," I said, attempting to look cool. "You're not bothering me." I picked up my water glass and took a long sip, hoping to hide any smile.

"Oh, I'll bother you alright," Rhett muttered under his breath. He slipped his hand up my thigh and I nearly dropped my glass.

"Wait a sec," Travis interrupted, angry. "Don't I get any say in this?"

"No," Naomi said, turning her attention to him. "No, you don't. I'm still ahead of you in the chain of command, and the decision has been made." Her eyes softened. "You're killing yourself, Travis. You've got to have some help."

"He *stole* from us." Travis's face showed pure outrage.

"And you need to learn to forgive and give people second chances," Naomi said, giving him a warning look. "It's not up for discussion."

Travis opened his mouth, then clamped his jaw shut. He finished filling his plate in stony silence, then announced he had a lot of work to do. He carried the plate with him and stormed off, letting the door bang behind him on the way out.

Chapter Twenty-Six

Rhett

Mom watched Travis storm out, her eyes revealing her surprise.

"Well," she said, clearing her throat. "I guess he's unhappy with my plan. Does anyone else have anything to say about me hiring Jimmy back?"

"Did you find out why he stole?" Cheyenne asked, surprising me by being the first to speak up. I liked it. It showed she was still comfortable with my family despite whatever was keeping her from being honest with them about us.

Mom nodded. "I think so. He said he was trying to help an old foster sister run away from a terrible situation. He needed the cash for her. I get that, even if he made several big mistakes. Stealing, obviously. Not going to anyone else for help." She shrugged. "He's not used to trusting people though. I think it will take him time to know he can fully trust us. Despite that mistake, he's always been a hard worker. He loves the horses and the job."

Cheyenne nodded in agreement. "He's been asking me to talk to Travis for him, but I didn't want to give my opinion when it hadn't been asked for."

Mom's face softened. "Oh, Cheyenne, your opinion is always welcome here. You should know that. You're one of the family."

I squeezed Cheyenne's knee again, letting her know I agreed.

"I think I'll go talk to Travis," I said, pushing away from the table.

Everyone looked up at me in surprise.

"Really?" Claire's eyebrows rose. "You're acting as the family peacemaker now?"

I rubbed my knuckles over her mess of blonde curls. "Maybe I am."

"Weird." She laughed. "That's Beth's job."

Beth smiled. "I'm happy for you to be the one to talk to Travis. He's been a bear lately."

"I can tell. I'll try to help him pull that giant stick out of his ass."

"Rhett!" Mom said, choking on her water.

I winked and gave her a kiss before heading out—and winked at Cheyenne, too, when no one was looking.

Travis was sitting at the desk in his office, doing something with the books in between shoveling down bites of food.

I plopped down into the chair in front of him.

"Yes?" He gave me a wary look.

"What the hell is wrong with you?"

"Excuse me?"

"You were pushing the line back there with Mom. And why do you have such a problem with Jimmy anyway?"

"He *stole* from us." Travis threw his hands up like it was that simple.

"How much? What are we talking here?"

"A couple hundred bucks."

I scoffed. "Is that all? You're willing to lose good help over that?"

"It's not good help if I can't trust him," Travis growled. "Now Mom's forcing me to work with him, and I'll have the added stress of feeling like I've got to keep all the petty cash locked up, and keep an eye on him all the time." He ran his hands over his face, the anger vanishing, replaced with a bone-deep weariness. "I don't need any extra stress right now."

I studied my brother. He looked ten years older than he had the last time I'd visited. New lines were etched around his eyes. Early gray was starting to pepper his temples. Beyond that, he seemed sad in a way I'd never seen him before.

"What's really going on?"

For a moment, he looked like he wanted to tell me that it was none of my business and to get lost. But he finally relented, burying his face in his hands.

"It's everything. Trying to keep this place in the black is ... stressful in the best of times. It's a seventy-hour a week job as it is. Then we lost Jimmy. Add Dad being down, and my workload doubled."

"That's rough."

"I've tried to keep it from affecting everyone else, but I feel like I'm losing my mind over here trying to make everything work. Trying to be in two or three places at once. Trying to be everything to everyone. Then, you got hurt—not your fault, I get that—and we were down Mom, too, and then Cheyenne. Rhett, I'm tired."

Tired was the understatement of the year. He was broken down and exhausted, and I felt terrible about it.

"I hate that I made things worse instead of better. I came here because I really wanted to help."

"I know," he said, leaning back in his hair and shaking his head. "And I feel like a total ass complaining about my work load when you nearly died."

"You've been acting like an ass." I gave him a little grin.

"That's what Missy says," he muttered.

Missy. I had a feeling she figured into this somehow. "What's going on there?"

His face went stony. "She's not following our custody agreement. She's keeping the girls from me and not bringing them around. Tries to say it's because I'm too stressed, too busy to be a real parent. But, Rhett, you know I love those girls more than anything. I drop everything any chance I get to be with them. Besides, they love being here on the ranch."

He choked up. "I'm missing my girls' lives and I don't know what to do about it, except take Missy to court. But to do that, I need some help around here. Because if I take a day off, it feels like the whole world is going to burn down."

"I get it. The weight of the world is on your shoulders. It's one reason why I never wanted this place."

"You and I are different that way," he admitted. "I love it. Love the work, love the land. But Mom's right. I'm drowning. I can't do it all myself."

"Well, you don't have to. Mom's right. Bring Jimmy back. And I should be able to work a couple hours tomorrow, doing whatever you need me to do. We'll keep doubling the time until I'm working full days again. Schedule a court date or whatever you need to do. I'll stay on until you get things handled on that front."

He swallowed hard. "Thank you. Really. That means everything to me."

"The girls matter." It was as simple as that. "As far as keeping an eye on Jimmy, let me handle that. I'll keep an eye on him."

"Why do you care so much?"

"You're my brother, you dopehead."

He rolled his eyes. "I meant about Jimmy."

I paused, knowing I was about to reveal something personal about myself. "Because I know what it's like to want a second chance."

He eyed me. "You talking about the ranch or are you talking about Cheyenne?"

"Both. Sort of, anyway. But I figure I should be straight with you." I looked away and took a deep breath before looking him in the eye again. "I don't plan on making the ranch my permanent job. I'll stay on while Dad recovers and you get things settled with custody, but I have plans after that."

Travis scoffed. "I'm shocked. Heading back to Austin?"

"No. I'm staying in Wildwood. But I'm starting my own thing." Telling my dreams to Cheyenne had been one thing. Admitting them to Travis was another. It made me feel nervous, afraid to fail. Afraid to do one more thing that made me a loser in his and Dad's eyes.

But the look on his face was curious, not judgmental. "What are you planning on starting?"

"Home renovations. Same kind of thing I've been doing down in Austin, only this time, I'll be working for myself. I'll take the kind of jobs I actually care about, do some historical restorations. Build homes for real people instead of commercial spaces and temporary rentals."

"Why here?" He looked puzzled. "Don't get me wrong. I'll be glad to have you back. We all miss you. But it seems like you'd have more opportunities elsewhere."

"Maybe I missed your ugly face." I grinned.

He shook his head. "Nah. That's not why. It's Cheyenne, isn't it?"

"Partly, yeah."

His face turned serious again. "Whatever happened between you two? No one ever really talked about it."

I toyed with the plaque on his desk, not knowing how much to reveal. "I left. That's what happened."

"Duh. But why? You two have some sort of blowup or something?"

I shook my head. "No. I had to leave to find myself. Figure out who I was outside of Dad and all this. Dad was pressuring me to take on a bigger role and I didn't want it."

Travis gave a look of understanding. "Dad knows how to put the pressure on for sure."

"Damn right. I didn't fit here the way you did, didn't grow up knowing my purpose the way you did. I had to find it. But I did, and now, I want to be here. Want to see my nieces grow up, want to be around to help. I even miss these damn mountains."

"And Cheyenne."

"And Cheyenne," I agreed.

"Think she's going to give you that second chance you're looking for?"

"I sure hope so."

This time, he grinned. "She'd be a fool not to. You're a good guy, Rhett. Even if I give you a hard time sometimes."

"I get it," I said, chuckling. "It's the brother code."

"So, we're cool?"

I nodded. "We are. But listen, I want to talk to you about something else."

"What?" He frowned, sensing the change in my tone.

"Has Dad talked to you yet?"

"Not today." He looked puzzled. "I've been out all day though. What's up?"

"You think Thomas could have sabotaged Dad's ladder?"

His face blanked. Then awareness slowly dawned. "You think his fall wasn't an accident?"

"I'm wondering. Where's the ladder? I'd like to take a look at it."

"I threw it out." All the color leached from his face. "It was a hazard. I didn't want anyone else getting hurt. It's gone now."

I grimaced. "Damn. Well, at least in good news, Thomas is in jail. So if it was him, he can't get to any of us now."

Travis was quiet for a minute. "What if it wasn't Thomas?"

"What do you mean?"

His eyes bored into mine. "Dad's accident was two days after I fired Jimmy. Jimmy was desperate to get his job back. What if he thought putting us down a man would make us bring him back on?"

"Shit." I leaned back in my chair and let out a breath that was half groan, half growl.

"If Jimmy sabotaged the ladder, then..."

"Then Mom just hired back the man who hurt dad."

Chapter Twenty-Seven

IF NAOMI THOUGHT IT WAS STRANGE FOR ME TO COME TO family dinner, she didn't let on. She acted like it was the most normal thing in the world for me to be there and didn't ask a single question about any potential change in my relationship with Rhett.

But a new softness in her eyes when she looked at me made me think she knew anyway.

It made me nervous, because if she knew, she'd eventually tell Walker. Who knew what would happen then?

Rhett cared about me. Maybe even loved me. But he had loved me before and he had still left. For all his good qualities, the man was not great at handling pressure. A relationship was apparently high pressure for him. And if Walker added more?

It could be game over.

When Rhett left the first time, I felt like it might break me. And in some ways, it had. I could see now though that it had broken me in a way that helped me build back, create something new. I was stronger because of all of it. So I tried to tell myself that, even if he left again, things would be okay. It would hurt, but I would rebuild. I would get stronger. I would become something new.

None of this felt reassuring in the least.

Rhett took his time coming back to the main house, so I lingered with the others, helping Naomi wash dishes and clean up. It was nice in a way that warmed my heart and made me think of holiday movies, where the scene was lit with a warm glow and the kitchen was filled with people who loved each other and were happy to be together. *Family.* It was something I had only really had here with the Hawkins crew, and tonight it felt like I fit in a way I hadn't since Rhett had left.

It was lovely and addictive, which made it dangerous.

Naomi nudged me as I dried our plates and put them away in the cabinet. "What are you thinking about over there? Seems like you're miles away tonight."

"Oh." I gave her a faint smile, then glanced toward the door. "I'm sorry. It's been a while since Rhett left, hasn't it? I wonder if we should go check on him."

"I'm sure he and Travis are still talking," she said, waving me off.

"We're done now." Rhett's deep voice came from behind me. Heat pooled in my belly and my heart fluttered, even as I felt instantly more grounded, more...*home.*

I turned and smiled at him. "How did it go?"

His face was serious. "Good. But I'm pretty tired. Ready to go?"

"Sure." I dropped the towel I was using to dry and gave Naomi a quick smile. "I'll take the patient home and let him get some rest."

"Good idea." She was clearly fighting back a smile.

I blushed, feeling entirely too seen.

After quick hugs with Claire and Beth, I followed Rhett to the door. He held it open for me, putting a hand on my lower back as he guided me outside. The moment the crisp night air hit my skin, I took a deep breath, feeling like I'd been underwater for hours and could finally breathe.

"Did you have fun?" he asked, glancing at me like he was as nervous as I'd felt earlier.

"I did," I admitted. "I wasn't sure what it would be like, but I enjoyed it."

"Felt like old times."

"Yes."

"Only better."

"Better?"

"Yeah. Better." He opened my truck door for me and brushed a hand along my hip as I got in. Then his lips found mine as he snuck a heated kiss in the dark that left me breathless before going around to his side.

"Why is it better?" I asked when he climbed into the truck.

"Because I know who I am now, and I don't have that dark cloud hanging over me, knowing that the end is coming."

"Did you always feel that dark cloud?" I looked over at him, curious. This was the first time I'd heard about that, and it surprised me. He'd always been so carefree as a teen. Sometimes moody, sure, but I'd never thought of him as dwelling underneath a dark storm cloud.

"I always felt this tension," he admitted. "I knew I was going to leave, and it always colored over everything."

"You always knew?"

"Yeah."

That was news to me, too, although it shouldn't have been. He'd always talked about going new places, seeing new things. But back then, I'd always thought it was the same as when I dreamed up a million dreams that I knew were completely unrealistic. Dreaming was fun, but I'd always assumed that, deep down, he was as grounded to this place as I was—which was why it had shaken me to the core when he ripped those roots out of the ground and left without looking back.

It made me realize I hadn't known him quite as well as I'd thought back then.

"You're awfully quiet," Rhett commented as I pulled into my drive.

"Sorry," I said, sighing. I threw the truck into park and leaned my head back on the headrest.

Rhett hopped out and came around to open my door, but he didn't move for me to get out. He put one hand on the steering wheel and another on the headrest, essentially trapping me.

"What's going on?" he asked, his tone demanding. "Did someone say something while I was with Travis?"

"No."

"Then what?"

"I'm just tired," I said, gently pushing him away so I could hop down.

"No."

"Excuse me?"

He shook his head. "No secrets. I know we just got back together, but you know as well as I do that relationships don't work without communication."

I crossed my arms. "Is that what this is? A relationship?"

He jerked his head back like he'd been bitten. "Damn right it is. What the hell is wrong with you?"

Tears sprang to my eyes. "I'm happy—that's what."

"You're ... happy." The look on his face was utter confusion.

"Yes." I turned on my heel and started walking to the doorway.

He walked behind me, muttering, "Could've fooled me with that attitude."

"You don't get it."

"You're right. I don't. How can I if you won't explain it to me?"

I sank down onto the steps of the porch instead of going into the house. "Have you even thought about what's going to happen if we break up again?"

"Nope." He put his hands in his pockets and gave me an exasperated look.

I shook my head. "Of course you haven't. Because for you, nothing will really change, right? But for me, it affects my whole world. My job." *My family.*

He sat down beside me, looking as if he was trying to exercise patience. "What do you mean?"

"You left. Gran died. I had *nobody* here. I was nineteen years old, living alone in a log cabin in Wyoming, a thousand miles from my closest family member—not that she would have filled the void anyway."

He put his hand on my back, stroking up and down my spine. "I'm sorry."

"Claire was my family. Travis was my family. They checked on me, helped me put together a plan. Your mom always kept the door open, even offered me a cabin so I didn't have to stay here alone."

"I didn't know that," he said softly.

I shook my head. "I turned her down. Couldn't bear to be on the ranch the first couple of years. But the point is, *your* family has been *my* family, too. Without them, I have Alma and Sam and that's about it. And I love my job at the ranch."

"I'm not seeing the problem," he confessed. "Doesn't it work out nicely that you get along so well with my family?"

"*Your* family. That's the point." I swallowed hard. "They were there for me, but it didn't require them to split loyalties, you know? You weren't around. But you're putting down roots here again. If things end between us, it will be different this time. I'll be the outsider."

Rhett chuckled. "Whatever."

"This is serious."

He shook his head. "You're getting all worked up over nothing. That's not like you, Cheyenne."

"It isn't 'nothing.' You don't know what it's like to be alone."

"Sure I do. It just doesn't bother me." He shrugged. "But why are you even worried about this? If you decide to break things off with me, I'm sure they'll understand. They all know you're too good for me anyway. But as far as I go? I'm in this. I'm not going anywhere."

"That's what you think now," I said quietly, staring at the ground. "But what if Walker starts putting pressure on you again?"

"Is that what this is about? My dad?"

"How did today go with him?" I searched his face, looking for signs of stress.

"It went great, actually. He was glad for the company. Plus, I took over a hundred off him in poker, so that was fun." He grinned. "Want to blow it all somewhere crazy with me?"

I couldn't help but smile as a little of the tension I'd been carrying melted away. Rhett's confidence was reassuring. "Yeah. I do."

He leaned in for a soft kiss, his lips brushing mine in a way that made me ache for more. But he pulled away, whispering in my ear. "Maybe we should take it to Vegas. Mom will be pissed we didn't give her a wedding here, but how fun would it be to surprise them all with a ring on your finger?"

I pulled away. "Don't say things you don't mean."

"Who says I didn't mean it?"

I forced an awkward smile before standing and brushing off my jeans. "We should go inside."

"Wait." His powerful voice stopped me in my tracks. "If you don't want to go to Vegas, that's fine. Hell, if you don't want to marry me at all, that's fine, too. I'm not the kind of man who's going to pressure you into something you don't want. But don't blow it off like I didn't mean it."

"You're being silly," I said.

"No." He stood, walking toward me. "I'm not. See, I think you're still convinced I'm going to run the first chance I get. The first little sign of pressure, the first fight, the first time I get a wild hair. Isn't that right? That's what you think of me."

I crossed my arms again. He was right, but wasn't that fair? He'd never given me a reason to think otherwise.

Anger flared in his eyes. "I'm not going anywhere. Got it? I'm not a kid anymore. I know how to handle pressure, how to stand up for what I want. And I want *you*. We were always meant to be together. You know it. I know it. My family knows it. So I'm making you a promise. I'm in this. As long as you want me, I'm here."

Hope and love flooded my heart, but I cut it off. I shook my head and turned to move into the house. "We barely know each other. You can't make a promise like that yet. It's too early."

He spun me around and forced me to look at him. "Yeah, I can. Cheyenne, when I make a promise, I damn well keep it. I'm not your father. He broke his promises to you. I didn't, because I never made you one back then. Remember that? But I'm making you one now."

"Don't," I whispered, trying to take a step backward.

"You don't get to decide what I promise," he said, stepping with me and refusing to back down. "You can make your own choices. But I get to make mine."

"This is crazy."

"I'm not asking you to promise me anything in return. But I'm promising you. Cheyenne, I love you. And I'm going to love you for the rest of my life. If you'll let me, I want to wake up with you every morning. Want to go to bed holding you every night. I want everything you'll give me. But that will be up to you."

I searched his face and saw he meant every word. And he was right. He'd never made me a promise he hadn't kept.

Rhett Hawkins was a wild soul. But he was also a man of his word.

I opened my mouth to tell him I wanted that too, but words I never meant to say tumbled out of my mouth instead. "Alma told me I should settle down with someone like Pete. Someone loyal, kind, and sweet."

He frowned. "Am I not loyal, kind, and sweet?"

"You are," I said, nodding. "That's the thing. You're all of those things. But you're not like Pete."

He shook his head. "No, I'm not."

"Pete's a golden retriever. You're a wolf."

He smirked. "Which do you prefer?"

"I think you know."

Chapter Twenty-Eight

Rhett

I WOKE UP BEFORE DAWN THE NEXT MORNING, A CONTENT smile on my face. Cheyenne hadn't actually promised me anything in return, but that didn't matter. I didn't expect her to. This was new, and she was right—it was more complicated for her.

For me, it was the simplest thing on earth. I had Cheyenne back and I had a second chance at life. I wasn't going to screw it up.

She was still sleeping, but I was ready for coffee, so I slipped out of bed and left her there while I went to turn on the pot. But when I opened the bedroom door, I could already smell it.

Sure enough, there was a hot pot already made. I grinned, realizing Cheyenne must have set it up on a time delay so it would be ready when she got up. Efficient. I liked it.

I poured myself a cup and, on impulse, poured her one, too, in the mug she'd kept tucked away in the back of the cabinet. I carried it back to the bedroom and set it gently on her nightstand, then got back into bed with mine.

She stirred and opened her eyes, smiling. "Good morning."

"Good morning, beautiful." I tucked her hair behind her ears and marveled at how gorgeous she was. I loved her like this, with her hair all a mess and her eyes still soft and sleepy. It was a version of her that the rest of the world never got to see. I felt damn lucky to be the man who got to wake up next to her.

"Do I smell coffee?"

I nodded. "Brought you a cup."

She glanced over at the nightstand, then stilled. "Oh."

"You kept it."

She sat up, pulling the sheet with her, and took the mug into her hands, staring at it. "Yeah, I did. It was special."

"Yes, it was." I reached for her hand, interlacing her fingers in mine. "And now we get to make a whole lot of special together."

She smiled. "Yeah." Then she sighed.

"What is it?"

"You know... At first, I grieved for the time we lost. But..."

"Yeah?"

"Will it hurt your feelings if I tell you that part of me is glad you left?"

I shrugged. "Will it hurt your feelings if I tell you I'm glad I left, too?"

Her face flushed with relief. "Don't get me wrong. I do hate that we missed so much. But I also know that I would never have joined SAR if you had stayed. Between that and living independently in Wyoming at such a young age... Well, I learned things. It made me stronger. More confident. And I like who I am."

"I like who you are, too. I liked you then, but I like you even more now. And I'm still glad I left, because if I had stayed and worked the ranch all these years, I'd be a miserable, unhappy person."

"Yeah," she agreed, nodding. "That's something else I was thinking about last night, after we talked. I got so nervous yesterday about the pressure of dealing with Walker. I can't imagine you having to deal with that day in and day out for years."

"It would never have worked," I admitted. "But I still wish Gran would have told you the truth. Maybe we could have made it work long-distance."

She shook her head. "No. I would have moved to be with you. And who knows? Maybe it would have been wonderful and I would have built something amazing for myself there, too. Hard to know how it all would have played out. But I know for sure I wouldn't have what I have now."

"We can't change the past. But we can decide what the future looks like."

She took a long sip of coffee, her smiling eyes peeking at me from over the mug. "What if I don't want Vegas?"

"I told you. I made you a promise, but there's no pressure for you to make me one."

She shook her head. "That's not what I mean. I'm not ready for promises, Rhett. But...someday, if I do feel ready... I don't want to do it in Vegas. I want to do it in the woods. Or on a cliff. Or beside a water-fall, or even at the ranch. But not in Vegas."

I grinned. "We'll do it wherever you want. *Whenever* you want."

She gave me a little smile. "On another topic, I feel like I should give you a heads-up. Your mom is going to pull you away this morning to go shopping."

"Shopping?" My face blanked.

She nodded, a teasing look on her face. "There's a secret event coming up at the ranch, and your mom said you're not allowed to wear any of the five outfits you brought."

"She *counted my clothes*?"

"Apparently, yes. While you were in the hospital. According to her, nothing you have is appropriate for her party. She pulled me away last night while you were talking to Travis and filled me in."

I rolled my eyes. "I'm so sorry my tuxedo didn't fit into the saddle-bags of my bike. It's a good thing we live in a big city, where I can easily replace it at one of the many high-end shops in our shopping district."

She tossed a pillow at me. "One, do you even own a tux? Second, she didn't say you had to wear anything like that. She requested a decent dress shirt and a pair of casual slacks."

"Of course I own a tux." I tossed the pillow back to her. "Bought it for Cole's wedding, 'cause Mom insisted. Which was stupid, because it turned out to be a casual backyard thing and he wasn't even wearing one. Haven't worn it since. What is this event, anyway?"

"A surprise birthday party for Beth. Naomi started planning it before you even got to town. She's doing a fancy tea party on the lawn. It's supposed to have *Little Women* vibes or something like that."

"Ugh." I threw my head back and groaned. "That sounds terrible."

"Beth will love it. It's her favorite book."

"Pretty stupid of her to love a book where her namesake dies," I muttered.

Cheyenne laughed. "That's not why she loves the book. You know her. She really should have been born in a different era. Just be glad your mom settled on slacks and a dress shirt. She originally wanted us all in period costume."

I groaned again. "Costume? Fine. I'll stop complaining about dressing up. But no dress shoes. I'm wearing my boots."

"Me too," she said, winking. "In fact, after we get home tonight, maybe that's *all* I'm planning on wearing."

I put my coffee away, no longer in need of it, and grabbed her instead.

We pulled up to the ranch right in front of an old beater car. The car pulled in on my side; then a familiar figure got out. Shock was all over his face when I climbed out of the truck.

"Jimmy. Long time no see. How the hell are ya?" I stuck out a hand. I'd decided to play it friendly. I wasn't convinced he was the one behind Dad's fall—I still thought Thomas was the most likely culprit for that one—but I was going to keep a close eye on him just the same. Easier to keep an eye on him if he felt comfortable around me.

He stared at me, confused, then took my hand and shook it. "Um, hi, Rhett. What are you doing here? I thought…"

"I came back to town a week ago. Or longer, now that I think of it," I said, chuckling. "Time's a little fuzzy for me right now."

"But what are you doing *here*?"

"Heading to work, just like you." I clapped him on the shoulder.

He was still staring at me. "I thought you were dead."

"Dead?" My face jutted forward in surprise. "Oh, I guess you heard about the accident. Nah, I'm fine." But the way he was staring at me was making me feel damn uncomfortable.

Cheyenne walked around the truck, glancing at each of us in turn. She shot me a questioning look. I'd filled her in on Travis's theory, but she was adamant Jimmy would never do something like that.

"Hey, Jimmy," she said, squeezing his forearm. "Glad to have you back. I'm proud of you for telling Naomi the truth about the money."

"Yeah." His face turned bright red. "I'm real sorry about that. Nothing like that will ever happen again, I promise." His eyes shifted from her to me then back again.

I put a heavy hand on his shoulder. "We all make mistakes. But you got a second chance. I know something about that." I glanced at Cheyenne, who gave me a knowing smile.

"Yeah," Jimmy said, uncertainty painting his features. "A second chance. Exactly. Well, I better get to work. Don't want to make Travis mad by being late."

He walked off, and I looked back at Cheyenne. "Did that seem weird to you?"

She frowned. "Yeah. Yeah, it did."

I GOT IN A GOOD COUPLE HOURS OF WORK, ENJOYING THE feel of pushing my muscles again, before Mom pulled me away.

"I hate shopping," I groaned as we headed toward the main house.

"I know. And after seeing Cheyenne's face when I told her the plan, I realized forcing you to shop would be a terrible idea. So you're off the hook."

"Thank God." I let out a breath. "So you've made peace with me wearing my normal clothes to the party?"

Mom threw her head back and let out a loud laugh. "Hardly. But Travis agreed to let you borrow some of his clothes for it. You guys are about the same size."

"I'm bigger than him," I muttered under my breath.

Mom rolled her eyes. "Come sit with me while I prep the afternoon meal. You can make yourself useful by peeling potatoes. Deal?"

"Deal." And probably a good idea, considering the headache that was threatening to blow up again.

I opened the door for Mom and followed her inside. She motioned for me to sit at the bar, then grabbed two giant bags of potatoes and plopped them down in front of me. She pulled out a giant bowl and a peeler and handed them over.

"Wow," I said, eyeing the bags. "That's ... a lot of potatoes."

"Twenty pounds," she confirmed. "I'll admit I was happy to steal you away for a while. Peeling potatoes gets old."

"So do most of the jobs around here."

She pulled out a cutting board and began chopping onions. "You still feel that way?" There was a tinge of disappointment in her voice.

"Yeah," I said slowly. "I do."

She kept chopping, never looking up. "Seems like you and Cheyenne are getting along pretty well."

"Seems like someone's dead set on playing matchmaker."

She dropped her knife and looked like she'd been caught in the cookie jar. "I've been doing no such thing."

"Really?" I shot her a skeptical look. "We own a dozen cabins and you couldn't come up with a single place to put me except Cheyenne's house? You just *happened* to hire Jimmy back and gave him the loft right when I was physically capable of managing it again? I may have been too slow to realize what was happening at first, but my head's getting clearer every day."

She flushed red, but when she saw my grin, she relaxed. "Alright, fine. But I wouldn't call it playing matchmaker. Just ... giving fate a push, that's all. The question is: Did it work?"

"I guess you'll have to wait and find out." Truth was, I was dying to tell her. But until Cheyenne was ready, I had to keep my mouth closed.

Mom gave me a knowing look. "I see. So that brings me to my next question. You know you have a job here at the ranch if you want it. But it seems your attitude about that is about the same as it always was. So..."

"I'm starting my own business here in Wildwood."

She smiled. "Well, okay, then. Have you talked to Cheyenne about that?"

"I have."

She held up both hands. "I'm not trying to change your mind. You need to do what you want to do. But it can take a while for a business to become profitable. If you'd like to work here in the meantime—even part time—you can."

"I'm not planning to leave you guys in a lurch," I said. "I know it will be a while before Dad is back in the saddle, and I promised Travis I would stay on while he works some things out in his own life. You can use me as long as you need me, as long as we all know it's not forever."

"I understand and agree," she said, nodding. "And I mean it when I say we're grateful you're going to hang around and help out. I have a proposition for you."

"What's that?"

"With Jimmy back, Travis finally has some help. I could really use Beth in the kitchen, and Jonathan hates the trail rides and would rather work cattle. Why don't you take over as Cheyenne's partner for now? It will be easier on you physically while you recover. Plus, it will make your time here on the ranch more enjoyable." She winked at me.

"Playing matchmaker again, are we?"

She grinned. "I think the match has already been made. I'm simply offering you a job that benefits everyone involved."

"I'll take it," I said, tossing a freshly peeled potato into the bowl. "As long as Cheyenne approves it, that is."

"Based on how starry-eyed she was yesterday, I'm pretty sure she'll be thrilled," Mom teased.

Chapter Twenty-Nine

LIFE FELT LIKE A DREAM. IT WAS A CLICHÉ THING TO SAY, BUT there was no other way to describe it. Every morning, I woke up in Rhett's arms. We had coffee together on the porch while Ash ran around outside. Then we went to work together, where Naomi had arranged for Rhett to be my partner on the trail. I'd always loved my job, but sharing it with him made it a thousand times better. Plus, the patrons loved it. All the little kids wanted to get their picture taken with the "real cowboy."

A few of the women wanted that too, and one even went so far as to tuck her number into Rhett's back pocket.

All it did was make me laugh. I couldn't blame her. He was gorgeous, sexy, and—most importantly—he was mine.

I never officially told anyone we were together, other than Claire. But I didn't need to. It was obvious in the way he looked at me—and by the way we couldn't keep our hands off each other. After the first few days, I gave up trying. Without even thinking, I slipped a hand on his knee during lunch one day, and his arm automatically wrapped around my shoulders. When I realized what we were doing, I looked up and saw Naomi giving me a knowing smile. After that, I relaxed and stopped worrying about it.

Family dinner became a regular thing, and we stopped trying to hide our relationship there, too. The first time Rhett kissed me in front of everyone, I was startled. But then I realized no one seemed to care. We didn't need a big announcement. We were together, and it was as natural and normal for everyone else as it was for us.

When Thursday rolled around, I was actually disappointed about missing the family dinner.

"You ready?" Claire asked, waltzing into the barn, still wearing her sheriff's uniform.

"Almost," I answered, leading Diablo back to his stall. Soon, he'd be able to stay out in the pasture if he wanted.

We'd had to keep him in the barn full-time at first while we monitored his recovery and got his weight up to where it should be. The poor horse had been horribly malnourished and injured when we'd gotten him. But today, he looked sleek, healthy, and confident. He wasn't nearly as skittish and had even let Rhett saddle him without bucking.

It was such an interesting thing. Diablo was still uncooperative with Travis and Jonathan, even though neither of them would try to "break" him the way old-school cowboys did. Everyone on this ranch followed Walker's rules, which included a strong respect for the spirit of a horse. Even so, Diablo clearly preferred to be handled by women. But he had become comfortable with Rhett since we'd gotten together, as if my trust in Rhett made Diablo trust him, too.

Rhett walked in, his face lighting up as soon as he saw me. My face lit up at the sight of him, too. I couldn't help it. Those black boots, that long hair hanging down underneath his cowboy hat. That sexy grin and swagger. My heart felt like it could beat right out of my chest every time I saw him.

"You have it so bad," Claire said, laughing as she elbowed me.

"I sure do," Rhett said as if she had been talking to him. He swept me off my feet into a giant bear hug, then planted a loud kiss on my lips right in front of her.

"Hi," I said when he put me down. "That can't have been good for your ribs."

"Worth it," he said, winking. "I wish I could come with you tonight."

"Really?" I cocked my head. "Why?"

He shrugged. "I think what you do is cool, and it's a huge part of your life. I'd like to see it in action. If you played a sport, I'd want to cheer for you at your games, right? Same thing."

"It's not the same thing at all," Claire interjected, rolling her eyes. "You can't compare search-and-rescue to a sport."

"But if you really want to come, you can," I offered. "We let civilians observe or train with us for a night to see if they're interested in joining."

"Really?" His eyes lit up.

"Yeah, sure." My heart fluttered all over again, knowing that he cared about something I was so passionate about.

"Awesome. I'll tell Mom I won't be here for dinner after all." He turned to leave, then stopped. "Wait, they have food, right? You're eating there?"

"No," Claire said, straight-faced. "Hunger is part of training. We all skip dinner in order to simulate what it's like on a real search."

He hesitated, rethinking his decision.

"Claire's kidding," I said, rolling my eyes. "Yes, there's food. Hank's wife cooks the team dinner every Thursday. We eat, then train for a couple of hours. She cooks enough to feed an army, so there will be plenty for you, too."

"Perfect." He threw me a wink, then disappeared out of the barn.

THE SUN HAD ALREADY SET WHEN WE ARRIVED AT HANK'S and let ourselves in the gate to their backyard. The team had long outgrown Hank's small house, but it was tradition to meet there before training. So Hank and his wife, Jackie, had installed multiple picnic tables in their backyard and lit the space with hanging lanterns. The effect was as beautiful as it was practical.

Hank and Jackie both welcomed Rhett with arms wide open. As far as Jackie was concerned, the more the merrier. She, like Naomi, loved playing hostess and always enjoyed a crowd.

Hank, meanwhile, was always looking for more people to add to the team. He would see Rhett as a prime candidate: strong, experienced on horseback, and the kind of person who liked to push himself. That was something everyone on the team seemed to have in common. You didn't sign up for this kind of thing unless you wanted to see what you were made of and continually challenge both your mind and your body.

I slipped my hand into Rhett's as I introduced him to team members. It gave me a thrill, knowing that even though I hadn't said anything, we were officially going public with our relationship. I'd never brought anyone to training before, and I had certainly never held hands with anyone in public. It was new territory for me, but it felt right.

It always felt right with Rhett.

Everyone seemed happy to see Rhett except Sam. He glanced at our intertwined hands and gave me an unreadable look. I smiled at him, trying to let him know that I was okay—that everything was good. But his disapproval spoke loudly, even though he didn't say a word.

Jackie had set up a taco bar for dinner, so we all feasted and laughed before diving into training. The camaraderie of the group was an important part of how we functioned. We all needed to be able to trust each other and feel comfortable with each other out in the wilderness.

Rhett fit in right away, which brought unexpected relief. I hadn't realized how nervous I was about mixing these two parts of my life. Search-and-rescue could be incredibly hard on relationships. We frequently dropped everything to respond to callouts and were often put in dangerous situations, coming home bruised, sore, and exhausted. That was hard on loved ones back home. I'd seen more than one relationship fail because of SAR—and I'd seen more than one person drop from the team in order to make their relationship work.

I didn't want to be in either of those camps. I wanted this to work well so I could have both. Rhett fitting in so easily with the group, laughing and cutting up with them over dinner, felt like a step in the right direction.

When we wrapped up the meal, Hank stood and clapped his hands for attention.

"Alright, folks. Don't forget, we're here to train. Tonight we're working on swift water rescues. Grab your gear and let's head down to the creek."

There were a few groans—though they were accompanied by grins. Water rescues were neither our specialty nor our favorite thing to do. But it was a crucial skill in the mountains, and we did whatever was necessary.

Rhett whispered in my ear as we began the short hike from Hank's place to the creek. "Thanks for letting me come."

"You're welcome." I smiled up at him.

"You guys really are like a family."

"We are," I confirmed. "A pretty dysfunctional one sometimes. You get a mix of personalities on the team. Occasionally, someone will join who doesn't jive with the rest or who wants to take charge. It can cause some conflict. But in the end, we all come together for the mission."

"So what are we about to do?"

I grinned. "You'll see. And I mean that—you're limited to observing today. But if you ever want to think about joining the team..."

He chuckled. "Hank suggested the same thing."

"You'd probably be good at it. It's a big time commitment though. Something to think about."

"Yeah." He looked thoughtful. "It is."

Hank put us through our paces at the creek. We worked on shallow water river crossing techniques, reaching for subjects with a pole, throwbags, swimming out to subjects, and belaying. By the time we finished, we were exhausted.

Rhett was grinning from ear to ear when Claire and I exited the water for the last time.

"That was amazing," he said. Pride sparked in his eyes. "You both kicked ass."

"Of course we did," Claire laughed.

"I mean it," he said. "You two are the best on the team. I don't know why that would surprise me, but seriously. Fantastic job."

"Thanks," I said, pulling my helmet off and wringing out my ponytail. Despite my gear, I shivered in the cold night air. I was more than ready to shed these clothes and get warm—preferably with Rhett.

"Wait until you see us descend out of a helicopter," Claire said, punching him on the shoulder. "Then you'll really be impressed."

Rhett's eyes widened. "You guys do that?"

I nodded. "Yeah. Sometimes. Our county doesn't own a heli yet, but once per quarter, we have longer training days where we go to some of the counties that do. It's a big part of what happens here in Wyoming."

"Why don't we own one, then?" He frowned.

Claire shrugged. "Lack of funding. We're working on it. We've increased our fundraising efforts and are stashing away anything we raise for one."

"You mean the *team* has to buy it?" He looked shocked.

"Yeah," I confirmed. "We buy all our own gear."

"So you're volunteers who give up work without pay *and* buy all this gear I'm seeing out of your own pockets to save the lives of strangers?"

"Basically," Claire answered, nodding. "I get paid now because of my role at the Sheriff's Office, but everyone else is a volunteer."

"Wow." He shook his head in disbelief, then slung an arm around each of us. "You two might be the coolest people I know. How close are you to the helicopter funding?"

"Oh, we just need another half a million," Claire said, laughing. "For now, there are some private agencies we can contract with if we need one for a search. Or sometimes, one of the other counties will help us out. But, hopefully, someday we'll have our own."

"Hopefully," I agreed. "Although, I definitely prefer being on the ground."

Rhett grinned. "Afraid of heights?"

"I'm not afraid of anything," I teased. "But we all have things we're better at, and I'm better on the ground. It's what I do. Up in the air, you're scanning with your eyes, hoping to spot something—or heading straight to where you already know the person is. On the ground, I can get into the mind of the missing victim. Figure out what moves they might have made. Look for the small clues you can't see from the sky—a broken branch, or a torn piece of clothing. Ground searches are my specialty."

Hank came up and slung an arm around me. "That's right. Cheyenne's got the best instincts of anyone on the team."

Rhett's eyes shone with pride. "That doesn't surprise me at all."

When Hank walked away, Rhett pulled me into a tight embrace, wet gear and all.

I sank into his arms, feeling totally at peace.

Until I saw Sam staring at us with disgust all over his face.

Chapter Thirty

Rhett

Settling into my new life felt so easy and natural it almost felt wrong. For the first time ever, I started enjoying working on the ranch. Mom's idea of partnering me with Chey for the trail ride side of the business was brilliant. Since I could do it full-time, it freed Jonathan, Beth, and Claire up from the rotation, which meant Mom and Travis both had consistent help. And being out on the trails with Chey made my new role a pleasure instead of a drag.

She was incredible. Patient and gentle with the horses *and* their riders. Always found ways to make the experience new and exciting. Kept everyone safe, taught them a bit about horsemanship, and showed them Wyoming's natural beauty all at the same time. She was a natural guide, able to answer any of their questions about the landscape around them. Full of great stories about the history of the Bighorns. And she had a way with the horses that put even her most nervous riders at ease before it was over.

It was no wonder half her riders seemed to fall head-over-heels in love with her by the end of every tour.

Beyond that, she'd amazed me at SAR training. Watching her navigate the swift water rescue techniques with ease had impressed me more than I could say. I'd grown up in this country, had white water rafted and spent summers splashing around the creeks and rivers, but I wouldn't have managed those exercises half as well as she did. It was incredible.

I was damn proud of my girl.

When we got back from a morning tour, I pulled her aside before we headed to lunch. Wrapped my arms around her waist in the barn and pulled her in for the kiss I'd been imagining all morning. Loved feeling her body pressed up against mine and running my hands through her hair.

Still couldn't believe this was my life.

"What was that for?" she asked when she pulled back, breathless.

"Missed you."

"You've been with me all day," she teased.

"I've been *sharing* you all day," I corrected. "All week, actually. I miss being alone with you. Let's not stay for dinner tonight. Let's go out. Me and you."

"Alright," she agreed. "Where do you want to go?"

My mind instantly wandered to all the places I'd love to take her in Austin. Our options were pretty limited in Wildwood. But it didn't matter.

"I don't care," I said, shrugging. "I just want time with you."

"Is the bar okay?"

"It's great."

But there was worry in her eyes, clear as day.

"What is it?" I asked.

"I hope Pete's feelings aren't hurt."

I shrugged. "If they are, that's his business. He asked you on one date that didn't even happen. Any feelings he has about that aren't your responsibility."

Her mouth twisted into a wry grin. "You make everything seem so easy."

I shook my head. "Nah. Life's hard. I just don't see the point in complicating it needlessly."

"And yet, you're here," she said, staring up at me with those big brown eyes. "Complicating your life to help your family. Complicating it more to be with me."

"Some things are worth it."

Her face relaxed. "Yes. They are."

TRAVIS HAD TAKEN CARE OF THE TIRES ON MY BIKE WHILE I was recovering, so I talked Cheyenne into taking it to dinner. When I suggested it, the concern on her face was clear, but I reminded her that I'd been riding a horse all week and was doing just fine. My headaches were pretty much gone and I was nearly back to full strength.

Besides, if I couldn't manage the bike, I knew she could. I told her as much and won another smile.

"Fine," she said. "We'll take the bike." She glanced over at it, a wistful expression on her face. "It's been a long time since I've been on one."

"How long?"

"Since you left."

That stabbed. She'd always loved riding with me. I hated that she'd missed it all these years. "We've got a lot to make up for."

But she smiled. "You've been doing a pretty good job so far."

"I don't guess you still have your helmet?"

She shook her head. "No. But Claire has one. I'll borrow it."

I stopped cold in my tracks. "Since when does my sister have a motorcycle helmet?"

Cheyenne laughed. "I guess you missed that. She briefly dated a biker a couple of years ago. It didn't last, obviously, but she enjoyed the ride."

I frowned. "Hmmm. I don't know if I like that."

She rolled her eyes, grinning. "You're one to talk. You ride cross-country on these things."

"I wasn't talking about the bike part."

She gave me a quick kiss. "I know. I'll be back in five. Then we can go."

"I'll be waiting."

I watched her walk off with a feeling of immense satisfaction.

Coming back to Wyoming had been the best decision of my life.

Half an hour later, we pulled into the parking lot of Pete's bar. Cheyenne hopped off the bike and pulled the helmet off her head, shaking out those gorgeous brown locks. Her cheeks were pink and her eyes were bright.

"That was awesome," she said, her whole face lit up in a grin.

"Yeah, it was. I always love riding, but having you on the back of my bike, holding on to me? Makes it ten times better."

Those cheeks pinked even more. "Come on," she said, grabbing my hand and dragging me toward the door.

"You hungry?"

"Yes. But I'm also thinking that the faster we eat, the faster we get to go home." She winked.

"I like the way you think." I grinned. "And I love that you can't wait to take me home with you."

She threw her head back, her laughter lighting up the night like sweet music. "I'm just ready for another ride—on the bike, I mean."

I held my fist to my heart. "Way to break a man's spirit."

"Oh, there's nothing broken about your spirit," she said, grinning again. "That's part of why I love you." The moment she realized what she'd said, she turned white and tried to backtrack. "I mean—"

"I love you, too, Cheyenne." I put my hands on her face and stepped close, keeping my eyes locked on hers. "I've already told you that, but I'll tell you again. I love you with every ounce of my being."

Her hands came to my wrists, holding on like she was holding for dear life. "Really?"

"Really. Always have. Always will."

And right there in the parking lot, she wrapped her arms around my neck and kissed me in a way that made me know she finally believed it.

It should have been perfect. But when she pulled away, flushed and happy, I felt an uneasy prickle on my neck.

I glanced around the parking lot and didn't see a thing out of place. But that didn't stop the cold fear from creeping up my spine.

Chapter Thirty-One

Cheyenne

My heart beat wildly as I kissed Rhett in the middle of town for the whole world to see. It was more than just a kiss—it was a declaration. One more part of my life where I was being open about our relationship.

But as we broke apart, I felt a shiver run through me—a feeling that, somehow, something was wrong.

That something was coming.

I glanced around the edges of the parking lot. Daylight was fading quickly, and the shadows in the trees seemed more ominous than they should. It sent ripples of fear through me that I couldn't explain.

"What's wrong?" Rhett asked, frowning as he pulled me closer.

"I don't know. Let's ... let's go inside."

"I agree."

Inside the bar, I felt better—for a moment at least. Pete's station was empty, and something felt off. I slipped my hand into Rhett's without even thinking, needing to feel the connection.

We walked up to the bar and waited. A couple of minutes later, Pete emerged from the back. He jumped when he saw us.

"Oh, sorry," he said, flustered. "Didn't realize you guys had come in."

"That's okay," Rhett said smoothly. "You know what you want, Chey?"

I nodded. "Same old, same old. Water to drink, please."

Pete gave me a small smile. "Got it. What about you, Rhett?"

"I'll take the burger I had last time—the one with the barbecue on top—and a whiskey."

I put a hand on Rhett's and gave him a little head shake.

"Make that water," he ground out.

I rewarded him with a smile. I knew that Rhett could hold his liquor, but this was his first time on the motorcycle since his accident. It wasn't a good idea to complicate things with alcohol.

Besides, I couldn't shake this feeling. And if something was coming, we needed to be alert.

Pete didn't seem up for conversation, so we paid quickly and excused ourselves to a booth. When Rhett slid in across from me, his brows knit together.

"What's going on?"

"I don't know," I said, sighing. "When we kissed in the parking lot, I felt like someone was watching us. It freaked me out."

His eyes narrowed. "I felt the same way."

"It may have been my mind playing tricks on me," I admitted. "It's strange, you know, going public with our relationship. Everyone was so quick to judge you for leaving. So angry at you for the way it broke my heart. I feel like I'm betraying them by getting back together with you."

"Well, that sucks." An unhappy look settled onto his face.

I put my hand over his. "It's my problem, and I'll deal with it. I love you. It doesn't really matter what anyone else thinks, does it?"

"No, it doesn't. I'm only worried about how *you* feel."

"It's going to take some time to adjust. It was nerve-racking at first on the ranch. But everyone has been supportive and not intrusive at all."

He snorted. "Come on. Mom practically forced us together. That's about as intrusive as it gets."

I smiled. "Yes, it is. But it came from a good place, and she's been great about giving us privacy."

"They've been great," he admitted. "Maybe you're wrong about everyone else. Honestly, people tend to think less about us than we believe. People are busy with their own drama. Who cares if we're together?"

"You're right," I said—even though I didn't believe it. I'd felt the weight of Alma's disapproval, of Sam's... And I could feel the tension in the bar as Pete eyed us from the cash register.

Rhett had lived away for a long time. He'd forgotten how tight-knit our little community was and how protective we all were of each other. He was an outsider now—an outsider who had scorned our town and broken my heart.

They wouldn't forgive him so easily.

But right after Pete delivered our food, the front door swung open and I began to realize I was wrong about the source of my foreboding.

Thomas Smith stepped inside, and the look he shot us was aimed to kill.

He marched over to our table and placed his fists on it. Rhett straightened, broadening his chest.

"Back off," Rhett said smoothly. "I don't believe you were invited to this party."

"Invited or not, I've got some things to say," Thomas growled.

"I wouldn't," I warned him, pulling out my phone and hitting Claire's number. I put it on speaker and sat it on the table.

Thomas tried to snatch the phone away, but I was quicker than him. When Claire answered, his face turned red.

"Fine. Let her hear this, too," he snarled.

"Thomas?" Claire said, instantly alert. "Is that you?"

"Yeah, it's me. You listen up." He jabbed his finger toward Rhett. "I don't know what kind of sick game you're playing, but I wasn't the one who attacked you. Wish I was, as every single one of you deserves a hell of a lot more than what you got. But it wasn't me. Seems you're intent on framing me though, so let this be a warning to you. If I'm going down for what happened to you, I'm going to make it worth it. Know what I mean?"

He glared at Rhett, then turned his eyes toward me. A sick, twisted look was in them as he dropped his gaze to my chest.

"Get your eyes off of her," Rhett growled, tensing.

I squeezed his hand in warning. I could take care of myself, and the last thing I needed was Rhett getting into any more trouble.

"Back off, Thomas," I warned. "Or you'll regret it."

"Oh, is that a threat?" His eyes glinted cold.

I shook my head. "No. You're the one threatening me. I'm letting you know you don't want to follow through with it. Trust me, it won't go well for you."

He leaned down and whispered in my ear. "I'll be seeing you again. Soon."

Chapter Thirty-Two

Cheyenne

"Cheyenne?" Claire's breathless voice came through the phone, along with the sound of a car door slamming.

"I'm here," I said, picking up the phone and shaking myself a bit.

"I'm on my way. Is he gone?"

"He's gone."

"Stay there. I don't want you guys even walking out to the parking lot. I'm calling the sheriff and we'll meet you there, okay?"

I met Rhett's gaze and he gave me a small nod. "Okay."

"Alright." She let out an exhale. "Hang tight."

I ended the call and put my phone down on the table. Rhett's hand instantly came to mine, covering it.

"You okay?" he asked, worry in his eyes.

"I'm okay."

The worry was replaced by fresh anger. "I can't believe that guy." He gripped my hand tighter. "I'm sorry I got you caught up in this. But I won't let him hurt you."

I shook my head, giving him a small smile. "He's angry because of me, not you. *I'm* the one who should apologize. If I hadn't reported him, he wouldn't have so much anger toward your family."

"This is not your fault," Rhett insisted. "He's hated us for years. Always figured he was jealous of what my family had built."

"Well, I certainly didn't help things. But there's nothing we can do about it now, except whatever it takes to stay safe."

Pete called out from the bar. "You guys okay?"

"We're okay," I called back.

Rhett tensed as the door to the bar flew open again. But I relaxed when I saw that it was the sheriff. McGrath strode straight to our table, a sour look on his face.

"Claire called me," he said before either of us could say a word. "I came straight here. Hoped I'd catch him in the parking lot, but he's already split. You two okay?"

"We're fine," I said.

"Claire said it sounded like he was threatening you," Sheriff McGrath said, looking me straight in the eye. "That right?"

"Yes." I shivered as my mind flashed back to the twisted look on his face. "He said he wasn't the one to hurt Rhett, but that if he was going down for it, he would make it worth it."

Sheriff McGrath rolled his eyes. "I see he's still proclaiming his innocence."

"He is," I confirmed. "Then he..." I swallowed hard, not knowing how to say it.

"Yes?" McGrath waited.

Rhett filled in the blanks for me. "He looked at her like she was a porterhouse steak and he was a dog who hadn't had a real meal in a week. Then he told her he'd see her soon."

McGrath's face turned hard. "I see."

"What is he doing out of jail, anyway?" Rhett demanded.

"He made bail," McGrath said flatly. "Judge went soft on him. I don't like it any more than you do. Don't even know where he came up with the money, but he did."

"Can we get a restraining order?" I asked.

McGrath nodded. "Yeah. I'll take care of that. But that's just a piece of paper," he warned. "Don't know if it'll do much to stop a man like Thomas."

"So what are you going to do about it?" Rhett was furious.

McGrath stayed cool, letting Rhett's anger wash over him without a visible reaction. "I'm going to send my deputies over to his house to take him in and lock him back up."

"Good." Rhett relaxed—slightly.

Claire ran in, her shoulders sagging in relief when she saw us. When she came over to the table, McGrath excused himself and said he was going to make that call.

Claire slid into the booth. "I'm sorry. I was off work today and didn't know he'd made bail or I would have warned you."

"It's fine," I said, giving her a quick squeeze. "We're okay."

"What about you?" she asked, throwing an anxious look toward Rhett.

"I'm fine," he said.

I looked at him closely, relieved to see that it was true. His hands were steady and the look on his face was pure determination. Despite the anxiety responses he'd had right after his accident, Thomas hadn't rattled him.

If anything, the run-in seemed to have strengthened him. He looked like a man ready for battle. And I couldn't help but like it.

"Eat," Claire said, gesturing to our food. "Before it gets cold. Hey, Pete?"

He jumped up and ran over from where he'd been watching from behind the bar, clearly uncertain as to whether or not he should get involved in this whole mess.

"Yeah?"

"Did you hear Thomas threatening them?"

He shook his head. "I was on the phone, taking a to-go order. Saw him come in but couldn't hear what he said. I was watching though. Figured I should wrap up the call and get the sheriff over here, but he left quickly and they said they were okay."

"That's fine," Claire said. "Cheyenne called me while he was here. I just wanted to know what you'd witnessed."

"Alright. You want a drink or something?"

She shook her head and snagged a couple of my fries. "Nah. I have a feeling I'm about to be on duty."

Sheriff McGrath walked back in, shaking his head. "Bad news," he said as soon as he got to our table. "Thomas isn't home. No one is, actually. The front door was wide open, so Burns went inside to do a welfare check. Looks like Thomas's wife packed up and left with the kids while he was in jail."

"That's not a bad thing," Claire interjected.

"Maybe not," McGrath said. "Except it means Thomas just lost everything. If we thought he had a reason to be angry before..."

He didn't finish the sentence, but he didn't have to. Claire, Rhett, and I all exchanged looks. Thomas was a snake on his best days. On his worst?

I couldn't even imagine.

Claire's phone rang. "It's Travis," she said, glancing at McGrath before answering. Her face went white at whatever Travis was saying. "I'm on my way," she finally said, sliding out of the booth before she even hung up.

"What now?" McGrath asked, bracing himself.

She looked at me, sorrow in her eyes. I felt sick, afraid of what she was going to say.

"Diablo's missing. Someone stole him right out of the barn. And there's blood."

Chapter Thirty-Three

Rhett

The look on Cheyenne's face when Claire had told her Diablo was missing played over and over again in my mind as we rushed back to the ranch. We ran into the barn and found Travis pacing, waiting for us.

Cheyenne turned white when she saw the empty stall. The wood railing held fresh dents and fractures from Diablo's hooves, and bright-red blood was smeared on the wall. More blood was on the ground, marking a trail toward the pastures.

"How did this happen?" Cheyenne cried out, devastation all over her face.

Travis shook his head. "I'm sorry, Cheyenne. You know the gate stays open for guests. I never thought he'd be brazen enough to come here and steal his horse back."

"It's not his horse anymore," Sheriff McGrath said angrily. "He lost that right when he abused it. This will add more to his charges." He put a hand on his gun belt. "Claire, we need to follow that blood trail, see if we can catch up to him."

"We should go on horseback," she said, moving toward a stall. "We'll make better time. Travis, who's still saddled up?"

"Shadow and Juniper," he said, springing into action. "I'll help you get them."

"Wait," I said.

Travis turned around, impatient. "What?"

"Where's Jimmy? Wasn't he supposed to be bringing the horses in tonight?"

He blinked twice, then realization dawned. "Shit. I haven't seen him since before dinner."

"I'll check the loft," Cheyenne said, turning to head toward it.

"Not alone, you won't," I muttered, catching up to her.

She climbed the stairs to the loft apartment and knocked.

No answer.

She knocked again, casting nervous eyes my way. "You really think he was involved in this?" She kept her voice low.

"I hate to think it of him," I said slowly. "But it wouldn't be his first mistake, would it?"

She knocked again, harder this time. We waited. But when three full minutes had passed, she turned toward me with sorrowful eyes. "I think he's gone."

I cursed, kicking his door.

After a thorough search of the stables, the barn, and the pastures, we headed back to the main house to wait for news from Claire. Travis was already in the kitchen with Mom. Her face was white and pinched, and as soon as we walked in, she grabbed us both in a fierce hug.

"I can't believe any of this is happening," she said. She turned toward Travis. "And I suppose I owe you an apology for hiring Jimmy back when you were so against it."

"No," he said, shaking his head. "You were doing what you always do. Giving someone a chance. And you were right. I was drowning. It's not your fault this turned out badly."

"Maybe we're wrong," Cheyenne said, though her voice was marked with doubt. "Maybe he went out for the night and he's going to come back soon and be as surprised as we were at Diablo's disappearance."

Travis grimaced. "I don't think so. His car is in the parking lot and he's not much of a walker."

"What if Thomas hurt him? If Jimmy was in the barn when Thomas came to take Diablo..." Cheyenne looked sick.

Travis and I looked at each other. His face mirrored the anxiety I felt.

"I didn't even think of that," Travis admitted. He ran his hands over his face. "Oh man. If he's innocent, I hope Jimmy is okay."

"Breaks my heart," Mom said. "Whether he was involved or is a victim, it's a tragedy either way. All we can do now is wait for news."

We waited an hour. Then Claire and Sheriff McGrath came to the house, looking weary and disappointed.

"We lost him," Claire said. "The blood trail stopped about a thousand yards from the barn. We tried to keep following the horse tracks, but, well, this is a horse farm. There's countless tracks out there."

Sheriff McGrath popped in. "Looks like he was heading toward the forest, which makes sense. He'd want to get undercover as quickly as possible. We did a quick search in the tree line, but we need more manpower and better light. I hate to tell you this, but we might be at a crossroads until tomorrow."

Mom flattened her lips, angry and worried. "I understand. Chey, Rhett, I think you're going to have to stay here tonight. He has his horse back. I hope to God he doesn't hurt Diablo—or Jimmy, if Jimmy is innocent in all of this. But I don't think he'll come back here."

Cheyenne straightened. "I can't stay here. What if he goes after Wildfire or Ash? He wants to hurt me, and he knows hurting my animals is an easy way to do it." She rose from her chair. "I didn't even think about it until now, but I bet that's where he went. I've got to get back to my property and make sure they're okay."

"Where Chey goes, I go," I said, standing. I gave Mom a look to let her know that it wasn't up for discussion.

"I'll go with you," Sheriff McGrath said, flicking his eyes toward Mom with a nod. "Make sure everything's okay over there so they aren't walking into anything alone. Claire, can I count on you to stay on guard here?"

"Of course," she agreed.

Travis came up to me, keeping his voice low. "Can we talk for a minute?"

"Now?" I gave him a blank look.

He nodded.

"Just a minute," I told Cheyenne, squeezing her elbow. "I'll be right back."

I followed Travis to Jonathan's room, where he closed the door and pulled the pistol from the holster on his hip.

"Here," he said, flipping it and handing it to me. "Wasn't sure you had a gun with you. If Thomas is out looking for revenge, I want you to have one."

I took the pistol and gave him a dark nod. "Thanks."

"Wish you guys would stay here."

"We can't."

"I know." He nodded. "I get it. You can't leave her property free for the taking. I'd come with you, but—"

"But he's angry at you guys, too, and Dad isn't in any shape to defend this place."

"Exactly."

I clasped his arm. "Take care of Mom and the rest."

"I will. And Rhett?"

"Yeah?"

"If Thomas Smith sets foot on Cheyenne's property..."

I looked him dead in the eye. "I'll shoot to kill."

Chapter Thirty-Four

Cheyenne

I climbed onto the back of Rhett's bike, grateful for the chance to hold on to him for a little while. I felt sick. I'd promised to protect Diablo, but Thomas had gotten to him anyway. And now, Thomas was far beyond his normal angry self. He was furious, and Diablo would pay the price.

Like he could read my mind, Rhett reached back and squeezed my thigh, a gesture that had always meant "everything's going to be okay."

But I didn't believe it. The sick feeling in my gut wouldn't allow me to.

As we got close to my property, the scent of smoke hit my nostrils. I sat up and searched the sky, my heart falling when I saw the plume of smoke rising from the direction of my home. Rhett dropped his head and twisted the throttle, rushing toward home.

Sheriff McGrath apparently saw the same thing we did, because he put on his lights and zoomed ahead.

I breathed a momentary sigh of relief when Rhett pulled into my driveway and I saw my home still standing. But the relief was washed away in a moment when I realized the truth.

The barn was on fire.

"Wildfire!" I jumped off the bike before Rhett had fully stopped, threw my helmet to the ground, and raced toward the flames.

"Cheyenne, no!" Rhett yelled.

I ran blindly, smoke choking me. Strong arms grabbed me and pulled me back.

"You can't run into it," Rhett yelled hoarsely into my ear.

"I have to save her!" I cried. Hot tears stung my face and nausea rose, threatening to overtake me. I fought against his arms, tried to break free.

"Stop," he said, holding tighter, pulling me away. "She's okay. Look."

He pointed toward the pasture, where Wildfire was running. She was anxious but very much alive. I nearly collapsed in relief, my legs unable to hold me. Rhett half dragged me away from the barn.

"The hose! Get the hose. Maybe we can save it." I tried to pull away again.

"No." Rhett held me tight. "Cheyenne, there's nothing you can do. Not now."

The truth of it finally sank in. The entire structure was engulfed. Red flames flicked angrily toward the sky and lit up the barn from within, glowing between the gaps of the boards that remained. The roof had already collapsed on one side.

My world was burning down, and there was nothing I could do about it.

Sheriff McGrath was already on the phone with the fire department, but we all knew the truth. By the time they got there, it would be gone, nothing but embers on scorched earth. The old wood and hay were perfect kindling. We'd never had a chance.

"Fire truck is on the way," Sheriff McGrath said. His face was lined with frustration. "I'm awfully sorry, Cheyenne. We'll get him. I promise you that."

I nodded, numb. "I-I need to check on Ash," I said, choking out the words.

Rhett tensed. "You're not going inside the house alone. What if he's still here? He could be inside waiting for you."

"Rhett's right," Sheriff McGrath said firmly. "Give me your keys. Let me check it out."

I fished my keys out of my pocket, too tired to argue.

McGrath pulled his weapon and headed toward the house. I sank back against Rhett's chest and watched my world burn.

"My grandfather built that barn," I whispered as a single tear fell down my cheek.

"I'm so sorry, baby." He wrapped his arms around my waist and held me. "I know it's not the same. But I'll build you a new one."

I pulled his arms even tighter around me. "All that matters is that we're all safe." But the words felt hollow.

A few minutes later, Sheriff McGrath came back and tossed me my keys. "Everything looks fine inside. Ash is a little stressed out, but she's unharmed. Doesn't look like he was in the house at all." He looked toward the barn and shook his head. "I hate this so much for you. But I hope it means he's done. He got his horse back. Got some revenge and left. He could have pushed it further, but he didn't."

"Unless the only reason he stopped is because we showed up with lights and sirens," Rhett growled.

McGrath nodded. "You have a point there. Speaking of which..."

We could hear the fire truck sirens. They'd made record time, but it didn't matter. We all knew it was a total loss.

I was just grateful Wildfire and Ash were okay.

The next few hours passed in a blur. The fire was extinguished, leaving a mess of charred wood and ash behind. There was nothing that could possibly be salvaged. It was all gone. My grandfather's legacy, wiped away in a single evening.

It didn't take long for the fire investigator to declare arson. Shortly after, Sheriff McGrath found an engraved lighter with Thomas Smith's name on it half buried near the rubble.

It burned hot in my soul and made me feel an anger and hatred I'd never experienced in my life.

When everyone was finally wrapping up and ready to leave us on our own to pick up the pieces, McGrath came back to us.

"I've got everyone looking for Thomas. We'll find him, Cheyenne. We won't rest until he's caught. I'd like to suggest that you guys go back to the ranch and stay with your family." He cut his eyes toward Rhett. "The more people around, the better. I don't think Thomas will come back here tonight, but you never know, and I'd feel safer knowing you were at the ranch."

I shook my head. "No. If I would have been here earlier, this wouldn't have happened."

"You don't know that," he pointed out. "He could have snuck onto your property and torched your barn before you knew what was happening. Only difference is that he might not have stopped there."

"Ash would have told me he was here," I insisted. "Trust me, if he comes back? I'll be ready for him. I'm not abandoning Ash and Wildfire."

"I'm not asking you to abandon your animals," he said, exasperated. "Claire's got a horse trailer. Get her to pick Wildfire up and take everyone over there."

"No." I clamped my lips and shook my head again. "I'm not abandoning my home, either. Sheriff, this house was built by my grandfather, just like that barn was. I don't have much in the way of a family legacy, but I had his barn and I have this. It matters to me. I'm not leaving it for Thomas to burn too."

He gritted his teeth. "I hope you don't have an objection to me stationing a deputy out here tonight, then."

"None at all. In fact, I hope you do. I also hope you understand that if Thomas Smith steps foot on my property again, I'll shoot him."

He knew me well enough to know I meant what I said. He lowered his voice and leaned in. "I'd think less of you if you didn't."

WHEN EVERYONE WAS FINALLY GONE—MINUS THE DEPUTY stationed out front in his car—Rhett and I took flashlights out to the remnants of the barn to take a closer look ourselves. Without the others there, I finally let the tears I'd been holding back come.

"Oh, baby," he said, pulling me into his arms again.

"I know it was just a building," I said, sniffling. "But when I moved here from St. Louis, that barn was my first refuge from the world. A place where I learned who I really was and what I really wanted in life. I fell in love with horses in that barn and connected with a part of my family tree I'd never known. It was as much my home as the house is."

"I know," he said, kissing the top of my head. "And I know right now you're probably not ready to even think about rebuilding. But I'm here when you're ready. I promise you, Cheyenne. I'll build you another one. It won't be the same, but it will be a new legacy. Yours."

I swallowed hard, taking comfort in his words. My mind drifted as I tried to make sense of all of this. "I guess I need to be a lodgepole pine."

"What are you talking about?" He chuckled and kissed my hair again.

"Lodgepole pines. It takes fire for their cones to open and their seeds to spread." I pulled back and looked at him, showing him I was serious. "Without fire, the forest wouldn't thrive. There would be no new growth."

He nodded. "That's right."

"You know, I look back at my life and the darkest moments felt like scorched earth and ashes. Dad leaving. Picking up and moving from St. Louis to Wyoming. You leaving." I paused, swallowing hard again. "They all felt like tragedies, and they were. But they were also the birth of something new. I can only hope this will be the same."

"It will be." He took my face into his hands and stared deep into my eyes. "I don't know what's next for us, Cheyenne. Seems like life is always a mix of good times and bad. But this time, all the bad stuff brought us back together. And no matter what the future holds, I want to face it with you."

Tears pricked my eyes and I nodded. "I want that, too."

Chapter Thirty-Five

CHEYENNE WANTED TO SIT UP ALL NIGHT IN THE LIVING room instead of going to bed. I agreed but managed to coax her into falling asleep in my arms there. Losing Diablo and her barn had sapped the last of her energy, and she was in a state of grief and exhaustion, even if she wasn't ready to admit it. I assured her that, with the deputy out front, Ash guarding the back door, and me staying awake with the rifle at my side, it was safe for her to rest for a few minutes.

Thankfully, that few minutes turned into several hours of deep sleep, until her cell phone rang. She instantly jarred awake.

"Who is it?" I asked, tensing. Someone calling at four in the morning couldn't be good news.

"It's Claire." She shook herself and jumped up, answering the phone to have a mostly one-sided conversation while she paced the room.

"What's wrong?" I asked, my heart accelerating when she finally hung up. If Thomas had hurt someone in my family...

"It's a lost kid." Conflicting emotions warred on her face. "A five-year-old out hunting with his dad. He wandered off from the tent in the middle of the night. The dad didn't realize he was missing until half an hour ago and has no idea how long he's been gone or where he went."

"Shit. That's not good."

"No, it's not. Claire is required to respond. She told me it was fine for me to not come, but…"

"But that's not who you are."

"None of us make it to every callout," she said like she was trying to convince herself. "The team would understand."

"But it's a missing kid."

Her shoulders dropped. "Exactly. And, honestly, this kind of thing is my specialty. If it was a lost hiker who had hit his GPS distress signal or a hunter who radioed in from a known location, that would be different. But it's not. It's a kid, and he's lost in territory that I know like the back of my hand. They're calling in a canine team from another county, but it will be hours before they can get here. And with a kid? Every minute counts."

"Go," I said firmly. "I'll be fine, and I'll stay here and guard the house. How long do you think you'll be gone?"

"You never really know. Average time is about five hours, but that's meaningless. They could find him before I even show up, and I could be back in an hour, or I could be gone for three days." She sighed. "I probably shouldn't go, should I? It's volunteer. They'll understand."

But it was clear from the look on her face that not responding went against her very nature.

"Go, Cheyenne. You know you want to. That kid needs you. "

She bit her lip, considering. "I thought you would try to talk me out of it. Insist that I stay here where you can protect me from Thomas."

"Are you disappointed I'm not?"

She smiled, despite her exhaustion. "No. Not at all. I love that you support what I do."

I stood up and put my hands around her waist, pulling her to me. "Will I worry about you? Of course. But I saw you in action the other night. You're amazing."

"Thank you."

"Plus, that team? They've got your back. Honestly, I figure you'll be safer out there than you will be sitting here at a house Thomas has already targeted once. You'll carry a weapon though, right?"

She winked. "I carry all sorts of things that can be used as a weapon."

I kissed her gently. "Then go do your thing. Save lives, and kick ass."

"You're sure you'll be okay?"

"I'm doing better than that poor kid is. Go find him."

"Okay," she said after taking a deep breath. Her face took on a resolve I'd never seen before. Cheyenne in warrior mode.

I loved it.

She typed out a message on her phone. "I'm letting them know I'm clear to respond." She took another breath and looked me in the eyes. "I love you, Rhett."

"I love you, too, Cheyenne."

Then she went into action mode, throwing on her hiking gear and getting her pack ready. And I tried to pretend I felt as confident as I was acting.

Chapter Thirty-Six

Cheyenne

As I changed into my SAR gear and double-checked my pack, my respect for the team members who regularly left their families behind to do this work skyrocketed. It had always felt so easy for me to compartmentalize and focus completely on a callout—until now. I felt torn between two worlds, knowing that this child deserved one hundred percent of my attention but also worried about everything I was leaving behind. Rhett was more than capable of protecting my home—*our* home now, I realized with a happy jolt. But leaving him felt like leaving half of my heart. At a time when we faced a very real threat, it went against everything in my body to leave instead of staying to stand beside him.

I closed my eyes, forcing myself to picture this child lost and alone in the woods. My place was with Rhett, but it was also on the team I'd dedicated my life to. Thomas might be miles away by now, content with the destruction he'd wrought. But this kid was in a life-or-death situation. It had to be my priority.

I kissed Rhett goodbye when Claire pulled up in her truck to get me. Even though this search location called for a horse team, Wildfire wouldn't be coming—my tack had burned along with my barn. But Claire had loaded up Stormy for me, so we were set.

"You made good time," I said, swinging into the passenger seat of her truck and shoving my backpack onto the floorboard.

"It's a kid," she said, frowning. "Any other call and I might resent having to leave this morning, but…"

"I totally get it. I have a whole new appreciation for some of our teammates. It's so much harder to do this when you're leaving someone behind who needs you too."

"Rhett will be fine," she said, her voice softening. "No sign of trouble here last night after you left. I think Thomas did what he set out to do and is laying low now. Sheriff McGrath has everyone out looking for him though. They'll get him."

"Yeah," I said, though I realized I didn't really believe it despite having told myself the same thing earlier.

Something in my gut didn't feel right. A little whisper that I couldn't pay too much attention to or else I wouldn't be able to force myself to go on this call. But I knew, if I didn't go and this child died, I would never forgive myself. So I shoved my misgivings down deep and tried hard to focus on the job ahead of me.

"Tell me about this callout," I said, propping an elbow on the door.

"Dispatch said the dad called nine-one-one about an hour ago, frantic. Cell service is pretty bad up there, so some of it was garbled and patchy. But it sounded like he took the kid on an overnight turkey-hunting trip. Dad thinks the kid left the tent to relieve himself in the night, but the dad slept right through it. Woke up because the tent flap was open and he got cold. Realized the kid was missing. Looked around the site briefly and couldn't find him."

"Kid's name?"

She grabbed the notepad sitting in her dash and checked it quickly before handing it to me. "Dispatch said it sounded like Tim or Timmy, but it wasn't clear and she couldn't get the last name. She's confident on the age though."

"Do we know what he's wearing?"

"Blue pajamas."

"Do we have a GPS location?"

Claire nodded. "Dispatch traced the phone. It's off the beaten path. Looks like they skipped the designated campsites and set up in the backwoods."

A fresh trickle of unease floated through me, but Claire's phone rang before I could voice it. She answered, responding in short tones, then hung up.

"Everything okay?" I asked.

She let out a frustrated growl. "Yeah. But that was Sheriff McGrath. He said that, under the circumstances, he wants me to stay at base camp with Hank instead of going out with the team."

"Why?" I was surprised.

"They've got a lead on Thomas's location and are hoping to bring him in. The sheriff wants me to stay close to my vehicle in case I'm needed. Two crises in one day is a stretch for our small team."

"Good point," I admitted, hiding a sigh. The entire SAR team was a family, but Claire and I had known each other so well for so long that we practically worked as one. All it took was a head signal or a hand gesture for us to be on the same page, and our skills meshed perfectly together. A search for a missing five-year-old was already potentially difficult, and I hated that I wouldn't have her by my side.

WE GOT TO THE TRAILHEAD THAT WOULD ACT AS OUR BASE camp, where Hank was already setting up a command station. Sam was waiting, and at least three other responders were on the way but hadn't arrived yet.

"You made good time," Claire said to Sam, grinning as she hopped out of her truck.

He nodded and gave us a small smile. "I was close by."

I went straight to Hank. "Have you talked to the dad?" Although dispatch had given us a report, we always preferred talking to whoever had called in ourselves. Information often got lost in translation, and dispatch didn't always know the questions the search team would find relevant. We also needed the dad to gather items for a scent pack before the canine unit arrived—unless we managed to find the kid first.

Hank frowned and shook his head. "I've tried. I've called the number dispatch gave me four times, but it's going straight to voicemail. I'm guessing the guy's battery died."

"Maybe." My concern grew. It wouldn't be the first time someone's cell battery died after they called in. But if he was out frantically searching for his kid, then we might have two victims to search for instead of one.

"You three good to go ahead and head out?" he asked.

"I'm hanging with you today," Claire said, shrugging. "Sheriff's orders."

"I'm ready," Sam said, jumping in. He looked at me. "I've already got the GPS location plugged in. Looks to be about a twenty-minute ride from here to where the call originated from." He pointed at the map. "It's up on a ridge, so good thing we brought the horses. They'll climb it quicker than we will."

I looked at the map, my heart sinking. The topography out here was rugged, and it would be so easy for a small child wandering around in the dark to tumble right off the side of one of these ridges. I wanted this to be a quick, successful search. But everything within me said today wasn't going to go like that.

The sun rose, brightening everything around us as we took our horses single file up the narrow switchbacks toward our destination. I was grateful for the light. My heart nearly stopped every time we came to a sharp corner and I imagined what could have happened to a child in the dark without a flashlight.

Things widened and flattened out as we came to where we supposed the campsite to have been. Sam came up beside me on his horse as I stopped.

"What's wrong?" he asked.

I double-checked my GPS. "This clearing makes the most sense for their campsite location. But there are no signs of camping. Not recently anyway. No tent, no fire."

He looked around, frowning. "The dad searched a bit on his own before calling in. He may not have called from the campsite."

"Maybe not," I agreed. But that whisper was turning into a roar. Something wasn't right here.

I swung down from Stormy's back. "I'm going to look around for tracks. Maybe we'll find the dad's footprints at least—or some indication that we're in the right area."

"Good idea." He swung down too and started following me as I scoped out the ground, using my headlamp to illuminate it. The sun was rising, but the light was still low, and I didn't want to miss anything.

Unfortunately, it didn't seem like there was much to miss.

"So, you and Rhett are back together," Sam said, throwing me an awkward glance.

"Yes."

"You sure that's a good idea?"

Irritation flared, but I tried to tamp it down. As upset as I was at Sam for scaring Rhett off years ago, I knew he had my back. He was practically family.

"Yes, I do," I said, my voice coming out a bit firmer than I meant for it to.

"He broke your heart," Sam started, but I interrupted him.

"Yes." I turned and looked at him, wanting him to see the resolve on my face. "He did. But there were pretty big misunderstandings on both sides. Nothing that happened ten years ago matters anymore. We've worked it out and we're good."

He shook his head. "I think you're getting swept up in puppy love again, and as your friend, I have to tell you I think it's a bad idea."

I choked out a laugh and turned my back to him, scanning the ground. I'd finally located some tracks up here, but they weren't the boot prints I expected from a hunter—they were horse tracks.

"Puppy love? Me? You're kidding. I'll admit there was some of that when I was a teenager, but I'm not a kid anymore, Sam. You know I'm not the kind of person to get swept away in a fantasy."

"Could have fooled me," he grumbled, following me again.

"Maybe you don't know me as well as you think."

He grabbed my arm and spun me around. "I know you better than he does, that's for sure. He's been gone for a decade. But me? I've been here, by your side, day in and day out, waiting for you to notice me. But you've never given me a second glance. How is it that someone like him can waltz back into your life and into your bed in no time at all, when I've been here all along and you've never even noticed?"

I took a shaky step back. "What are you talking about, Sam? You have a girlfriend."

He shook his head. "Emily? She doesn't mean anything to me. Isn't that obvious? I can't wait for her to get tired of this place and go back home. *You* matter to me."

He stepped toward me, his arms outstretched like he wanted to pull me into an embrace.

I saw the danger coming. And I froze.

Chapter Thirty-Seven

Rhett

I FOUND MYSELF ODDLY RESTLESS WHILE I WAITED FOR Cheyenne to get back. I knew better than to worry about her. She could take care of herself. Had been doing it for years.

But reminding myself of that did nothing to change how worried I felt waiting for her to come home safe. I kept picturing all the things Mom had told me about SAR: Cheyenne dropping out of a helicopter to rescue someone from the top of a mountain, or taking a horse through bear country with nothing but a can of bear spray for protection. Rock climbing to perform a ropes rescue, or going deep into the earth because someone got lost in a cave.

The woman was a superhero. But her job was dangerous, and I worried about her. And that wasn't even taking into account the fact that Thomas Smith was still on the loose. I wasn't too worried about him though. Truth was, there was some comfort in knowing that Cheyenne was out of his reach. He wouldn't know where she was or what she was doing, and there was safety in that.

Plus, there was safety in having her surrounded by her team. That was one bad-ass group of people, and I knew they had her back.

I wouldn't leave the house because I'd promised to protect Ash and Wildfire. But sitting around doing nothing was driving me nuts. So I found her toolbox and took the time to fix the leaky sink in her kitchen. Changed a lightbulb in the living room and shaved down her screen door so it would close tight. Checked all the locks on the windows, pleased to see they were in good working order.

I looked around some more and started making a list of supplies I'd need to spruce the place up. The house wasn't in terrible shape, considering its age, but I could upgrade it significantly without losing any of its character. The legacy would matter to Cheyenne. I wanted to be the one to restore the cabin to its original glory, the way I wanted to build her that new barn.

Mom and Dad would offer us land to build a house out by the ranch—I knew that. But I also knew we'd never take it. Cheyenne belonged here, in the woods, on the land she loved. I couldn't imagine her living anywhere else.

The hours ticked by slowly. I knew better than to text Cheyenne or Claire and distract them on the search, but I shot Travis a message to check on the family. They were in the clear, too, though struggling to make things appear "normal" for the tourists without splitting up and dispersing over the property. They'd canceled the trail rides for the day, using search-and-rescue as an excuse, with a promise to make it up to everyone. Had managed to get Dad outside, where he was sitting out back, entertaining the guests with wild cowboy stories— while also keeping watch on the property with a pistol tucked into his belt.

With nothing else to do, I looked over at Ash. "Hey, girl. You probably need to go outside again, don't you?"

Her ears pricked.

"Let's go, then." A change of scenery would do me some good.

I walked to the front door with Ash following me and looked down at her.

"You don't need a leash, do you?" I knew that Cheyenne didn't use one, but then again, Ash was *hers.* Didn't know how she'd respond to my commands or if she'd come back if I called. Hoped she didn't take off, looking for her master.

Ash gave me a look that I imagined had a few colorful words in it.

I chuckled. "Okay, then. Don't make me regret it. Chey will kill me if I lose you."

I opened the door and she bounded out, energized by the great outdoors. Couldn't blame her. I felt better too, getting some fresh air and sunshine. I sat down on Cheyenne's porch, noting how she'd painted it a deep green shade that matched the pine surrounding it. It was fitting and totally her.

It was also starting to peel and needed to be redone. Half a dozen boards needed to be replaced entirely. I made a mental note to pick up some lumber. And then a second mental note to either borrow someone's truck or buy one for myself so I could do things like that. I'd always used the company truck in Austin, but if I was starting my own business here, I'd need one of my own.

The idea excited me. Crazy. At eighteen, I couldn't wait to get out of Wyoming. Now, I couldn't wait to settle down and build something here that I could be proud of.

Ash relieved herself, then played for a bit before joining me on the porch. She plopped down beside me, staring up with big blue eyes.

"Are we friends now?"

In answer, she nudged my hand. I stroked her fur and decided maybe she wasn't so bad after all. She looked scary, but she was a sweetheart. And, hell, Cheyenne had been a single woman living alone in the mountains. She needed a scary-looking dog. Ash was probably a damn good deterrent when it came to troublemakers.

Like she could read my mind, she lifted her head and let out a low growl.

I heard a car engine in the distance. I glanced at my watch. "It's probably your mom," I said, petting Ash again. "Maybe they wrapped up the search and she's on her way back home."

But Ash let out another growl, lower this time.

"Hmm. Does that not sound like Cheyenne?"

A few seconds later, a silver car rumbled into view.

I frowned. "Nope, not your mom. You were right," I murmured, keeping a hand on Ash's back. I was suddenly glad to have such a scary-looking dog beside me.

But I relaxed when I saw who was driving the car. Alma jumped out in her acid-washed jeans, snakeskin boots, and a brown poncho.

"Rhett," she called, gasping for breath. "You have to come quick! It's Cheyenne. She's hurt."

My entire world stopped.

"What do you mean she's hurt?" I was already moving, already running toward Alma with Ash by my side.

"She fell down a cliffside during the search this morning." Alma's hand was fisted at her chest, gripping so tightly her knuckles turned white. "She's hurt bad. Needs emergency surgery. Claire sent me to pick you up, take you to the hospital. She knew you'd be a wreck and didn't want you driving your motorcycle up there."

"Okay." I braced my head in my hands, trying to stay calm even though all I wanted to do was rush to her side. "Let me put the dog inside and lock up."

"Do you have keys?"

"No," I realized, shaking my head.

"It's alright. I do. I take care of Ash when Cheyenne's gone." Alma patted my arm. "Go ahead and get in the car. You look like you're going to pass out if you don't sit down. I'll lock up, and then we'll go straight there. Everything's going to be okay."

"Okay." I took a deep breath and did what she said.

But my entire body was screaming at me that things were not okay at all.

Chapter Thirty-Eight

Cheyenne

"Don't move. Don't come any closer." I tried to be strong, but the words came out in a whisper.

Sam gave me a weird look. "What are you talking about? I'm not going to hurt you, Cheyenne. I love you. That's what I'm trying to say."

I shook my head, realizing he still didn't understand what was happening.

"She's not talking to you. Get your hands where I can see them." The voice came from behind him, and Sam went rigid, slowly raising his hands into the air.

I lifted my hands. "You don't have to do this."

Thomas moved toward us, pistol in hand. "Oh, yes I do." His eyes were crazy. "I lost everything because of you. Now you're going to lose everything, too."

"What's going on?" Sam's voice was steadier than mine. He turned slowly, facing Thomas.

"There's no missing kid, is there?" I asked. "You called this in to get me here."

Thomas nodded proudly. "That's right. You always were a sucker for kids and animals. Knew you'd be ready for me at your place, but you wouldn't be expecting me out here. All I had to do was get up high where I could watch the response and keep an eye out, make sure I followed the right team. It's you and me now, and you're going to suffer like I've suffered."

Sam stepped toward Thomas. "I don't think so."

Thomas aimed his gun and pulled the trigger. The sound echoed through the canyons, and Sam sank to his knees, clutching his shoulder.

I ran to him, supporting his weight as he fell backward. Dark blood seeped through his shirt. His skin went white and his eyes widened in shock, but he was still breathing.

"We've got to get him help," I cried.

Thomas shook his head. "He's on his own. You're coming with me." He motioned to his horse. "Get on."

"Think this through," I urged, hoping to reason with him. "If he dies, it will be so much worse for you. There's still time to make this right. We need to radio for help. There are supplies in my bag. I can give him medical attention in the meantime."

"No." Thomas's voice was sharp. "I don't care if he dies. I've already lost everything anyway. My wife, my kids, my livestock. Now I'm being framed for something I didn't do."

"Thomas, it doesn't have to be this way."

But his face was as hard as a stone. "We both know I'm not going to make it out of this alive. But before I go, I'm going to make sure you understand what it feels like to have everything taken from you, too. Now, come on. Get on my horse."

My heart sank as I saw the truth in his eyes. There would be no reasoning with him. He didn't care what happened to him in the end—all he cared about was hurting me.

I blinked back hot tears as I realized how stupid I'd been.

He'd set a trap. And I'd walked right into it.

Chapter Thirty-Nine

Rhett

Alma came back and got into the car with me, giving me a tight smile. "All locked up," she said. She glanced around like she half expected to see someone else, then pulled out and turned her car toward the highway.

My pulse raced and cold sweat dripped down my back. At first, I thought it was fear for Cheyenne's safety. But I closed my eyes and had a flash, a memory. Something hazy and broken, a piece I was trying to grab on to.

"Looks like you need a ride."

I turned around, relieved. "Man, am I happy to see you. But the ranch is out of your way. You sure you don't mind?"

"Not at all. Hop in."

Alma. Alma had offered me a ride that night.

But she wouldn't have... Would she?

It didn't make any sense. She was practically Cheyenne's second grandmother.

Cheyenne's second grandmother. I suddenly felt sick. She had been best friends with the woman who had deliberately sabotaged my relationship with Cheyenne ten years ago.

"Hey, do me a favor? I need a smoke. Grab my cigarettes from the glove compartment?"

The pieces kept coming back. I'd been in this seat and she'd asked me to get her cigarettes. I'd leaned forward and then my head had exploded in pain before everything went dark.

Alma Moore had tried to kill me. And she'd tricked me into getting back into her car again. I was in trouble. The realization sank in like a lead weight in my stomach.

I glanced over, wondering about jerking the steering wheel out of her hands, fighting for control of the car. But we were already going too quickly down the switchbacks that led to Cheyenne's place. One wrong move and I'd send the car over the side of the mountain. It was too risky.

"Cheyenne's not really hurt, is she?" I asked, gripping my knees with my palms.

Alma glanced over. "No. She's not. Your memory coming back to ya?"

"Yep." The words were tight. "Why did you do it?"

"Because I made a promise."

"To Gran?"

She nodded. "That's right. A promise to watch over Cheyenne when she couldn't. She didn't want you and Cheyenne together. You're no good for her. So I'm keeping my promise by making sure you're out of the picture."

Alma was crazy. She didn't want me and Cheyenne together, so she was going to *kill* me? Thomas I understood. But this? This was insanity.

"Shouldn't Cheyenne get to make her own decisions?" I asked.

She looked at me sharply. "She does make her own decisions, or at least she did before you came back. But when it comes to you, she can't see clearly enough to know what's good for her. You've always been nothing but trouble, and you dragged Cheyenne right into it. Underage drinking, sneaking out to spend nights with you, letting you in her window at night. Oh, we knew all about it. Could have gotten her knocked up and ruined her whole life. Barb was worried sick about what might happen to Cheyenne after she was gone, and she knew the most important thing she could do for her was to get rid of you."

I shook my head in disbelief. "We were kids. Kids do stupid stuff."

"No." She shook her head. "*You* did stupid stuff. Getting into fights, acting like rules didn't matter. Too wild for our girl. And Barb was right. Once you left, she straightened right up. Made a good life for herself."

"I've made a good life for myself, too. I grew up, Alma. I'm not a kid anymore. I love Cheyenne, and I'm going to take care of her, be the man she deserves."

Oh, God, give me that chance. It was a prayer I'd prayed more than once since waking up in that ditch, but the stakes were higher now. I watched the road carefully, looking for a chance to take control. But Alma was driving like a maniac. I couldn't risk it.

Alma snorted. "You're not good enough for her. I tried to warn you. You should have left when I told you to."

"The note?" My jaw dropped.

She nodded. "I watch the bar from my shop. Had a bad feeling when I saw your bike out front and watched Cheyenne go in anyway. She was a wreck when she walked back out, after seeing you again. Hoped you'd leave town, but you didn't. Knew you were going to be trouble. And I was right, wasn't I? You hadn't been in town a week before you got into that fight with Thomas Smith."

"So you tried to *kill* me?"

"Thought I had," she admitted. "You didn't seem to be breathing when I pushed you out into that ditch. Never thought you'd make it, and I'll admit I was sweating when I heard you were in the hospital. But I'll do things right this time."

She spoke matter-of-factly, like we were talking about mundane chores, not murder. Ranch life could harden a person, that was certain. Managing things on her own for so long had probably toughened her up quite a bit. But even the tough ranchers I knew were still human. She didn't seem to have a heart.

"They found the tire iron in Thomas's car," I said, putting the pieces together. "You framed him?"

She nodded. "Had to. Once Cheyenne told me that fight was about him threatening her, I knew I needed to keep her safe from him, too. Easiest way was to make it look like he attacked you."

"How'd you do it?" *Keep her talking. Think—there has to be a way out of this.* Maybe when we turned onto the flat highway roads, I could take a chance, get the wheel.

But she didn't head toward the highway. She turned off onto a narrow side road that went back up the mountain. We were heading toward her place: a desolate ranch in the middle of nowhere.

"Thomas never keeps his vehicle locked, so it was easy as pie to put the tire iron in there," she bragged. "Swiped his lighter, too, in case I needed it. Glad I did. That came in handy. Couldn't finish the job until he got out on bail, but now they'll have more than enough evidence to put him away. And Cheyenne will be safe from both of you."

"You burned Cheyenne's barn?" My jaw dropped. I couldn't believe it. This woman who claimed to care about Cheyenne had destroyed something that meant everything to her.

But Alma blew it off. "That old barn needed to come down anyway. It was a piece of junk. Cheyenne will rebuild and be better off for it."

"You're crazy," I said, the words slipping out before I could think better of it.

She gave a hoarse laugh. "You have to be to survive out here alone."

"But you're forcing Cheyenne to do the same. I love her, and she loves me. I want to take care of her, build a life with her. You may not think much of me, but I know you think highly of her. She's decided I'm worth a second chance. She loves me. If you kill me, you'll hurt her far more than I did by leaving."

She scoffed. "You're still a child. You've been back together, what, a week? If that? She'll get over you faster this time than she did the first time around. At least now I'll never have to worry about you coming back here and stirring things up again. It will be over for good this time, and I'll have fulfilled my promise."

She pulled up to her house, a lonely one-story ranch sitting in the middle of a thousand isolated acres of red soil dotted with stones and sagebrush. It was somewhere no one would ever think to look for me.

This time, Alma never intended for me to be found.

"Get out," she said, pointing a small revolver at me. "We're going for a walk."

Chapter Forty

Cheyenne

I HAD TO KEEP THOMAS TALKING. I COULDN'T GET ON THAT horse with him. Claire would already be on her way here. I'd pressed the emergency button on my GPS while Sam's body was blocking mine, and the team would have heard the gunshot. No way would Claire hang behind knowing I'd signaled for help. If I could keep him here long enough for her to get here, she could take him down before he ever saw her coming.

"What did you do to Diablo?" I asked, my voice shaking.

Thomas grinned. "You really are a sucker. I've got a gun pointed straight at you and you're *still* worrying about that damn horse. Shows you haven't suffered enough in life. Don't worry. Soon enough, you'll be in so much pain that you'll understand what it's like for the rest of us."

Sam's blood seeped through my fingers. He was losing too much, too fast. I put more pressure on the wound, praying for Claire to get here. How long had it taken us to get up this mountain? Only twenty minutes or so. She'd be moving even faster, but I had to keep him talking.

Or I'd have to end this myself.

"You didn't answer me," I said, letting my voice quiver. He thought compassion was a sign of weakness. Let him think that. It would catch him all the more off guard if I had to make a move.

"You're stalling," he said, waving the gun at me. "Think I can't see that? Don't worry about Diablo. I offered Jimmy five hundred bucks to get him back for me. *Jimmy's* the one you should worry about, since I don't actually have the money." He laughed out loud. "Told him I'd double it if he took Diablo to your house and kill him, leave the head in your bed. I'm guessing the kid was too weak for that though."

Blood pounded in my ears. The man was evil.

"Wasn't it enough to burn down my barn?" I cried. "When's it going to be enough for you, Thomas?"

He threw his head back and laughed. "Now, I didn't know about that one. Jimmy must be trying to earn that extra money after all. I hope he locked that damn horse in there before he lit it on fire."

Sam groaned. I looked at him and tried to somehow communicate that help was on the way and he would be okay.

But Thomas was done waiting. "I told you to stop stalling," he warned. "I'll shoot him again if that's what it takes. He's got a chance now, but if you don't get over here, I'll make it to where he doesn't. I know Claire Hawkins was at the foot of the mountain and that she had to have heard that gunshot."

His tone had changed. He wasn't laughing anymore, and he glanced around nervously, knowing Claire could be there any minute.

It wasn't much. But it was something.

"Alright, I'm coming," I said, faking surrender.

"No," Sam groaned. "Don't go with him, Chey." He tried to sit up.

"I have to." I squeezed his hand and gave him a tiny nod. He saw the look in my eyes and gave me an almost imperceptible nod back.

I pushed to my feet, brushing the dirt from my pants.

"Get your hands in the air," Thomas warned.

My heart beat wildly. I began to slowly raise my hands, looking for an opening. All I needed was one split second.

A squirrel rustled in the bushes. Thomas jerked his gun toward the sound, thinking it was Claire.

I drew the pistol hidden on my hip, aimed, and fired.

"NICE SHOT," CLAIRE SAID, CONGRATULATING ME WITH A grin as she took custody of Thomas. "Not many people can shoot a gun straight out of someone's hand. You're a real Annie Oakley, my friend."

"What are you talking about?" I scowled. "I was aiming for his head."

She threw her head back and laughed. "I'm going to pretend I didn't hear that."

"Me too," Sam said, attempting a chuckle. "If you end up in court, we'll all vouch for you." His voice was weak and his face was strained with pain, but he was going to make it.

The entire team had arrived on Claire's heels, and together we'd stopped the bleeding and loaded Sam onto a stretcher. He'd grumbled the entire time, saying that it was a shoulder wound and he could still walk, but we insisted on giving him the same first-class treatment he'd given so many others. Besides, the blood loss had made him weaker than he wanted to admit, and he needed to save his strength.

Sam was a good guy. I hated that he had feelings for me I'd never noticed, but maybe it was better that way. We could pretend that this conversation never happened and hopefully stay friends and teammates. Someday he'd realize that it never would have worked out between us anyway. He deserved someone who would adore him for who he was.

The only man I would ever adore was Rhett. And I couldn't wait to get home to him.

But between getting Sam taken care of and debriefing with Claire and Sheriff McGrath, it felt like I was never going to get home. Alarmingly, the trickle of unease I'd felt since that morning never went away. If anything, it was growing stronger by the moment.

I impatiently answered the sheriff's questions again, arms crossed as I watched Claire take a phone call out of ear's reach. When she hung up, she came back over to us with a grin on her face.

"Diablo's fine," she announced. "Travis found Jimmy hiding out with him on one of the trails on our property. Jimmy was never planning on turning him over to Thomas. He took him to keep him safe."

"The blood?" I asked, my heart racing.

"Jimmy's. Diablo didn't cooperate with him—shocker. Travis is taking Jimmy to the emergency room for stitches."

"He's sure Jimmy wasn't stealing the horse?" Sheriff McGrath asked.

She nodded. "Yeah. Jimmy confirmed that Thomas wanted to kill the horse to hurt Cheyenne. Travis may not have total trust in Jimmy, but he knows how much Jimmy loves horses. He believes him."

"What about my barn?" I asked. It was a loose end that was bothering me. I couldn't believe that Jimmy would do it, but Thomas had acted surprised by that one.

"Travis asked him about that. He was shocked and doesn't know anything about it."

"It was Thomas," Sheriff McGrath said, attempting to reassure me.

"I don't know. You've got him solid on shooting Sam and attempting to abduct me. Why would he not admit to hurting Rhett and burning my barn?" It didn't add up, and it only added to the anxiety I was feeling.

"Honestly? It's probably habit at this point," the sheriff said, shrugging. "He's been proclaiming his own innocence for years, and let's be honest. It's served him well. He should have gone to jail long ago for what he does to his wife, but he denies and she covers for him and he gets away with it. He probably thinks he'll get away with this, too."

"Maybe." But the more I thought about it, the sicker I felt.

"If you'll excuse me, I need to get Hank's statement now," the sheriff said, tipping his hat to me and Claire. "Glad you're okay, Cheyenne. And if I didn't say it before, I'll say it now: Nice shot." He winked at me.

"Again, I missed," I muttered under my breath.

But Claire didn't smile this time. She pulled me away, where no one could hear us. "What is it?"

"I just have this feeling."

"What feeling?"

"That this isn't over. Am I free to leave?"

She glanced at McGrath. "As far as I'm concerned, yes, but I'll need to check with him."

"Please do."

Her eyes narrowed as she saw the look on my face. "Okay. I'll be right back."

While she spoke with the sheriff, I tried to call Rhett.

But the call went straight to voicemail.

HALF AN HOUR LATER, CLAIRE AND I WERE FINALLY BACK IN her truck, headed toward my place. Rhett still hadn't answered his phone, and I was now certain something terrible had happened.

"Think it through. Who would want to hurt Rhett?" Claire asked, managing to keep her voice steady even though she was driving fifteen over the speed limit. Her hands gripped the steering wheel like she was holding on for dear life.

"I really don't know," I said, my mind racing as I tried to figure it out. "Thomas, obviously. I know Rhett rubbed people the wrong way as a teenager. Maybe someone who has a grudge from back then? But why now? It doesn't make sense."

Claire frowned. "When Rhett first got here, someone left a note on his door telling him to leave, that he didn't belong here."

"Are you serious?"

She nodded. "Yeah. Mom thought it was a prank. We all wrote it off. But..."

"But maybe it was a warning."

She took a deep breath. "Is there any chance Pete is holding a grudge, since he asked you out?"

Pete had been acting strange, and he had been there at the bar that night. But did he really have it in him? I couldn't see it.

"Maybe," I said doubtfully. "But I don't know."

"We have to drive through town on the way to your place anyway. We can look and see if Pete's car is parked behind the bar or not."

"Good idea."

But we didn't have to look. As we pulled into town, Pete was carrying a garbage bag out to the dumpster. He saw us and waved before heading back into the bar.

"He acts normal," Claire commented.

"Yeah..." But my mind was already off Pete, because I saw something that wasn't normal at all.

"What is it?" Claire's voice sharpened as she saw the change on my face.

"Alma's store. It's closed."

"Closed?" She whipped her head around to look. "She's never closed."

"Claire." I felt sick. I didn't want to believe it, but something inside me knew.

She turned and looked at me, horror all over her face as the realization sank in.

We raced to my place and confirmed that Rhett was gone. His cell phone was still inside the house and the door had been locked, but his bike was out front.

"You know Alma better than I do. Where would she take him?" Claire's voice was desperate.

I closed my eyes, trying to grab on to that connection with Rhett. Once again, it was like looking for a needle in a haystack. But I could feel him. He was alive.

And I would find him.

"She'll want to finish the job this time," I said slowly, thinking it through. "Honestly, the best place for that is her own property. It's private. There are a million places she could dump a body and it would never be found. And since she wasn't on anyone's suspect list, no one would think to look there."

"Okay. Let's go." We ran back to Claire's truck and pulled out. She called it in while I texted Travis to let him know what was going on—and prayed that we weren't too late.

The drive to Alma's felt like it took forever even though it was only a few minutes from my place. Claire slowed down as we pulled onto the long drive leading to her ranch house, scanning the area for signs of movement. Despite the warmth of the day, I felt chilled to the bones. I couldn't believe the betrayal. Alma, my second grandmother, had tried to kill the man I loved. Had probably helped Gran sabotage us so many years ago.

And she had him now.

"There's her car," I said, my heart catching as I caught sight of it in the distance. It was parked out behind her house, where the rocky flatland dipped down into rugged canyons.

Claire drove straight to it and parked, hopping out with me following right behind. The wind blew hard, whipping my hair into my eyes.

"Tracks," Claire said, pointing toward the passenger side. "Boots. Those look like Rhett's size."

"So he was still walking when they got here." I knew he was alive, could feel it, but it still gave me palpable relief to see the evidence of it right in front of me. I hugged my arms around myself, bracing against the wind.

"The tracks don't head toward the house," Claire said, snapping photos of them with her phone and pointing the direction where they headed. "Looks like she joined him and they started walking east."

"The canyon," I said, my heart in my throat. "Her property backs up to it on the east side. She'll force him over the edge. He'll never survive that fall, and odds are, he'd never be found."

"We've got to stop her," Claire said, sprinting that way with her gun drawn.

I ran after her, my heart throbbing wildly.

But it nearly stopped at the sound of two gunshots.

Chapter Forty-One

Rhett

Alma shoved her revolver into my ribs, prodding me toward the canyon. The wind picked up, blowing her poncho like a sail.

"Don't fret," she said like she was talking to an animal she was about to cull from her herd. "It'll all be over soon, and you probably won't feel a thing."

"You don't have to do this."

"We're past that," she said sharply. "I've lived a good, long life, and I plan on living out the rest of my days here—not in a jail cell. So you'll have to disappear."

"You won't get away with it, Alma."

"Course I will," she said, chuckling. "Everyone's ready to be done with Thomas Smith once and for all. They'll be all too happy to pin it on him."

We came to the edge of a canyon. She kicked a rock over and watched it fall to the bottom.

"Too many places where you could grab on," she muttered. "Can't take the risk. I'm afraid I'll have to shoot you first. But don't worry. That will make it easier on you anyway. I've had to put down more animals than I can count. I know how to do it."

My heart raced, but I knew what to do. I thanked my lucky stars for all the times I'd practiced moves with my brother Cole when he was training in martial arts. He'd taught me how to take a gun from an assailant—though I had to admit, it was a lot more nerve-racking when the gun was real.

"I'm sorry about this," she said, lifting the revolver and aiming it toward my head. "Maybe you want to turn around so you don't—"

Before she finished her sentence, I made my move, ducking my head out of the line of fire and grabbing her hand with both of mine, pushing the gun up. The gun went off instantly, like Cole had always said it would. I was ready for it. When Alma jerked back, I yanked the gun from her hands.

Enraged, she ran toward me, threatening to take both of us off the side of the cliff.

I pulled the trigger.

She collapsed to the ground, clutching her leg. "You shot me!" She looked at me with shocked eyes.

"You had it coming," I muttered.

Cheyenne and Claire flew over the hill, running straight toward us. I held the gun up, showing Claire, then backed up and put it on the ground, out of Alma's reach.

Cheyenne stopped in her tracks when she saw me, throwing her hand to her heart, before running and jumping straight into my arms.

"Careful," I said, chuckling. "There's a cliff right there, and I'd just as soon stay on solid ground if that's okay with you."

She covered my face with kisses. "You're okay. You're really okay."

I held her face in my hands. "I'm really okay."

"I didn't know..." She looked helplessly at Alma, then shook her head. "I didn't know."

"Me either." I wrapped my arms as tight as they would go around her and held her close. "I'm so sorry."

Claire had already slapped handcuffs on Alma and radioed for medical. "Nice shot," she said, smirking. "Non-lethal, but you stopped her in her tracks. Or are you going to tell me you missed?"

"Oh, I never miss."

If I'd aimed differently, I'd never admit it.

Chapter Forty-Two

Cheyenne

Summer came and went, but this time, Rhett stayed. There were people who seemed surprised by that, including Travis, who I think secretly always expected for him to leave again. But he didn't. He stayed and worked the trails with me, even as he began putting the plans into place for starting his own business the next summer. The trail guide gig grew on him though, and he admitted that he didn't want to totally give it up.

He also started training to join our search-and-rescue team, wanting to be a part of something that had helped save him, too—and wanting to replace Sam as my partner. To be honest, that was a relief. As grateful as I was for Sam trying to save me, things were never really the same between us after that day. He broke things off with Emily and apologized to me for the things he'd said. We managed to get along well enough to keep working SAR together, but I deliberately kept some distance between us. I hoped he would find someone else and be happy.

Walker recovered even better than the doctors had predicted, and was back at work, giving Travis the relief he desperately needed. Thomas admitted to being the one who had sabotaged the ladder in retribution for the ranch taking in Diablo. I was relieved it hadn't been Jimmy. Jimmy had already had a difficult life. I wanted only good things for his future.

Green grass grew in my field, slowly erasing the last traces of the fire. Rhett built me a new barn, as promised, finishing it in time to store our winter hay. The beautiful new space was big enough for Wildfire *and* Diablo, who moved to our pastures not long after everything had happened. Somehow, Diablo became Rhett's instead of mine. The change was fine with me. Wildfire was the horse of my heart, and Diablo was perfectly suited for Rhett. The chestnut mare and the black stallion made a pretty pair in our pasture, and I loved watching them.

Early one morning, in the crisp air that signalled the coming of fall, I sipped coffee by the barn and watched the horses graze. Rhett came up behind me and wrapped his arms around my waist.

"Morning, beautiful."

I laid my head against his chest and smiled. "Good morning."

"Looked like you were lost in thought out here. What are you thinking about?" he asked before dipping his head to plant a kiss on my neck.

I took a deep breath and bit my lip. "That this is the spot."

"The spot for what?"

I turned and smiled at him. "The spot where we make a promise to each other, in front of our friends and family."

He tipped his cowboy hat back and moved quickly, pinning me to the barn wall with a wicked grin on his face. "Are you saying what I think you're saying?"

I grinned back, then stole a quick kiss. "What do you think I'm saying?"

"Are you finally going to marry me?"

I nodded. "Yes."

"When?"

"Hmmmm." I pretended to mull it over, counting days on my fingers. "How about ... next month?"

He tipped my chin up and lowered his lips to mine, kissing me hungrily. "I can't wait."

THANK YOU FOR READING *WILDFIRE OMENS*! NEED MORE Rhett in your life? Sign up for my newsletter and get a bonus chapter about Rhett and Cheyenne's wedding!

The Wildwood series continues with Claire's story, *Shadow Sabotage*. I also recommend meeting Rhett's brother, Cole, in *Mountain Secrets*.

Reviews are invaluable to authors. If you enjoyed this story, I would so appreciate you taking the time to leave a review at your preferred vendor. It truly means the world.

Want to stay in touch? Connect with me on Facebook or Instagram. I love getting to know my readers!

Acknowledgments

When I was five years old, my parents made a decision that changed the course of my life. My dad accepted a research position in Bighorn Canyon National Recreation Area. We packed up our things into a little trailer and drove from Arkansas to Wyoming, where we lived for six months while my dad studied Peregrine Falcons.

Everyone called it an adventure. But to me, it was everything.

To say I fell in love with the spirit of Wyoming is a massive understatement. Despite being as young as I was, my memories of that time remain vivid and powerful—core memories that, in many ways, define my worldview even now.

So my very first thanks goes to my parents, who chose to say yes to an incredible adventure even though it was crazy and probably terrifying. Thank you for that experience, for everything it taught me, and for the ways it continues to shape me now.

As always, I'm so grateful for Brandon, my husband. Thank you for chasing adventures with me, for making me laugh every day, and for being the shore to my waves.

Any acknowledgements would be incomplete without mentioning my boys, Aiden and Will. I'm so proud of you both, and I'm grateful for the joy you add to my life.

Massive thanks to Mike Poulsen, real life search-and-rescue hero who has been working in the Wyoming wilderness for many years. Thank you first and foremost for your service on the SAR team. And thank you for taking the time to talk with me about SAR in Wyoming. You patiently answered so many questions for me, and I cannot thank you enough!

I'm so grateful for the team that helped with this book. Esther from

Meraki Cover Design did an incredible job of bringing the vision for this series to life. Thank you, Esther, for your beautiful work! And to Mickey Reed, my editor: you've become a dear friend and I'm so glad to work with you. Thank you for always being there!

I'd like to say a special thanks to my critique partner and writing friend of over fifteen years: Camille. Working with you on our novels last year was such an enriching experience. I'm grateful for your friendship and can't wait to see your books on my shelf!

Thanks also to my beta readers, Jessica and Deondra. Thank you to my writing buddy, Elsa, for those early morning sprints!

And finally, I'm grateful for YOU. Yes, you. Readers make all of the early mornings, late nights, and agony over the words worth it. Thank you for sharing this world with me—and welcome to Wildwood!

About the Author

Nicole Gardner lives in NE Arkansas with her husband, their two sons, and their two crazy dogs. If she's not at her desk, you'll likely find her either in the garden, or creating teas and tinctures in the kitchen.

Nicole's background is in psychology. This fascination with human behavior and relationship dynamics plays a significant role in her writing and the way she shapes her characters.

www.nicolegardnerbooks.com